Formula for Crime

Formula for Crime

Where racing meets racketeering, and speed hides sin

Aditya Aurora

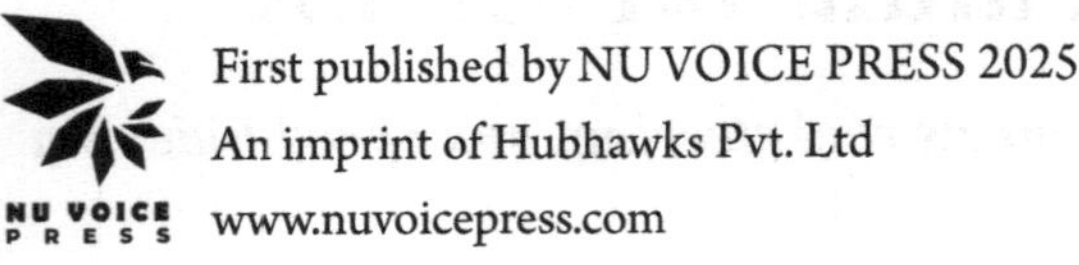

First published by NU VOICE PRESS 2025
An imprint of Hubhawks Pvt. Ltd
www.nuvoicepress.com

ISBN: 9788199505162

Typeset by: Pooja Sharma

Published by: Nu Voice Press

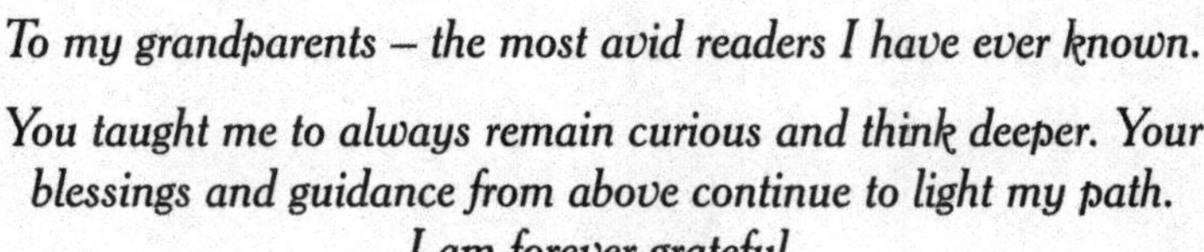

To my grandparents – the most avid readers I have ever known.

You taught me to always remain curious and think deeper. Your blessings and guidance from above continue to light my path. I am forever grateful.

Chapter 1

On 18 September 2008, at 5:45 am in San Francisco, Raymond switched on the television to watch the Formula One Grand Prix and wore his Ferrari T-shirt to support his favourite team. The race was set to begin in fifteen minutes, and he was rooting for Michael Schumacher and Ferrari to win. After all, Michael was the reason he followed F1 like a religion. He watched eagerly as the cars took to the circuit and slotted into their grid positions. The mechanics prepared the cars—fitting their choice of tyres, hard or soft, depending on the race strategy. Teams played tyre-poker with each other, speculating on what their rivals might choose. An indistinct chatter between the drivers and their race engineers was drowned out by the roar of the fans as they performed a Mexican wave. The grandstands transformed into a sea of red. After all, it was Ferrari's home race, and Michael Schumacher was the most loved. The fans were there to witness him being crowned world champion. If he won, he would secure his seventh world title, which, although almost certain, would be quite an achievement if accomplished in front of the *Tifosi* (a group of Ferrari fans).

The engines roared to life, and the fans cheered in appreciation. The five red lights were illuminated, and they went out to signal the race start. Michael led the race into turn one, closely followed by McLaren's Mika Häkkinen, his arch rival, and his teammate, Rubens Barrichello, behind him. As he approached the Ascari chicane, Michael was already one second ahead, and Rubens began to close in on Mika. The sound of the V10 engines reverberated through the town of Monza. Adrenaline was in the air, and the fragrance of rubber being laid down on the track mesmerised the fans as they watched Michael drive his heart out. Flawless and aggressive—that was his driving style. Lap after lap, he pulled away and extended his lead. The only chance anyone had of beating Michael was in the pit stops. But Ferrari's pitstops were a masterclass. Glory awaited Michael as he seemed destined to become the most successful Formula One racer of all time. The grandstands erupted in jubilation, and Raymond was euphoric. During the two pit stops, Ferrari continued to show their finesse with impeccable accuracy. The most successful team in Formula One history, coupled with the most successful racer, made a formidable and enviable pairing. No matter what was thrown at Michael that day, he was a class apart. Accurate and deadly, he swept past backmarkers like Monza was his backyard. The chequered flag was waved, signalling the end of the race with Michael securing his seventh world title by winning the race. He punched the air and celebrated his victory.

His engineer radioed in, "Michael, you are a seven-time world champion. This is history."

"Yes! Yes! Yes! Thank you, boys! Oh my god! We did it! We did it!" screamed Michael.

As he made his way into parc fermé (the part of the pitlane where the cars are parked after the race and scrutinised by the officials), he leapt into the arms of his team and triumphantly jumped on the podium, captivating the hearts of many across the world. The *Tifosi* made their way to the track, jumping over barricades just to steal a glimpse of their favourite racer and witness the iconic podium ceremony. Red smoke enveloped the circuit, and Ferrari flags fluttered everywhere. The German and Italian national anthems played in sync, and the crowd joined in the celebrations. They sang along while the strangers hugged each other as if they had achieved glory. After the race, the fans continued lingering on the track, many of them wrote their names on the tarmac, and some even had the fortune of meeting Michael as he made his way to the edge of the pit wall to meet his ardent fans. It was a win written in gold and would remain etched in everyone's hearts.

Although Raymond was thirty-one, he jumped on the couch like a five-year-old. His wife, Giovana, couldn't believe what she was witnessing. Her husband, who was generally controlled, elegant, and poised, now behaved like a gorilla gone mad. Anyway, this was a sight she had now come to terms with. After all, she was from Italy and could still remember her father and brother going berserk when Ferrari did win. Raymond had saved a bottle of expensive champagne, which he had decided to open once Michael won the world championship. Champagne was popped simultaneously in Italy and San Francisco, and Giovana was drenched. Raymond kissed her and celebrated as if they had won the lottery. He knew the church bells near the Monza circuit would soon start ringing, and it only meant one thing: a Ferrari racer had won the grand prix. The entire town of Monza turned into a party. And why not? After all, Ferrari was nothing short of a religion in Italy.

After celebrating the day's joys with champagne and cleaning up, it was time for bed. Raymond, a successful attorney on the verge of becoming a partner at Roth & Gotham, one of the world's largest law firms, was known for his work with banking and investment management clients. A top law graduate from Stanford University, he possessed an exceptional memory and towering stature, drawing attention wherever he went. Standing six feet three inches with an athletic build, his green eyes and blonde hair gave him a model-like appearance. Always well-groomed, he exuded the confidence of a top-tier lawyer. He was decisive in his professional dealings; he knew how to get things done. As a fifth-year Senior Associate handling the crème de la crème of the firm's clientele, he was poised to become the youngest partner at Roth & Gotham. He was a steady and dedicated man, happily married to his high school sweetheart, Giovana.

Giovana's family had moved to the United States when she was in sixth grade, and although she had not been in favour of the move at the time, she had eventually settled in well. She had the native Italian features: blue eyes, light hair, and a light skin tone. She could have easily entered a beauty pageant, but opted instead for the academic way, similar to Raymond. She had a degree in mathematics and chose to spend her time as a professor at Berkeley University. She was writing her dissertation and was on the verge of securing her PhD. She was a well-respected professor, and over the past few years, had delivered lectures around the world. They were a power couple. Successful in their respective fields, down-to-earth, and well-liked in their friend circle.

The next morning at 5:00 am, Raymond was already dressed in his joggers, ready for his gym session. After an hour and a half, he returned and got ready for work. Raymond and Giovana lived in Burlingame, about seventeen miles from San Francisco. He drove his Mercedes C-Class AMG across Bay Shore Highway, reaching the office at 456 Mission Street in approximately thirty minutes. He arrived around 7:30 am, earlier than most, and at 8:30 am, his secretary, Astoria, informed him that Andrew Roth, one of the firm's Managing Partners, wanted to speak with him. Raymond understood it was important; otherwise, the message would have been relayed by a junior partner.

Andrew was fond of Raymond; they both had studied at Stanford and enjoyed discussing racing. He often bantered with Raymond about how NASCAR was better than Formula One. Andrew was now fifty-eight and still going strong. He was about five feet nine inches with a receding hairline, but a mind as sharp as a sword. His dark brown eyes were trained to look through a person's soul. A sharp judge of character, coupled with a knack for winning cases. He had spent most of his years behind a desk defending clients and dealing with the District Attorney. Many times, one would find him in his office quietly sipping scotch and reading the latest provisions on financial or criminal law. He was ruthless in court and had even won cases in the Supreme Court. He was known to be calculative and always prepared. When he spoke, the clients listened. His word was sacrosanct, and he ensured no one took him for granted. On the other hand, he was accommodating towards his colleagues and believed in leading by example. He, along with Ron Gotham, had built one of the largest law firms in the world.

Raymond entered Andrew's office and noticed Ron, the senior partner, sitting there. It was the corner office on the twenty-third floor, and in the evenings, in the distance, one could see the carnival at Pier 39. During the day, the Oakland Bay Bridge stole the spotlight, gleaming in the sunlight like a steel crown stretched across the water. Inside, the office was just as impressive, plush furniture, an ebony wood table that looked as if carved from luxury itself, and chairs so comfortable even your back would forget it needed support.

Ron Gotham was almost sixty-two years old and still came to the office at least six days a week. In contrast to Andrew, Ron was almost completely bald. Standing at five feet eleven inches with greying eyebrows and a clean shave. Although he wasn't the most athletic person, he compensated with a dynamic personality. He had grown beyond the hustle and bustle of the courtrooms and had mainly focused on liaising with the firm's platinum clients and leading the firm's Partner Advisement Committee. In his younger days, he had lit the courtroom on fire with his powerful and well-argued reasonings. He knew the loopholes in the provisions and ensured to bend the law to the extent possible to prove his point.

A meeting with two named partners meant he had either screwed up and it would be his last day in the firm, or he was going to be *awarded* a new sizzling case. Raymond was one of the hardest-working employees at Roth & Gotham, and he always believed the reward for good work was more work.

The firm's stalwarts greeted Raymond and signalled him to take a seat. Andrew extended a firm handshake while casually remarking, "I think your apartment would have turned into Italy yesterday after Michael won his seventh championship."

"It pretty much did!" Raymond skipped the story of the champagne-drenched apartment and greeted Ron with much more formality, inquiring about his family.

As the three of them settled in, Ron stood up and walked around the office, mapping the edges of the dark brown polished table with his finger. He looked at Raymond almost as if he was trying to read what he was thinking.

By now, Raymond knew he was not getting fired, but didn't know what the partners wanted from him. The anxiety was broken when Ron said, "Mr Holster, we have a new case for you!" Raymond had never been addressed as Mr Holster by anyone but Ron. Raymond knew Ron was quite a character. He strictly had a no-alcohol policy, but the rumour had it that he would enjoy an occasional drink of Jonnie Walker, Blue Label, King George V in the confines of his office.

"You'll need to drop whatever you're doing and hand it over to another associate. Andrew will fill you in with the details, and let me tell you, if you nail this one, we'll have the partnership agreement ready for you to sign immediately."

Ron had other pressing things to take care of and walked out of Andrew's office. Andrew mentioned to Raymond that their new client was a probable whistleblower and the case involved his two favourite interests, Formula One racing and investments. Raymond was now puzzled as to why he had to drop his regular client, who had assets under management of twenty billion dollars, and focus on a whistleblower. Although he was confused, the excitement of his legal work entering the world of finance and flirting with his love for Formula One was thrilling.

"Raymond, what I am going to reveal to you needs to remain in this room. All our meetings are to take place securely. You will be given a new encrypted phone, laptop, and a secure private internet connection." He now knew shit just got real because he had never heard of a technology update just for a case. It was as if they wanted him to operate off the grid.

"What are we dealing with, Andrew? I've never seen this level of security at the firm," said Raymond.

"Neither have I, Raymond, but our whistleblower is ready to pay our fee as well as any incidental expenses, so we do our job and don't question the methods if they are legal," remarked Andrew.

"Understood! Please tell me more about this case where I'll be dabbling with my two favourite subjects."

"Yes, so our whistleblower, let's call him Mr X for now, says he knows of a scheme where the results of various races in Formula One are being manipulated, and he needs our help with what to do next."

Raymond was dealing with a curveball! His mouth was open, and his eyes were glaring directly at Andrew. His skin went pale, and he blurted a "What" so loud it would make an entire city come to a halt. "Are you sure we have the right guy? I mean, it's not like baseball, where you can miss a swing and make it look like a rookie error."

"I was as shocked as you are, Raymond. Believe me, I had the same reaction when Ron brought this to my attention. However, this guy seems to have some concrete proof that *some* results are being manipulated, and not all. After all, you can't infiltrate all teams, drivers, and the officials at such a level."

"Well, the fact it's happening at some level makes me fucking sick to my stomach."

By now, he and Andrew were close enough to use the most sporting language in each other's company. After all, Andrew had hired him and was his career mentor.

"Look, Andrew, now I am curious to know how the results are being manipulated and which of these scumbags are involved."

"We knew this would ignite a fire in you; therefore, we chose you, Raymond. From today to the end of the week, work on handing over all your work to Gregory. He'll be filling in for you. Oh, and when it comes to the rest of the firm, you're on mandatory leave."

"First Gregory, and now I'm on a pseudo-leave of absence," exclaimed Raymond.

"You know he's always trying to piss me off, and if he thinks I'm on a leave of absence, he'll want my office and my secretary. You know how well Astoria and I work together, right? She's one of the highest-paid secretaries because she literally knows half the law, and all the clients love her. I have trained her, and I am not willing to give her up."

Andrew knew Astoria and Raymond were a great team. All the junior associates loved working with the two of them, and none of them complained when they were asked to work overtime. In fact, they stood up for them when push came to shove because of how respectfully they were treated.

"Well, in that case, you'll get to keep your secretary, and she, too, will be on pseudo-leave of absence with you. She's been asked to hand over all of her work to Shana. You can choose one junior associate and two paralegals, and all of you will be working from the top floor of the Marriott Marquis."

"The Marriott Marquis? Isn't that the hotel right around *Tropisueno*, the Mexican eatery? Also, how are we supposed to work from there?"

"Easy, cowboy! You probably don't know my sister in-law is one of the investors in the hotel. And we have their top floor on permanent lease. That's where we work on all our top-secret cases. You and Giovana will have the presidential suite to yourselves with a butler and two errand boys at your disposal."

"Wow, that's some royal treatment," blurted Raymond.

"Yes, it is! Also, you and Giovana will be given a chauffeur. She can travel to Berkeley to deliver her lectures while you and the team work on this new gig. Oh, and royalty comes at a price our top-secret clients are willing to pay," said Andrew, with a smirk, meaning money was not a problem.

Andrew could see the excitement and nervousness on Raymond's face. He would inform him of the dangers associated with this case in the upcoming week. For now, he needed Raymond to operate without a gun to his head, hand over his clients, and prepare for the case of a lifetime.

Chapter 2

As Raymond arrived in his driveway, he wondered how to tell Giovana about the enforced vacation. They both cherished their cosy three-bedroom, 2,500-square-foot home. Still, he thought, *you've got to do what you've got to do.* He entered the passcode to unlock the security door, followed by his vintage-looking key for the main entrance to the drawing room of his apartment. Inside, Giovana was eagerly waiting. She had prepared a beef steak and kept a bottle of their favourite red wine, Chianti Classico Riserva, ready for him.

"What's with the elaborate spread?" questioned Raymond, knowing that once he revealed to her how their life was going to change, she might want to break the bottle on his head. The last time they had to move out of their apartment was two years ago when their home was under renovation. For an intermittent period, they had to occupy a rented apartment, during which Giovana went mad and threw a tantrum almost every other day.

"Well, you remember the dissertation I was working on?" said Giovana.

"You were working on a dissertation, darling! I didn't know that," joked Raymond.

She knew Raymond was pulling her leg. After all, she was talking about it for the last eight months. "Well, I am going to ignore what you just said because it was a lame attempt to piss me off. Coming back to my dissertation, it just got approved!" As she said this, she flung into Raymond's arms and kissed him like their first kiss after they got married. "Thank you for all your support over the years. I know there have been days and nights when I have lost my cool and poured my frustration on you."

"Wow, honey, that's fantastic news! This calls for a celebration," remarked Raymond.

He decided to enjoy the moment and went to the bar cabinet that had its in-built cooler to keep the champagne at optimum temperature. He pulled out a bottle of Dom Perignon, which was used only for special occasions. He popped the champagne, which they enjoyed while discussing how long and arduous her dissertation journey had been. Raymond decided to focus on Giovana's achievement for now; nevertheless, at dinner, he would have to tell her how they would have to move into the city at the end of the week.

As they ate, Raymond's expressions got serious, and Giovana caught on. "Is everything okay? You seem tensed and distracted, as if something is eating at you. Please tell me what's bothering you, Raymond?"

"Well, Giovana, today Andrew and Ron called me to their office and instructed me to drop all cases and work on a new case. If I nail this one, I will become a Partner at the end of the appraisal cycle."

"Wow, that's great news, Raymond! And since you look concerned, I think there is a catch. Please tell me we're not moving to another continent."

"We're not moving to another continent!" exclaimed Raymond.

"But we're moving?" she asked with one eyebrow raised. Almost reminding him of what had happened the last time when they had occupied the rental accommodation.

Without diving into too many details for now, Raymond explained how Ron and Andrew brought him up to speed on the new case and how it was so sensitive that the two of them needed to move into the Marriott Marquis. The thought of occupying a presidential suite, although exciting, was met with equal disappointment since Giovana loathed having to move. However, she knew how hard Raymond worked, and a promotion meant a much better standard of living. Although her father approved of Raymond, her mother always doubted whether he would make it in his career. She would finally be satisfied to tell her mother she had married the right man.

"So, what's with the secrecy? Why is this case so important, and why does Roth & Gotham have the top floor of Marriott Marquis on permanent lease?"

"Giovana, there are some questions even I don't have the answer to right now. After all, I am just a Senior Associate and not a named partner. But I'll tell you what I do know."

He explained the gravity of the case to her and why it was extremely important. She knew she was sworn to secrecy and had to remain tight-lipped about everything Raymond discussed with her. Being married to a star-studded lawyer like Raymond, Giovana thought she had developed the skills to beat a lie detector test. She kept all the information regarding Raymond's work under wraps. If anyone ever quizzed her, all she said was, "Raymond is sworn to attorney-client privilege, and he does not breach it for anyone, including me."

The next morning, Raymond reached the office at his usual time of 7:30 am. Andrew had instructed him not to change anything about his routine. Astoria arrived at 8:00 am, barged into his office, and said in a serious yet concerning tone, "Boss, I wanted to talk to you about this leave of absence I'm forced to take. Have I done something wrong? Did I fuck up, and am I subject to an internal investigation at the firm? Please tell me so I can prepare myself mentally and look for another job, if needed."

"You're fine, Astoria," said Raymond in a calm and composed voice. Hearing the tone, Astoria knew she did not need to worry, but also understood this was something important. "I, too, have been put on a leave of absence from the beginning of next week. But we won't be on leave. We'll be working on a secret client from the top floor of the Marriott Marquis."

"From the Marriott Marquis? And what's so secret about this mysterious client?" asked Astoria.

Raymond said, "I have scheduled a meeting with you, Shane, our junior associate, as well as Laura and Jordan, our paralegals."

"What do you mean by *our*?" asked Astoria.

"All secrets will be revealed at our 11:30 am meeting," remarked Raymond.

Raymond was making his way up to Andrew's office to discuss how much detail he needed to give each person on the team. On the way, he bumped into Gregory. "Ahh! if it isn't Mr Leave of Absence. What did you do this time, Raymond? Did you swindle money, or did you try bribing the District Attorney? Doesn't matter, I'll be working on your clients now, and I'm going to make sure they sing my laurels. Looks like someone is not going to be in contention for partner this year, and that makes my life so much easier," said Gregory with an evil smile. Gregory was stout with a big mouth. He wasn't the most pleasant person in a professional environment. Most of the people at the firm tolerated him, but he more than compensated for it with those unparalleled research skills. Although he wasn't the best at being diplomatic while dealing with clients, senior partners always wanted him as co-counsel on their cases since he was abreast with the latest provisions and applicable case laws.

Although Raymond never paid attention to the office gossip and always felt bad for Gregory, this time, he wanted to tell him to shove it or maybe even take a swing at him and break his jaw, but he knew better. He used passive-aggressive tactics and, in a composed tone, said, "You want a proper handover, right! So, make sure you treat my team well, or else you're going to have to get all the details from the client, and they're not going to be happy. And guess whose laurels will be sung and who will actually make Partner." Gregory went silent and quietly walked away with his tail between his legs. *What a pussy!* thought Raymond.

As Raymond entered Andrew's office, Andrew asked him to sit while he was completing a phone call with a client. Raymond took the liberty of making the two of them a cup of coffee as he stared at the Oakland Bay Bridge and watched cars go in and out of the city. It all seemed like a rat race. He had begun to wonder if he was cut out for this case. He'd almost had a run-in with Giovana last night and thought about taking a swing at Gregory this morning. Once Andrew finished his call, the two of them sipped coffee, and Andrew said he had a free hand when it came to revealing information to Astoria and Shane, but the less Laura and Jordan knew, the better. He did not want to overwhelm the paralegals for now, but as time passed, they both knew the light would dawn upon them as well.

"When they catch on, Raymond, we'll have them moved into the Marriott Marquis as well. For now, it's your family, Astoria and Shane, who will be given accommodation." He joked, "I hope you guys rack up enough points and nights to become platinum members."

"You know this is scary, right, Andrew! I mean, I've never heard of this arrangement, and now everyone around me has to move. It's like a safe house but in the open," said Raymond.

Andrew looked at Raymond and realised he had caught on. This was not just a case; it was a mission. Soon, international courts and law enforcement agencies across the globe would be on the hunt for the perpetrators. As they navigated this ordeal, lives could be lost, secrets exposed, and loyalties severely tested. Trust would become a rare commodity. Andrew needed his best team far from the reach of anyone who could jeopardise their safety. Over the years, he had learned that one of the most effective disguises was hiding in plain sight.

"Raymond, there is something about me that only a handful of people know. I used to be a police officer at one point in time. I got tired of the mess and the corruption in the system, so I left the force for good. But the instinct never left me," said Andrew.

"What! You were a cop?" remarked Raymond.

"Why do you sound scared? Have you been on the wrong side of the law?" joked Andrew.

Raymond instinctively defended his expression and responded, saying, "I'm not scared, Andrew. I'm just appalled. You know, you don't give out the cop energy, so to speak."

"Well, once you take on the black coat and start working behind a desk, a certain sense of refinement sets in, but the instinct remains."

"So what does your instinct say?"

"My lawyer instinct says this case is a gold mine. If we hit the nail on its head, our firm will be swimming in money."

"And your cop instinct?" asked Raymond.

"Don't get killed," responded Andrew, with both eyebrows raised, signifying he meant what he said.

Raymond went cold. His eyes widened in disbelief, and the hairs on his arms stood on end. His life had never been in danger.

He was happy dealing with the SEC, the courts, occasionally with the Cayman Islands Monetary Authority, and the banks. But this… this was something else. International criminals? Warlords who put bounties on people's heads? This wasn't the world he'd signed up for.

"I'm not telling anyone about this conversation. I neither have any intent on having my wife live her life having one eye in the rear-view mirror to see who is following her, nor forcing my team to work in fear. If lives are at stake, Andrew, I suggest we leave Astoria, Shane, and the paralegals out of this mess. Since I am the only one working the case, I'll assume all the research and communication at my end. Nothing is ever perfect, and I cannot sleep at night knowing each decision I take has the possibility of endangering the lives of my team."

"I trust your judgement, Raymond. And, Ron and I are always going to support you. Our lives are at as much stake as yours. So, I believe you are making the right decision," said Andrew.

Raymond knew it was horse shit. If their lives were in danger, they would be operating from a corner of the world he hadn't even heard of. But he needed to be civil and knew the next few weeks were a test of his patience. In a calm voice, he said, "Looks like we're going to have each other's backs like always."

"Always, Raymond! Take care, my friend."

Chapter 3

If Vegas was the home of gambling, then New York was the home of hedge funds. There were stark similarities between a gambler in Vegas and a Hedge Fund mogul in New York, both wanting to make a fortune, fuelled by greed. They both had one goal—winning it all by risking it all.

Mike Frazier was a mathematician by profession. He had thick brown hair and stood at a height of six feet one inch. He was clean-shaven and a marathon runner. Damien Brown, a thirty-six-year-old Harvard finance graduate, stood at six feet with black hair and a salt-and-pepper beard. Gary Hughes, a Chartered Financial Analyst, was moderately tall at five feet eight inches. He, however, was the sharpest of them all and spent his spare time lifting weights at the gym. The three of them were the General Partners of Lions Star Capital that handled investments amounting to about $300 billion. They had two offices, one in New York and the other in San Francisco. Their hedge funds operated from New York, and their office in San Francisco controlled their private equity portfolio.

The three of them met at a bar and discussed stocks and trading strategies. Soon, they realised they had much more in common than alcohol, and in the summer of 1995, they founded Lions Star Capital. All three of them had their sights set higher than the stars.

They wanted nothing to do with modesty and had dreams of being so rich, that if they wanted to clear out an expensive car showroom in a day, they could do so without batting an eyelid.

For thirteen years, the firm had dominated the investment advisory landscape, outpacing competitors with unmatched prowess. Known as 'The Gifted Investors', the trio at its helm had built a formidable reputation on Wall Street. Their Midas touch ensured every venture yielded substantial returns, delivering consistent returns to investors even amidst market volatility.

The firm's relentless pursuit of excellence left no strategy unexplored, whether strictly legal or skirting the edges of propriety, to ensure its funds consistently outperformed both competitors and the broader market. Entry to their exclusive funds was reserved for the elite: investors must boast a minimum net worth of twenty million dollars, with a baseline investment of at least one million dollars.

Their investors came from all walks of life: real estate moguls, highly paid C-Suite executives, others with generational wealth, and some even from questionable backgrounds. Like their investors, each of them had different methods in which they conducted business. While Mike and Damien were more involved in the private equity business in San Francisco, Gary was the caretaker of the hedge fund portfolio in New York. The three of them met once a month to discuss valuation and business strategy, and also share a few drinks.

It was 15 September 2008, when the three of them met to discuss business operations and future strategy. The housing market had just crashed five days earlier with the bankruptcy of one of the largest banks, exposing various players at all levels in the US market to risk levels that were unheard of since the Great Depression. The subprime loans had been exposed, and the amount due on most of the mortgages exceeded the value of the homes. The American public had defaulted on its loans, and the banks foreclosed on the properties. Little did they know they were sitting on a pool of real estate with no buyers, resulting in falling valuations.

Since the market crashed, the hedge fund portfolio of Lions Star Capital had nosedived about twenty per cent in five days. Many of their competitors had declared bankruptcy, and the only reason they survived was that Gary had liquidated about fifty per cent of the positions based on a tip, he received from a close associate working at the US Federal Reserve.

As the partners discussed the future, Gary suggested a contrarian strategy where they sit on the cash for a while and slowly pump the money back into the market to take advantage of falling valuations. Both Mike and Damien agreed it would be the optimal strategy for the hedge fund portfolio.

However, discussions about the firm's private equity arm revealed a startling oversight. Gary was stunned to learn neither Mike nor Damien had initiated efforts to liquidate any positions or signal intent to sell existing investments, raising concerns about the portfolio's liquidity and strategic alignment.

Gary shot to his feet, his chair screeching backwards. His face flushed with disbelief as he said through gritted teeth, "Are you guys out of your minds? I told you about the tip before the markets collapsed, and you could have easily liquidated some of the positions since we always have takers. What were you thinking?"

Mike responded, "We could have, but we believe we can weather this storm. The world of private equity will take it better than the others."

"Why do you think so? Most of the private companies have leverage in their capital structure and have taken loans from these exact banks. Now that the banks are collapsing left, right, and centre, they too will feel the heat."

Damien intervened and tried to play the peacemaker between the two of them. He apprised Gary about the conversation they had with their major investors and informed them that everyone was caught off guard. They assured the investors they didn't need to worry about their money, and Lions Star Capital would be able to weather the storm.

"I doubt it has helped, because Roman, one of our longstanding investors, called me yesterday and wanted to pull out fifty per cent of his money from all our funds, which includes about two billion dollars from the private equity side."

"Roman is our longstanding investor, but he's not our biggest fish," said Damien.

"Well, what about the big fish?" asked Gary.

"They are swimming well," responded Mike.

Gary looked perplexed and began wondering why the two of them were downplaying such a huge, catastrophic event. They were fighting him tooth and nail for indecision on their part. He mellowed down and asked, "Okay, guys, what's going on? How are you so confident our major investors won't pull out?"

Mike and Damien looked at each other, and it seemed Gary was not privy to something brewing between them. Damien requested that Gary take a seat and calm down. He said, "Well, we've sort of been funnelling money through our funds. We kept this hidden from you because we know it is difficult for you to turn a blind eye when it comes to doing something questionable."

"Questionable is an understatement! Is there dirty money in our funds? Since when has this been going on, and how much are we talking about?"

Damien pulled out his phone and looked at Mike and said, "It's close to ten billion dollars as of this morning. But we didn't move this amount of money around. Since the value of all investments increased, this pool grew along with it."

"Ten fucking billion dollars. Billion with a B? You guys have got to be kidding me. That's how you're able to buy two mansions, two Ferraris, one Lamborghini, and an Audemars Piguet in five years?"

Mike had heard enough about moral policing. He was the short-tempered one and said, "First of all, none of this is our money, and well, you're not a saint either. You sold investments based on *advice* you received from your friend at the Federal Reserve, which is worse than insider trading. Where was your morality then? You're just jealous of the success we have had. And don't forget, you get a share of the carried interest (bonuses paid to the management upon achieving higher than expected returns) and management fees from the private side too."

Gary knew Mike had a volatile personality, but he had never seen this side of him. However, he was right; this was not the first time the firm had acted on inside information. The only difference was that he had done it for the investors, and everyone had benefited. But what they did was abominable.

Damien signalled to Mike to take a walk. He knew the three of them needed to stick together in these trying times. As Mike was smoking a cigarette, Damien put an arm around Gary's shoulder and said, "Look, we know what this looks like, okay. This started a few years ago when Mike lost about twenty-five million dollars in one night while betting. This wasn't even an online bet; he went up against the most notorious gang in the country, *The Draconian Infarction*, colloquially known as "*The Draconists*."

"I thought the *Draconists* were just a legend," said Gary.

"Well, apparently not! And to put it lightly, gambling isn't their only source of income. Of course, ninety per cent of the time, they know what's going to happen, so winning the bet is almost a virtual certainty for them. They manipulate one side of the bet by bribing and then wager their money accordingly. It's cheating, but no one knows about it. Even the bookies are involved, and they get their cut."

What Damien told Gary next made his eyes pop in utter shock. Mike had been beaten and was released not only after paying the twenty-five million dollars but also agreeing to a pact where he would add them as Limited Partners and funnel their money through Lions Star Capital."

"Okay, Damien, humour me now. So, the eight billion dollars round we had in 2004 was actually all the dirty money?" said Gary.

"You caught that one pretty fast, Gary. But not all of it. Some of it was definitely dirty."

It was not difficult for Gary to decipher this since he had a keen eye for detail. He remembered all the money that had flown into the funds and where it was invested—or at least that's what he thought.

"So, now what? Where do we sit now? How are we supposed to tell these knucklehead gamblers that part of their money has vanished?" asked Gary.

"That's where we need your help and all the financial and accounting artillery you have stored in that big brain of yours."

"You want me to cook the books? It's something we've never done. We've exited and entered positions based on tips, but we've never cooked the books. And in this tardy market, we'll get caught too easily. Imagine we're the only firm whose valuations have not fully tanked. On the hedge fund side at least, we have the cash, so not everything is in the ground."

"That's what we were banking on. Can you push some funds from the hedge funds into the private funds, and we can probably appease the *Draconists?*" asked Damien.

The true purpose of the emergency meeting became clear to Gary—it wasn't about the firm's future strategy but a desperate bid to rescue Mike from the grip of the country's most notorious gang. Gary realised Mike's plan to funnel money from the hedge funds into the private equity portfolio was a risky manoeuvre to address his predicament. As Mike entered the room, Gary met him with a sympathetic glance but also raised a critical concern: such a transfer would almost certainly be flagged by auditors, especially with the SEC's inspection looming this year. The firm's reputation and compliance were now at stake, complicating their next moves.

Mike, too, looked concerned now. He had forgotten about the SEC investigation, which was due later in the year. In a perplexed voice, he said, "What do we do now, guys? I guess I fucked it for everyone. Gary, I know Damien has given you an overview of my situation, and I am sorry I brought this upon all of us."

The three of them looked at each other for a few moments, and Gary suggested, "Should we inform Roth & Gotham and request their help in this precarious situation? They have been our longstanding lawyers, and there is no way we're going to get through this alive by ourselves. It's a double-edged sword, and the only way to beat it is to break it."

Although the three of them were doing well, their personal liquidity was not enough to recoup the loss and pay back "the *Draconists*". Mike shivered a bit, thinking about what the *Draconists* would do to him and his family if they found out their money was devalued. He agreed they should come clean to their lawyers, and Mike decided to call Andrew's office.

"Andrew, we're fucked in a way we never thought it was possible. We need immediate assistance," said Mike in a concerned tone.

"Alright, Mike, let's have a chat tomorrow. I'll have my secretary set up some time for you guys."

"Thank you, Andrew!"

"Anytime, Mike, we're always at your service. Talk to you tomorrow when we meet in my office."

Chapter 4

The next day, all the General Partners of Lions Star Capital entered Andrew's home office at 8:00 am. The meeting was scheduled at a place where no one from the office would be around. As they entered, Andrew served them coffee, bagels, eggs, and muffins. The guests were quite happy with the breakfast, but honestly, they didn't care much for hospitality at this time. They were here to tell Andrew how they had shot themselves in the leg and now needed advice on how to cover their asses.

Andrew broke the silence by addressing the three of them, "So, gentlemen, how can I help you?" He assumed they were here about the Wall Street fiasco. He was ready to offer them what he'd told other clients: if bankruptcy seemed inevitable, either find a bootstrapped investor to play white knight, or take the hit and declare bankruptcy. If they chose bankruptcy, they had three options. One: appoint an administrator to turn the business around or sell it. Two: file under Chapter 7, shut down completely, and let a court trustee liquidate assets to repay debts. Three: file under Chapter 11, restructure, and present a repayment plan subject to court and creditor approval, keeping the business afloat, but under watch.

Mike took the lead on behalf of Lions Star Capital and informed Andrew about the dodgy business taking place at the firm. How he got involved in the betting scandal, and how his life was in danger. Due to this, he agreed to sell his soul to the devil.

Andrew stared at him, stunned. His jaw slackened as the words sank in. A betting scandal? Threats to his life? He couldn't fathom how any of this had slipped past their top-tier auditors. After all, they had appointed the best auditors in the world.

"Well, Andrew, when you admit a questionable limited partner, and they invest in your business through a shell company in the Cayman Islands, the anti-money laundering checks come clean, so no one can find out if something was amiss. Plus, it's not the auditor's job to audit the limited partner. They generally send us a sanctions checklist, and we ensure none of our investors are sanctioned investors. We took great care to ensure the auditors don't even get a sniff of what's going on."

"I see! So, this was intentional," remarked Andrew.

Damien intervened and said, "Well, he didn't want this to happen. He had to do this because there was a gun pointed at his head."

"I see you two are quite aligned on this matter," Andrew said, his gaze shifting to Gary. "Gary, were you aware of these colourful and mystifying activities taking place in your San Francisco office?"

Gary looked Andrew right in the eye and said, "No, Andrew, I was not. I was informed yesterday, which is when we decided it would be wise to get you on board. After all, we've been your clients for a long time. I still remember you were the one who drafted our Limited Partnership Agreement, and we trust you and your firm above everyone else."

Andrew asked them whether they wanted to break up the firm and pursue an individual case or fight it out together. The three of them agreed they would fight it together as they always stood by each other, no matter what.

Andrew then moved on to informing them that he would need to take up the matter under advisement and would need to update his longstanding business partner, Ron. He also told them the case would be led by Raymond, who was one of the firm's brightest Senior Associates, and he had immense experience in the financial fraud space. He was up for making Partner, and just about twelve months ago, Raymond had saved one of his clients about one billion dollars in penalties. He assured he would be in constant touch with them, and Raymond was the way to go. The three of them agreed to work with Raymond as they trusted Andrew's impeccable judgement.

"I'll introduce you to Raymond after a week, as he would need time to hand over his ongoing cases to other colleagues. In the meantime, I suggest you entrust the day-to-day activities to some reliable associates, and you three focus all your time and energy on ways to get out of this mess. I don't know how you will do it, but then again, it is the need of the hour. Also, Ron, Raymond, and I will be on this one together, and might I suggest, the fees are going to be much more than usual since we're going to be liaising with various government authorities and dealing with lawless miscreants who might just put out a bounty on your heads."

The meeting lasted over an hour, and after they left, Andrew wished he could execute Mike. But the businessman in him had a smirk on his face. A case like this meant a windfall of money for the firm, and these people were ready to do anything to come out clean. His next order of business was to onboard Ron, but before that, he began researching various laws on money laundering. He knew the three of them had not told him everything, and he had a hunch Mike was hiding much more than what he was ready to divulge. He would need to get Raymond to win Mike's trust so they could help them. It was going to take time, and that's what they didn't have. He knew they needed to act fast. In light of the precarious circumstances their client was in, he scheduled a meeting with Ron the same day at noon.

Andrew entered Ron's office at five minutes to twelve. He was known to always arrive before time. Andrew cut right to the chase and updated Ron as to what he had learnt that morning. One of their most prestigious clients was funnelling dirty money through their funds, and now their lives were in danger. Ron shook his head in disgust and simultaneously agreed with Andrew's plan to onboard Raymond. They decided they would call it a Code Red, which meant the team involved in this project would work from a place other than the office, but hidden in plain sight. They had not activated Code Red in eight years now. The last time it had happened, they had lost their senior associate to murder, and they did not plan on reliving that experience.

"Andrew, once we get Lions Star Capital out of this mess, I won't blame you for referring them to a lower-tier firm that doesn't mind taking this kind of risk. The safety of our people is paramount and more important than any other client."

"I agree, Ron! For now, we'll keep them and get them out of this. It will be a lot of legal fees, and I'm afraid some of it may be dirty."

"Well, it's not our job to check where our clients get their money. Make sure all the money we get from this case runs through the books, and we report every dime in our tax return."

"Got it, Ron! I understand your reasons; we don't want the IRS (Internal Revenue Service) knocking on our doors. And I think this will be the last time Lions Star Capital does something like this."

Andrew entered his office and began researching various provisions of the Anti-Money Laundering Act, SEC rules, CIMA provisions, and then it struck him: this would also fall under criminal law, so he'd have to involve the US government and possibly even have discussions with the Motor Sport Council and the *Fédération Internationale de l'Automobile* (FIA). He realised the case might be heard simultaneously in the USA as well as the High Court in England. Reality dawned upon him—his firm would be dealing with a plethora of legalities, and every department would be circling their heads like a flock of birds. He needed to get Raymond involved immediately, or else he would perish under the mountain of work this case entailed.

Chapter 5

As Raymond was handing over his work, he realised Gregory wasn't that bad of a person after all. Over the course of the week of coordinating with Gregory, Raymond learnt he'd been dealing with mental health issues, and he used his curt mannerisms to cover it up to ensure it didn't hamper his work. His personal life was not stable, and he had not been in a proper relationship for a while. This made Raymond feel sorry for him, but now he had other things demanding his attention.

"Okay, Gregory, thanks for taking up these clients and cases. I'll see you in a few days." The two men bid each other goodbye and headed home.

On his way home, as Raymond was driving his Mercedes across the Oakland Bay Bridge, he realised how much he enjoyed driving. Soon, he was going to be confined to a hotel with five-star service at his fingertips. Luxurious, yes, but it wasn't freedom. It wasn't *this*.

On impulse, he took the long route, veering off and driving an extra thirty miles into the open night. When the road finally cleared, he pressed his foot down hard on the accelerator. The car surged forward, the speedometer climbing past eighty, ninety, then a hundred. He didn't care if a cop pulled him over. Right now, he wasn't a man boxed in by meetings, deals, or deadlines. He was a motorhead chasing velocity, the kind who still tore up go-kart tracks on weekends and followed Formula One like a gospel.

The engine roared, deep and primal, and Raymond smiled. For a fleeting moment, it wasn't about where he was going, but that he *was* going. Fast. Free. He exhaled, the tension bleeding out of his shoulders, and let the night wind rush over him like absolution.

It was finally time to end this escapade, even though he wished he could continue driving for all of eternity. He knew it was going to be at least a few weeks before he would be able to venture out so freely. The case he was asked to work certainly had innumerable intricacies, and he may have to pull off multiple all-nighters. He took an exit and turned his car around to drive back home to Giovana.

It was Friday evening, and the two of them had to pack their bags and move into the Marriott Marquis in the wee hours of the morning. Away from the public eye. As he entered, he was welcomed with a lavish home-cooked meal of salad, roast duck, and chocolate mousse. He opened a bottle of wine, and the two of them discussed how many bags they would need to take.

They knew it was going to be a few weeks. Raymond packed three suits, and Giovana took almost half her wardrobe. It was almost midnight, and Raymond had packed two suitcases with clothes, a laptop, a few books on financial laws, and some light reading material. Giovana, on the other hand, had almost emptied her wardrobe and packed it in four suitcases.

"Looks like someone is planning on a long vacation," remarked Raymond.

"Well, I'm not the one whose client got entangled with thugs. If I'm going in hiding with you, I'm making a vacation out of it."

"You're still so hungry for adventure, G. That's what I love about you."

"Don't push it! You knew I would find this enthralling."

"Knowing your husband is part of a secret mission that can endanger his life is enthralling? My god, what creature have I married?" joked Raymond.

Giovana gave him a sly smirk and threw herself at him. Adventure aroused her, and she didn't shy away from making her intentions clear. The two of them made love as if it were their first night after marriage. They slowly slipped into slumber and were woken by the loud alarm clock that brought them back to reality, realising they had to leave for their *new home*.

They showered, and as Raymond was getting ready to load the bags into the car, three armoured Lincolns showed up in their driveway. Raymond and Giovana were taken aback. Raymond shoved Giovana behind him to cover her from any harm. His eyes pinned on the three Lincolns. Meanwhile, Giovana held his arms and couped up behind him. "Mr and Mrs Holster, we're here from the security department of Roth & Gotham and have come to escort you to your hotel," said one of the security personnel. Raymond looked puzzled because he didn't remember Andrew or Ron talking about Z-level security. Amidst all this commotion, his vibrating phone gave him palpitations. It was Andrew.

"Raymond, I believe our security personnel have reached you. They are your personal security officers for now. They will be leading you to The Ritz at Half Moon Bay. Do not repeat what I just said. Just follow the instructions of the security officers. They will hand you a piece of paper. Treat the information with discretion."

One of the security officers handed Raymond a piece of paper and put a finger on his lips, signalling him to remain quiet. Raymond read the note, "It is possible your residence, car, and phones are being tapped. There might have been a leak, and someone may be aware you're taking on this case. One of the security officers will be taking your car and parking it at the office while you ride with the others. He will be taking your phones with him, and you both will have to use the encrypted ones we gave you a few days ago."

Raymond looked up at Giovana and then at the security guard. They were ushered into the vehicles and asked not to speak a word till they left the driveway. On the way to The Ritz, Raymond called Andrew to ask what the hell was going on.

"How on earth did this get so hot so fast? I mean, we're lawyers performing our duties and doing everything legal," said Raymond.

"I don't know, Raymond! I just got a tip from our head of security, Mark, your car may be bugged. While he was reviewing the security footage of the parking lot, he noticed a mysterious man bending down and extending his arm under your car," replied Andrew.

"When did this happen? How was an unknown man allowed to enter the building? Every day, I am frisked at the entrance as if I'm a fugitive, but an unknown son of a bitch can bypass security like a ghost."

"These guys are good, Raymond. Anyway, we caught on to it, and you're going to be safe now. We made a similar arrangement at The Ritz in Half Moon Bay. We had to pull a few strings, but the safety of our people is of prime importance. Make sure you and Giovana enjoy the luxuries of this fine hotel," said Andrew.

"Fine hotel, my ass," thought Raymond. He ended the call by thanking Andrew in an agitated voice, but he now knew he had to have an eye out for anything that looked amiss and everything that didn't. The security guard, Joe, told them that since their car was bugged, they suspected the phone lines could be bugged too. He agreed this was an uncomfortable situation to be dealing with, and he sympathised with the Holsters. Two of the other security guards would be checking to see whether their residence was bugged or not.

The Ritz was about a thirty-minute drive from their home, and Giovana always wanted to visit for a weekend, but not under such compelling circumstances. As they crossed San Mateo, the car took a right onto J. Arthur Younger Freeway. Joe said they would be entering through the back entrance away from the public eye. He would be disguised as one of the hotel's security guards and would be on duty and ready to defend them. He said he was a former US Marine but could not reveal the missions he had been part of. Raymond and Giovana were glad they had Joe by their side. Raymond had forgotten all about his Mercedes and began strategising how he would defend his client. He also realised they needed an exit strategy in case things got out of hand.

Meanwhile, Ron had already arranged for the General Partners of Lions Star Capital to meet Raymond at a secluded spot. He had convinced them that the meeting place would be secret and they would be transported in three different lorries owned by the firm. Additionally, they would need to keep their phones at the office of Roth & Gotham to avoid being trailed. They looked like ordinary delivery lorries from the outside, but inside, the comfort was nothing short of a private jet. It was business class on wheels with seats so comfortable anyone could sleep like a baby and a bar so ostentatious it had almost every expensive bottle of single malt. They had their catering staff set out a luxury buffet for the clients.

Behind all this luxury, Mike, Damien, and Gary didn't realise the view of the outside world leading to the meeting point had conveniently been blocked. Ron knew the three of them were suckers for luxury, and no one could resist free food and alcohol. But he didn't care about the cost, as all of this would be billed back to them as out-of-pocket expenses. He had found a way to transport these three schmucks without them knowing where they were going and without being asked too many questions.

As Raymond and Giovana reached The Ritz, they were hidden under a kitchen trolley and escorted to the hotel's Firepit suite. The suite was 1,000 square feet of pure luxury. The linen was as soft as velvet, and it came equipped with an onyx dining table, comfortable dining chairs, a couch setting for four, a sixty-five-inch television with two lounging chairs, a table, and a fireplace on the balcony. The bathroom was decked with white marble, and it came with a luxurious tub. Raymond and Giovana looked at each other and realised they could get accustomed to this luxury, but in a few days, Giovana would long for the comfort of their home.

As they walked onto the balcony, they noticed the surrounding area was rich with natural resources and beauty. The hotel pamphlet stated guests could savour the Northern California sunset, and Raymond and Giovana decided to sip some wine while overlooking the setting sun, especially with such a dreadful start to the day. Giovana decided to get a massage at the spa, and Raymond decided he would utilise the gym and take a nap. Arrangements were made so the two of them would not come into contact with too many hotel guests. A separate spa and gym were arranged for the two of them. And although that was not something they particularly fancied, they preferred safety over socialising.

Andrew apprised Raymond that the meeting with the mysterious client would take place at three in the afternoon at a secluded place. He would be transported in the armoured Lincoln, and he was supposed to keep the details of his whereabouts a secret. There was a secure internet connection set up in the suite for the two of them, and they were asked not to connect to the hotel Wi-Fi. The couple was slightly terrified, but at the same time, happy that every possible area of security was being covered.

Each call with Andrew made Raymond more aware of just how deep the hole was—and how much trouble he was truly in. And this was *before* he had even met the client.

Chapter 6

As Andrew, Mike, Damien, and Gary were making their way to the meeting place, Raymond heard a knock on the room door. Joe was on the other end and said they needed to leave in thirty minutes for the meeting. Raymond showered and got dressed. He threw on a white shirt and his black suit, paired with a grey and maroon tie. He was ready in twenty minutes, and Joe accompanied him through the back entrance into the car. Once Raymond was in the car, Joe informed him that the meeting was going to be held at a secluded location, and the client wasn't aware of its exact address. He updated Raymond about the arrangements Ron had made to ensure this place remained hidden from the client.

"At this time, Mr Holster, we cannot risk anyone knowing where you are staying. Since your car was probably bugged, we are to believe the *Draconists* know you are the lawyer representing the client," said Joe.

"Do you know the name of the client? "questioned Raymond.

"I don't know the name of the client. In fact, I don't know which vehicle is carrying the client. I am only told to ensure your safety and take you to the places you need to be taken," responded Joe.

"Thank you, Joe."

"Anytime, boss."

Andrew and Raymond reached the facility before the client did. This was orchestrated on purpose so the client remained unaware of the vehicles used by Raymond and Andrew. The facility was situated on the outskirts of the city of Modesto, California. Ron had built a luxury getaway on the piece of land owned by his family. The house was spread across twenty thousand square feet, and it had a parking lot that could accommodate about ten vehicles. It came with a front lawn and a backyard with plush green grass, a swimming pool, and a barbecue.

The mansion's entrance featured a stony path stretched from the parking lot to the main door. At the heart of the manicured front lawn stood a majestic fountain adorned with angels, its design echoing classic Italian architecture. But they didn't go through the front. Instead, they were led around to the backyard and down into the basement.

To Raymond's surprise, the space was a near replica of the firm's San Francisco conference room. In the centre stood an oval-shaped, polished oak table surrounded by ten executive chairs. An eighty-five-inch television was mounted on the wall, and a high-speed internet connection ensured everything ran smoothly. Through Andrew, Raymond learned many of the firm's meetings with the platinum clients were held here, away from the noise and scrutiny of the city.

The clock struck three when Mike, Damien, and Gary entered the room. The five men shook hands, and Andrew introduced Raymond to the three of them.

"Raymond, they are Mike, Damien, and Gary. They are the General Partners of Lions Star Capital. Gentlemen, this is Raymond, our most charismatic and dynamic senior associate, who will be handling your case and working full-time on it. Of course, I am always available for you," said Andrew.

"I have heard of Lions Star Capital, and you're literally one of the most profitable asset managers on Wall Street. I look forward to working with you," remarked Raymond.

The three of them smiled, knowing how much was based on inside information. However, they accepted the compliment nonetheless. Once Andrew had made the introductions, he excused himself, saying he had to take care of some other business, and the three of them were in safe hands with Raymond, who would stay in touch with all of them. Once Andrew left, Raymond told them how much he knew about what was going on, and he would need to know all the details of how and when the laundering started.

Mike lit his cigar and said, "Well, that is going to take some time, and I don't think one meeting is enough." Raymond had been warned by Andrew that Mike would try to be the arrogant son of a bitch he was, and there would be times he would need to put him in his place.

Raymond realised he needed to assert dominance in the meeting and said, "I think we would all agree time is one thing which is not in your favour. If you don't want the *Draconists* to drag you down to your grave, you would be smart enough to tell me everything. Because that's the only way I can protect you." Mike's eyes widened, and his blinking paused. He had never been spoken to in this manner. But he knew he was running on thin ice. He apologised to Raymond and began explaining how he got into the mess. He explained how one wrong bet of twenty-five million dollars had hung his neck on a permanent noose. This made him nothing short of a puppet.

"But twenty-five million is not a big amount for you, is it?"

"Well, I was short on cash at the time. Had the bet worked in my favour, I would have pocketed about $100 million. I had just bought a yacht and a mansion, so liquidity was tight."

Raymond realised that royalty, too, had a price. The flipside of this coin was vice. "Well, what happened once you paid them?" asked Raymond.

"It took me three days to arrange the money, and for these three days, I was tied to a chair in a place I don't know. I went through hell and met the devil. During my captivity, they asked me all sorts of questions and even beat me up to extract information about the firm. Once they knew I used to manage private equity funds, their leader, Victor, untied me but had his accomplice point a gun at my head," responded Mike.

'What happened then?"

"He told me he would give me a month to come up with a plan to transfer money through our funds for manipulating results in Formula One racing as well as other activities he did not want to talk about."

Raymond was curious why a notorious criminal was interested in manipulating the results of Formula One. He'd never heard of something like this. "Mike, did he tell you why he chose F1 to gamble his money?"

"You see, when there is a gun pointed at your head, your only concern is getting out alive."

Raymond nodded in approval, and as the two of them spoke, Damien and Gary were whispering between themselves. It looked like there were details of the story Mike had kept to himself. He got to know Victor had a younger brother, Jerome, whom he loved beyond his own life. He had a thriving real estate business in Florida, the Cayman Islands, and the British Virgin Islands. He devised a plan where some of the shell corporations controlled by

Jerome would become limited partners in the funds managed by Lions Star Capital. Raymond had enough experience to know this was a common practice.

"And Victor was to deliver the cash from illicit activities to Florida, right?" remarked Raymond.

Mike smirked and arrogantly said, "Looks like someone knows how offshore transactions work."

"To defend my clients, I need to think like them," remarked Raymond. He realised he'd won Mike's trust, and this was a big win for him.

Mike understood Raymond was not naive, and Andrew had given them the best. He explained that once the cash reached Florida, Jerome would use a *hawala* transaction to transfer the money to the Cayman Islands. His associates in the Cayman Islands would then break down the money into small portions and deposit it into various bank accounts operated by individuals. These offshore corporations would then, in turn, transfer the money to other entities and finally enter the bank account of Excalibur Investments, the offshore corporation controlled by Jerome and Victor. This entity was one of the Limited Partners in Lions Star Capital.

"What happens once you guys receive the money?" asked Raymond.

"Well, Victor gives me names of various entities to *invest* in. He told me these funds were linked to other investment funds owned and controlled by the bookies, as well as some people who are connected to Formula One Teams."

Raymond was perplexed, and his mouth was half open in complete bewilderment. Mike continued to explain that all money was broken down into various investments, and finally, they reached a few investment funds having single owners. Once the money reached these funds, the owner could do whatever he wanted with the money. They would mostly invest it in companies which, after a few years, would go bankrupt out of the blue. These bankrupt companies would be owned and controlled by the relatives of the single owner's funds, so money remained in the family.

"Initially, the valuation of these companies would grow exponentially to the point where the investment manager preferred to keep the cash invested. This was, of course, just in the records," explained Mike.

"Why would the investment manager want to remain invested?"

"Because he, too, got a cut in the form of cash. In case the manager was not easy to reach, the money would be transported through a *hawala* transaction. Where this was not possible, anonymous charitable donations would be made to religious institutions that were falsely set up to launder money."

"You're saying this racket involves investment managers who have set up religious trusts and corporations just to keep the dirty money clean and rig Formula One results?"

"You see, manipulating Formula One results is just his way of having fun because he can. I just know he gets loads of cash, which he needs to wash up. Once he knows what is going to happen, he places his bets with various bookies and often collects the grand prize."

"What does he do with all this money?"

"Well, the money he wins from betting is then rolled into other illicit activities. The *Draconists* are known to be knee deep in every crime occurring in the United States."

Raymond once had a feeling there had to be more to this, and now his doubts were confirmed. Lions Star Capital was merely a pawn in the whole ecosystem run by Victor.

"Look, guys, all this is complicated and dangerous. What I don't understand is where Victor gets the cash from. He's got to be involved in a lot of shit," said Raymond.

"Yeah, the *Draconists* are infamously regarded as the brokers of crime. They broker deals for the drug cartels, terrorist groups, and anything illegal requiring some *professional intervention*."

"How much money have you pushed through your books?" questioned Raymond.

"Well, all in, we pushed about ten billion dollars, and as of this morning, we owe them about four."

"But you were constantly moving it off to the funds they instructed you to, right? How then is such a big amount sitting in your books? Because you were the middleman, right!"

"Well, you see, although the firm got a cut of about one per cent, I convinced them to let me invest some of it so he could earn some money out of it, which also increased our management fee and share of carried interest. You've got to help us, Raymond; Victor told me he hates losses. If he becomes aware that his four billion is now worth two billion, he's going to have me murdered. The crash in the market resulted in the devaluation of the investments, and there is nothing I can do."

Damien and Gary looked as though they had just heard a death sentence. Mike turned towards his partners and said, "Guys, I am so sorry to have done this. I should have formed another entity and operated it by myself. But these guys were pumping in the money, and I let greed take over."

Gary shot back and bellowed, "Damn right you should have done this on your own." This was the first time in many years that Mike and Damien heard Gary lose his cool. And he was right in doing so. Even Damien was in the dark about the depths of these illegalities. To calm the two of them down, Mike said he would take full responsibility for it. If they decided to invoke the dissolution clause in the partnership agreement and ask him to resign, he would understand.

This wasn't the first time Raymond had to play the role of peacemaker in his professional life. Over the years, he had seen more than his fair share of partners and associates bickering across boardroom tables. Calmly, he laid out the recommendation from Roth & Gotham: come clean to the appropriate authorities, cooperate fully in exchange for immunity, agree to become confidential informants, and, if necessary, enter the witness protection programme.

After delivering the firm's stance, Raymond stepped out and gave them space to talk, argue, and decide what their future would look like.

Chapter 7

As Raymond walked out of the room, he contacted Andrew and Ron and stated he had advised their client to come clean with the authorities. He informed them the four billion dollars of dirty money had halved in its value, which was why these guys panicked.

Raymond continued, "Although the *Draconists* signed the partnership agreement through their offshore vehicle, Victor doesn't care about the valuation. He just wants his money. He's probably going to hang Mike by the noose if he doesn't get his four billion dollars back. I hope these three can stick by each other, or else we might have to pick sides amongst them, and that won't be a pretty place to be in. One good thing is, none of the hedge fund money was poured into the private side, so those funds appear to be clean."

Andrew was relieved to know they had the brains not to intermingle the hedge and private equity funds. He reminded Raymond they represent the firm and not the partners individually, so if the firm continues, then they represent the firm, and if any of them decide to go their own way, they will need to consult their own general counsel.

"Although we would extend support to the extent possible, our loyalty lies with the client and not towards any of these schmucks," said Ron.

Inside the room, Gary was still furious because he had been caught off guard, and even Damien looked confused because he didn't realise four billion was still sitting in their books. Although when compared to the size of the funds, it was barely five per cent, this five per cent could be the nail in the coffin for them. The three of them decided it was best to follow Raymond's advice and come clean. They would find a way to negotiate with the authorities and, in exchange, deliver the *Draconists*. It would be a win-win situation for them. There might be a fine for the management company, and maybe Mike would be banned from Wall Street for a few years, but that was better than getting killed by some scumbag.

Meanwhile, not much had shifted for the *Draconists*, but for Jerome, the ground was crumbling beneath his feet. The housing market crash had hit hard, and he was now neck-deep in a financial crisis spiralling out of control. His buyers, once eager and locked in, were backing out in large numbers.

Contracts were being torn apart, and Jerome was now legally obligated to return their hefty deposits.

The problem? He didn't have that kind of clean, liquid money lying around. Most of his money was tied up in future projects, locked into development timelines, or stuck with contractors who had no intention of paying him back. The cash flow had turned into a slow trickle, then stopped altogether.

Across the market, it was carnage. Customers were defaulting, banks were foreclosing, and real estate developers were left with unsold inventory that couldn't move. No one was buying, and no one could afford to. With nowhere to offload the foreclosed properties, banks were now saddled with rapidly devaluing assets;

ghost buildings with no takers. The entire ecosystem was choking, and Jerome was caught right at its breaking point.

Jerome contacted Victor and said the money was drying up because of the crash, and he needed some liquidity. It was the right time to call up their friend at Lions Star Capital and cash out that four billion. Mike's phone started buzzing, but he wasn't aware of it. Ron noticed it was Victor's call. He realised things could soon get out of hand. He instantly rang up his team at Modesto and informed Raymond that Mike's phone was ringing like a call centre, and it was Victor on the other end.

Raymond entered the room, and Damien informed him they had decided to go ahead with the advice of Roth & Gotham. But they would need full immunity in exchange for the information and evidence they supplied. Raymond thanked his stars that the client took his advice and requested some time to set up meetings with the relevant representatives. Once they reached a consensus, the authorities would reach out to the FIA and let them know of the betting scandal, and then see how they proceed.

"Guys, let me tell you, this is going to be dangerous. Each department has an ego as grand as the Colosseum. We're going to have to take it one step at a time. I know a couple of people at the SEC and believe Ron and Andrew are connected with some people on Capitol Hill. Also, Mike, we'll have to come up with a strategy for how you will respond to Victor. Your cell phone has been continuously ringing. Try and come up with an excuse for returning his call late," said Raymond.

Mike froze. Eyes bulging and heart racing. He'd never been this scared in his life. Ron had technical support on-site who set up a secure connection through which Mike contacted Victor.

Victor was the leader of the *Draconists*. His presence was intimidating, and his personality compressed the room into silence. He had a visible scar on his right cheek that showed he was a survivor. He was well-groomed and had a sharp goatee. He'd make the world bend in front of him. He never backed down from any challenge. He rarely blinked. He had a predatory instinct and made sure his opponents were intimidated. He barely had any weaknesses and was a personification of brute force.

"Where the hell have you been, you asshole? I've been trying to reach you for the last two hours," barked Victor.

"I'm sorry, Victor, my phone was on silent and I was in a meeting with my business partners."

"I don't care if you're in your grave. When I call, you answer, understand?"

"I understand, Victor."

"Now, Jerome tells me the markets have crashed, and everything has gone to shit."

"Well, the housing crisis..."

"Shut the fuck up, you little bitch! I don't care what happens in your world. In my world, you owe me four billion dollars. Now, I want to cash out. Start sending that money. My guys are going to send you the transfer details, and this time, we need the money in ten days."

"Ten days! That's not enough time for such a big amount. I need at least a month to spread those payments," said Mike.

"Hey fuck-face, I am the one who calls the shots, not you. Ten days means ten days," shouted Victor and ended the call.

Mike started crying, and Damien and Gary stood startled. This was the first time they had heard Victor's voice. Anyone would have wet their pants if they were in Mike's shoes. Raymond asked Mike how much money could be transferred, and he said all the funds held in cash were about two billion, and he had about half a billion in liquid assets. Damien and Gary had about $300 million each. They were still short by about $900 million, which was not easy to get in this choppy market, since valuations were falling and no one had the cash to buy investments.

"How do you guys have so much cash just lying around?" asked Raymond.

Gary was quick to respond, saying, "We cashed out some of our investments and are yet to deploy those funds."

Mike said the fund just received a huge transfer from Jerome's offshore shell corporations, and they had sold some public stock that was received as in-kind distributions. "I hope that answers your question about the large cash balance," said Mike.

Raymond, too, began to look concerned and said, "Look, guys, the last call was recorded, so we have him threatening you on tape, but that's not enough to convict him since he is a limited partner and can demand his money back. I suggest you start transferring the money once they send the details so they don't get a whiff of what's going on. Meanwhile, you work on arranging the deficit from friends and family. I'll talk to Ron and Andrew to start working on arranging a meeting with the authorities."

Andrew, Ron, and Raymond met in his room in the Ritz. They agreed it would be better to inform the Department of Justice (DOJ) and the FBI first, and then speak with the SEC. They knew the SEC would not want to give up on Lions Star Capital. They would need the DOJ and FBI to pressure the SEC into catching a bigger fish.

Andrew placed a call to a long-time contact at the DOJ, while Ron got on the phone with the FBI's white-collar crime division, briefing them on a potential informant—one who was ready to flip and deliver someone sitting near the top of the nation's most wanted list in financial crimes.

The DOJ and FBI were intrigued to know the name of this group and were pushing them to reveal the identity of this fugitive.

But Ron and Andrew insisted they would first test the waters by meeting them, and only once there was consensus would they make the introductions with Lions Star Capital. The meeting was scheduled to take place at a black site operated jointly by the DOJ and FBI for the upcoming Monday. As a precaution, Ron and Andrew decided Raymond would sit this one out. The stakes were too high, and if the meeting went sideways, they couldn't risk exposing him—especially when his future role might require a cleaner profile.

Chapter 8

On Monday morning, just before dawn, Andrew and Ron were picked up outside their San Francisco office by two unmarked vehicles that looked like ordinary US mail delivery vans. Deceptively plain, but unmistakably secure. Without a word, they were ushered into the back, separated from the drivers by a reinforced black partition. There were no windows—just dim, overhead lights and a cold silence that made the thirty-minute ride feel like hours. The location of the black site was top secret, and they weren't taking any chances.

When the vans finally came to a halt, the back doors opened with a mechanical hiss. Two heavily armed operatives signalled them to step out. The air was thick with tension, the kind that comes from entering a place that doesn't officially exist.

Inside, the facility had clinical concrete walls, biometric scanners, and no sign of the outside world. They were led into a soundproof conference room where two men were waiting:

Walter and Gordon.

Walter, sharp-eyed and composed, held a presence that immediately commanded the room. A forty-five-year-old Yale law graduate and an expert prosecutor turned military strategist. He'd brought down drug empires and trafficking rings with surgical precision. Every win was logged, but few were ever publicised. He wasn't in it for glory; he was in it to clean the rot. He was well-groomed and had a light stubble. Standing at five feet and ten inches, his calm demeanour was a charade since his green eyes saw through the deeds of others.

Gordon, in stark contrast, was a storm in human form. A six-foot ex-Marine, lean and lethal, with the controlled energy of someone who'd seen too much and never let it show. A human predator whose file said "marksman," but on the ground, he was executioner, strategist, and blunt force all rolled into one. Even in a room full of armed agents, Gordon was the one people instinctively avoided making eye contact with. He measured the world through his killer instincts. With a short, neatly buzzed haircut and a couple of tattoos on his strongly built arms, his stiff jawline talked of military prowess.

Together, they operated the joint DOJ-FBI task force, unofficially dubbed *The Bounty Hunters*. Ruthless, efficient, and fiercely patriotic, their mission was simple: make America safer by any means necessary. In the past few years, they'd dismantled syndicates, locked away warlords in federal black holes, and executed high-value targets without hesitation. Their methods weren't up for debate. Their results were unparalleled.

Today, they weren't just meeting with Ron and Andrew—they were sizing them up. Trust had to be earned, and here, survival wasn't guaranteed.

The clock had started ticking.

The meeting started, and without exchanging too many pleasantries, Walter and Gordon got right down to business. They were facing a lot of heat from John Parx, the Attorney General, and the President due to the growing crime rate, and they wanted some of the heat taken off their backs. With the elections coming up in a few months, there was extreme pressure on all departments to deliver, and they needed to please their bosses.

Ron informed them that one of their clients was entangled in a mess where they were being forced to funnel dirty money through their books, and the money was being used to manipulate Formula One races. Also, the money that was being funnelled was definitely dirty, but they didn't know to what extent. If Walter was the brain, then Gordon was the brawn of any operation they undertook. Walter picked up on the scent and said, "So with the market crashing and cash drying up, your client is now willing to sell out their dirty friends? Easy, isn't it!"

"It might appear so, but the client was coerced and threatened with dire circumstances. The perpetrators would often threaten him with drastic actions, and he was being coerced," said Andrew.

"Well, why come out now, and who is your client going to deliver to us, the *Draconists*?" questioned Gordon.

With conviction and confidence, Ron exclaimed, "Yes, Gordon, they are going to deliver the *Draconists*."

"You're shitting us, right! The *Draconists* are the brokers in the world of crime," remarked Gordon. His gaze locked on Ron, and his jaw stiffened.

"Why would we involve you guys if we weren't serious?"

"The *Draconists*, huh?"

"Yup, the *Draconists*. We know exactly how they launder the money and which vehicles the money goes through. We know they use multiple offshore accounts which pump money into some private equity funds. These funds, in turn, invest, so to speak, in other funds and investment vehicles that the *Draconists* want. That's just a summary. If you agree to give our client full immunity and witness protection, our client is ready to give you names, account numbers, and transaction details. The ball is in your court now—take it or leave it."

Walter, not wanting to give out his intrigue, kept a stern face and, without blinking or flinching, said, "We will decide who gets immunity and who doesn't. But before that, we're going to need proof."

Ron, the ever-so-experienced lawyer, said, "If you can't even assure immunity for our clients, then we're walking off, and you get nothing. You can't search our office premises since no crime has been committed there, and we're not the perpetrators, so good luck. Further, we're bound by attorney-client privilege, so we know your threats are baseless."

Gordon and Walter looked at each other as if they had hit the jackpot, but they couldn't offer any deals until they received the go-ahead from up top. They said they would need to check internally and only then confirm if something could be worked out. Looking at their faces, Ron and Andrew knew the meeting had gone well, and they would soon be having another meeting to discuss the details.

As Ron and Andrew were being dropped off at the office, Gordon and Walter had already contacted the Attorney General's secretary, Frank, and requested a meeting concerning national security. No other details were revealed, but John knew these guys would never ask for an impromptu meeting unless it was significant. They took the next flight to Washington, D.C. and stayed overnight at the government guesthouse. They sipped bourbon while salivating at finally having a confidential informant against Victor and his gang.

The next morning, they were heading up the stairs of the Robert F. Kennedy Department of Justice Building, and as they entered the office of the Attorney General, they were asked to wait outside. After fifteen minutes, John greeted them and welcomed them into his office.

"So, what brings you both to my office, and what was the matter on national security that could not have been a phone call?" said John.

Gordon, in a composed voice, said, "We have a way to get them, Sir."

"Who?"

"The *Draconists*, sir! We have a meeting with a possible confidential informant who is ready to give us all the transaction details about how the *Draconists* are laundering money through various investment vehicles and manipulating the results of the Formula One races."

"Well, that means we'll have to involve the heads of Formula One, but that's just bribing."

Walter interjected, "It's Formula One betting for a start. But, sir, the proceeds of crime are being moved around. Once we have them for one thing, we'll be able to link all the other illegal activities. The rap sheet is going to be nothing short of a thesis. And we'll have them in for so long they'll be born in prison in their next life."

"We better ensure we get these guys. Next year is the election year and the President will want to flaunt this victory in his election campaign. Also, what is the name of the informant?"

Gordon and Walter informed the Attorney General about a complication. During their meeting with the informant's lawyers, Roth & Gotham, at the black site the previous day, they learned the client would only be willing to cooperate if granted immunity and witness protection. John looked displeased and remarked, "Well, you guys really know how to rile someone up and then tell them it's a negotiation." He however understood negotiation is always part of the process and with no quid pro quo, the world wouldn't revolve. He agreed to have his office prepare an immunity agreement, assuming the information was legitimate. If it turned out to be false, Gordon and Walter were to arrest the informant for money laundering, exposing their books and all the shady transactions that took place behind the shroud of a private equity fund. Although investor confidence would be lost, honesty would prevail.

The two of them boarded the 6:00 pm American Airlines flight from Washington, D.C. to San Francisco. On the way, Walter drank a Chivas Regal neat, and Gordon enjoyed a gin and tonic. They were not supposed to talk business on the flight since everything they did was confidential and a lot of it related to national security. They talked about baseball and discussed the upcoming elections while taking a few naps in the middle. As they landed in San Francisco, they made their way to their respective homes and reached the black site at 7:00 am the next day. By half past eight, they received the draft immunity agreements in their email from the Attorney General's office. They reviewed them to ensure everything made sense. All they needed to do was give the names of their confidential informant, and John himself would sign those agreements. This meant the President was on board, and now the success of this operation was going to be a key matter in the upcoming elections. By 9:00 am, the technical expert of the black site raised an alarm— he had just received a call from the President's office. It was patched to Gordon and Walter's receiver, and the President was on the other line.

"Good morning, gentlemen!"

"Good morning, Mr President."

"I believe you have received the draft immunity agreements. Now, I want this operation wrapped up before the voting commences for the elections. Remember, each incoming President reviews all the special task forces sanctioned by the outgoing President, so if you want to keep your jobs, you damn well know what to deliver.

I want the *Draconists*, and I don't care if you get them dead or alive."

"Got it, Mr President. We're trying our best," said Gordon.

"Your best better be enough. Thank you and good luck."

Once the call ended, Gordon said, "That guy thinks it's child's play, right? As if we're going to wave a magic wand and Victor is going to walk into our office and surrender himself."

"Well, I guess we have our work cut out. I'm calling Ron and telling him we have the immunity agreements ready. But their client signs it after they tell us everything," said Walter.

"What if they insist on signing it before?" asked Gordon.

"We tell them to shove it. If they came to us, it means their ass is already on fire," remarked Walter.

Walter contacted Ron and informed him that the immunity agreements were drafted, and the only detail left was the name of the informant. Once the informant reveals the information to them and they are satisfied with it, only then will the agreements be provided for signature. Ron blasted back, "Do you think we were born yesterday, Walter? If our client reveals everything and you don't present the agreements but instead show them the door to the jail cell, then we're fucked. The only way is that the agreements are signed first, and then the information is revealed."

Ron and Walter went back and forth for about five minutes but reached a truce: part of the transaction details of the *Draconists* would be presented first, and only once the government was satisfied would the agreements be signed. This way, if the government decided not to honour their end of the bargain, they would have something to go with and the informant's identity would remain hidden. Walter and Gordon were salivating at the thought of having some of the transaction details to scrutinise.

Andrew contacted Mike and told him about the conversation they had just had. Mike was relieved to know their names would be released only if the task force was satisfied with the information.

Over the next four hours, Andrew, Ron, and Raymond worked with Mike, Damien, and Gary to the obtain bank transfer details supplied by Victor over the past years. The wire transfer details that could be traced back to Lions Star Capital were carefully omitted. Once the document was ready, the lawyers suggested that they not give out the details of the names of shell companies in the Cayman Islands, as these were the limited partners in the funds and their details could lead back to Lions Star Capital.

Once the details were ready, Ron contacted Walter and informed him that some information was ready to be revealed. They were ready to provide twenty per cent of the names and account numbers controlled by the *Draconists*. Walter and Gordon instinctively connected with John and told him the informant was ready to share twenty per cent of the bank account details, and once they were satisfied, the immunity agreements would be executed. John was thrilled they were being supplied with some information for free. As the names and account details reached Gordon and Walter, they were able to pull up the information from the criminal database. Almost all of the names on the list were somehow connected to a crime somewhere in the world. Gordon and Walter realised they would need to contact the intelligence services of the United Kingdom as well.

John's secretary, Frank, was given strict instructions that if any call was received from Gordon or Walter, the same was to be patched immediately, even if he was talking to the President. Frank's phone rang once again. It was Walter. He swiftly patched the line to John, and Walter informed him the names given by the informant had raised alarm bells at the black site. Almost all the names were somehow linked to international crime; they would need to conduct a joint mission with America's CIA and the United Kingdom's MI6. John got the President online and updated him as well.

The President sounded delighted and said, "Let's get these guys their agreements and put them in witness protection. In the meantime, I will speak with my counterpart in the UK and try and get them on the same page as us. Although convincing them should not be a problem since Formula One is a lucrative sport for them. Catching the *Draconists* is going to be advantageous for everyone. It's a win-win, boys, great work."

Chapter 9

Ron and Andrew were relieved when the government finally agreed to sign the immunity agreements, and their clients would be placed in witness protection. They contacted the General Partners of Lions Star Capital and gave them the good news. Mike and Damien were picked up from their respective homes and escorted to the black site. Gary, who resided in New York and was temporarily staying at The Palace Hotel in the heart of San Francisco, was also transported there. The three of them could see the difference between the lorries provided by Roth & Gotham and the vans provided by the government: worn-out seats, creaking brakes, and a reckless driver operating the wheel. And even though these were not half as comfortable as those, there was a sense of calm that took over them. The fact that they were about to sign the immunity agreements and be transferred into witness protection until the *Draconists* were caught was rather comforting. They began to see some benefits of living on the right side of the law.

At the beginning of their journey, one of the agents blindfolded them to obscure their vision and ensured they could neither see the route nor the location of the black site. They were led underground along a staircase, and the black cloth was lifted once they were in the interrogation room. The air was thick and cold. The low ceilings and concrete walls were crammed together with unmarked rooms and corridors sprawling like a city hidden away. A few cramped interview rooms contained nothing but tables and chairs. The rooms were protected with bulletproof glass. Doors that could be opened only from the outside. The technology looked elite and previously unseen. Screens were turned away from sightlines, monitored by expert engineers and analysts. The staff consisted of tech analysts and fully-suited, well-built military operatives. Walter and Gordon watched as the rich kids from Wall Street struggled in their newfound environment. While this was transpiring, Andrew, Raymond, and Ron entered as well. They were transported in separate vans to ensure everyone connected to the case remained secure. They greeted Walter and Gordon, and Raymond introduced himself as the lead attorney on the case.

Mike, the ever-arrogant one, looked at Raymond and blurted, “What is this place? Why are we being treated like criminals?” Gordon glared at him with disgust.

Walter snapped, “Be happy you’re not in cuffs. The only reason you’re as free as you are is because you’ve agreed to provide information on someone who is far more important than you. Had you not agreed to this, we would have imprisoned you and made sure you went behind bars for at least ten years.”

Gary told Mike to shut up and behave. After all, they were now at the mercy of the government. Gordon and Walter closed the interrogation room door after Ron, Andrew, and Raymond entered. Gordon got straight to the point, saying they were satisfied with the information and wanted to discuss further what they knew regarding the *Draconists*.

Raymond interrupted him and said, “Our clients talk once the immunity agreements are signed. That was the deal. You yourself said you were happy with the information we provided, right?”

Gordon frowned and said, "Very well."

"Just doing my job, Gordon. No hard feelings," said Raymond.

Walter walked outside the room and returned with three immunity agreements. Ron, Andrew, and Raymond examined them in detail, and once they were satisfied, Gary, Damien, and Mike signed. With the formalities complete, Walter and Gordon briefed them, warning that everything they said from now on was confidential, and if they were to breathe a word of this even to their shadows, their lives could be in grave danger.

The recording tape was turned on, and Mike, Damien, and Gary stated their full names for the record and also that they were the General Partners of Lions Star Capital who had been coerced into laundering money for the *Draconists*. Mike informed the officers he was the one who had lost a twenty-five-million-dollar bet a few years ago, and till the money was paid off, he was held in captivity and tortured. That's when the *Draconists* discovered he used to operate a private equity firm. After realising this, Victor asked him to start laundering money for them. He held a gun to his head. The chamber was loaded, and the muzzle was pressed against his temple. Mike was left with no choice but to agree to the demands.

As Mike was recounting the events of the past, he began crying as though a weight was being lifted off his shoulders. Damien and Gary consoled him while Gordon and Walter did not flinch. Over the years, they had seen enough tears and remorse and had learnt to continue doing their jobs regardless of how emotional the perpetrators were.

Mike explained how Victor's brother, Jerome, operated several shell corporations registered in the Cayman Islands. They contained dirty money—cash Victor had acquired through various illicit activities. Once the funds were physically moved to Jerome's office in Florida, a *hawaladar* was brought in to facilitate the next step. Using this underground system, they discreetly channelled the money into multiple accounts spread across the Cayman Islands, effectively laundering it under the radar.

Once the money reached the island, the cash was deposited in small amounts within various accounts, which would be "*invested*" into Jerome's investment fund, Excalibur Investments. Excalibur Investments would then invest it into the funds operated by Lions Star Capital. After this, Victor would provide account numbers, names, and broken-down amounts where Lions Star Capital was to "*invest*" money. The money was mainly invested in privately owned businesses and funds. The owner could be a bookie or someone connected to Formula One who would play his part in manipulating the race. Once the appropriate people were paid, Victor would place his bets. About ninety per cent of the time, Victor would win the bet and take home a huge sum of cash. He bribed the bookies so they could manipulate the odds in a manner he would take home the maximum cash.

Mike was now tired of talking. Sweat from his brow trickled down his cheek. Nervous and scared, he gulped the water kept in front of him and said, "That's all I know, and that's all I have been doing. Damien and Gary were unaware of this, and we have not invested a single penny from the hedge funds into the private equity funds. So, the hedge funds are clean."

"What were you getting from all of this. I don't see you taking a cut," said Walter.

"Well, our firm would take the management fees based on the amount invested."

"So you did get a cut, rich boy," said Walter.

"Calm down, Walter. There is no point in taking digs at someone who is trying to help us," said Gordon.

Ron intervened and said, "It would be helpful if you guys stopped playing good-cop-bad-cop and allowed Mike to continue." Ron was a respected attorney, one with a clean record. Both Gordon and Walter backed off and allowed Mike some space to continue his story. Although the recorder was running, they were busy taking notes so they could provide John and the President with a summary.

Mike continued, "In the middle, I got a little greedy and convinced Victor to let me invest some of the money for a while and then return a higher amount to him. For some time, things went well, and his money grew significantly. But when the market crashed, I realised I had fucked up since I didn't have enough money to pay him back."

"What do you mean by invest some money?" said Gordon.

Mike explained he had started investing some of Victor's money into legitimate companies, hoping to achieve a higher return and even earn some carried interest for the firm. He started sobbing once again and wished he had not given in to his greed. Now that the market had crashed, the valuations of the companies had fallen, there were a handful of people with cash reserves, and there were no buyers left. So even though the companies had some value, the liquidity channels in the market had dried up, forcing the three partners to pool in money and return it to Victor. He informed the officers he had already started transferring some money to the accounts Victor provided, but they were short by $900 million.

"Short by $900 million?" blurted Walter. "You've got some balls to go up against someone like Victor. How are you still alive?"

"He doesn't know we're short. He thinks the money is invested, and all I need to do is sell the shares. But he doesn't understand how the markets work. I'm alive because we have already transferred two billion to him, and over the next five days,

I'll transfer another $1.1 billion. I don't know how I'm going to make up the deficit."

"So that's the reason you reached out to us. Because you didn't have enough liquidity to pay off the bastard!" said Walter.

"Let's see how you react when you have a gun pointed at your head, and you've been held hostage," barked Mike.

Raymond intervened, "Gentlemen, let's calm the nerves. We have a common enemy here. Let's focus on planning how to catch him and keep the trash talk at bay. We're on the same side and can't afford to bicker at each other."

Walter and Gordon made it clear they were satisfied with everything they heard. Raymond, Andrew, and Ron advised their client that it was time they provided the names and account details that secured their immunity agreement. Mike handed over a flash drive with one folder containing all the details from names, bank accounts, transaction dates, amounts, and even the original subscription agreements. Gordon inquired about the details of the *hawaladars* who rendered services to the *Draconists*. Mike said he was not involved with them and assumed Victor and Jerome dealt with them personally.

Damien was concerned about the safety of his partners and himself. He asked the officers how they would keep them safe and whether the safe house was reliable.

Walter drew on an analogy from the *Mahabharata*. He reminded them that, on the battlefield, Arjuna had wavered until Lord Krishna urged him to act without dwelling on gain or loss, victory or defeat—only on duty. "You've fulfilled your duty by coming forward with this information," Walter said. "Now we'll fulfil ours: we'll protect you, and the source of these details will remain confidential."

The entire meeting lasted about four hours, and by the end of it, Mike was exhausted, and Walter and Gordon had made enough notes to contact the Attorney General and the President and let them know they were holding a gold mine of information against the *Draconists*.

Mike, Damien, and Gary were ushered back into different vans that took them to their respective safe houses. The safe houses were situated in Snelling, California, about one hundred and thirty miles from San Francisco and roughly an hour's drive from Modesto. Each of them was placed in a different safe house and was provided with a new encrypted phone to be used to reach their emergency contact only, and no one else. They were instructed to work from there and not venture onto the streets without a disguise. The agency didn't want to take any chances and therefore didn't disclose the location of the safe houses to the lawyers either.

Chapter 10

Gordon and Walter were in conversation with John, and they disclosed to him the name of the informant and the information they had just received. The papers were sealed and stored in a safe known only to the agents and John. After the briefing, John contacted the White House, where he was patched through to the President. He informed the President that the immunity agreements were signed and the informants were currently being transported to the safe house.

The President and John were quite impressed with the brains of the informant, but at the same time baffled by how necessity can make a moral person commit immoral acts. Had these brains been used for the good of mankind, he would have probably won the Nobel Prize in finance.

The President was curious about the identities of the informants, and when he pressed the Attorney General for answers, the latter referred him to paragraphs 509, 510, and 533 of Title 28 of the United States Code. These sections outlined the Attorney General's Guidelines on the use of confidential informants, which strictly limited the circumstances under which such information could be disclosed. The President was frustrated; he disliked the Attorney General's stubbornness but respected his integrity. He instructed him to thoroughly examine the information and try to establish connections with every internationally wanted criminal.

Once that was complete, the President planned to reach out to the heads of the intelligence agencies in the relevant countries and propose a potential joint global intelligence operation. But before making those moves, he needed to inform Patrick, the Director of the CIA, that one of their top agents would be required to join this elite task force.

The President contacted Patrick on his private number. There were only five people in the world who had this number, and two of them were in the White House. The President informed him he needed one of the best agents, as there was going to be a joint operation between the CIA, FBI, DOJ, and MI6. Patrick was intrigued to learn this and wanted more information about the operation. The President reminded him that details of all ongoing investigations and special task forces were confidential and could not be disclosed.

The CIA Director let out a slow grunt and said he could assign Carter to the task force. Carter had just finished his current operation and, in the Director's words, was "looking to kick some ass." Patrick added that Carter had successfully executed missions in Mexico, Israel, and, most recently, in Russia. He was a weapons expert, skilled in everything from firearms to armoured vehicles. With Air Force training under his belt, Carter could also pilot any fighter aircraft in the US arsenal. "Don't be fooled by his sense of humour. He uses it to build a strong bond with his team. But once he's in the field, he's lethal and focused," said Patrick. The President nodded, visibly impressed. "Good! Lethal and focused is exactly what we need. He'll receive his instructions in the next couple of days."

The next order of business for the President was to contact the British Prime Minister and inform him of the fraud taking place in the UK. The President sat in his Oval Office overlooking the rose gardens. Through the corner of his eye, he could see the fireplace with a white mantelpiece located on the north end of the room. As his call was connected with the Prime Minister from the UK, all the ostentation of his office became a glimmer. Seriousness set in as the two leaders greeted each other, and the President walked him through what had recently been uncovered. The Prime Minister was appalled when he heard that the races of Formula One were being rigged, and even more disheartened to learn the people who assisted in laundering the money were given immunity and protection.

"If these people were in our backyard, I would have hanged them in public."

"Trust me, that's what I wanted to do as well. But when you're trying to catch a shark, you've got to sacrifice the fish. Anyway, these guys were coerced and their lives were in danger. I called to inform you that I am forming a special task force to deal with these sharks, and since a part of the laundered money is being funnelled into Europe, I think it would be beneficial to have an MI6 agent on board as well."

"Who are these sharks you are trying to arrest?"

"Have you heard of the *Draconists*?"

"Of course I have. If you're going to catch them, I have just the person for the job. Her name is Asha. She's one hell of an agent and is of Indian origin. She is well-versed in kung fu and can handle any type of weapon with extreme precision. She once broke a man's rib cage with her two fingers, which earned her the nickname 'Kill Machine'. Oh, and don't let her jovial side betray you. She changes colours like a chameleon and can instantly unleash terror on her opponents."

"Well, we need someone as badass as her. I am deeply indebted to you, and I think she will be perfect for the job."

"We seem to have a common enemy, and I'm happy we're collaborating once again."

"Oh, one more thing, we might need information from Admiral, and we're happy to provide the intel housed in Poseidon while this case lasts."

"Sounds like a plan. Consider it done!"

After a successful conversation with Patrick and the British Prime Minister, the President contacted Walter and Gordon and informed them he had secured the services of Asha from MI6 and Carter from the CIA. He was happy to learn Carter and Gordon had performed missions together in the past, and that they were partners, and they had always had each other's backs.

In a loud and proud voice, the President announced, "Gentlemen, we are going to call this new task force Sentinel, and since we have the cooperation of the CIA and MI6, we will be combining Admiral, the UK's secret spy system with our indigenous system, Poseidon. Once the link is patched between the two systems, we will be able to track everything, and nothing will escape our eyes. The *Draconists* can count their last few days. Also, we're going to call this combined system Nautilus."

After the conversation with the President, Walter looked at Gordon and said, "This guy is gloating like he thinks we've already caught Victor, and I didn't know you had worked with Carter in the past."

"There are a lot of things about me you don't know, Walter. It's called trade secrets. And now that we have Carter, and if Asha is even half as good as what MI6 portrays her to be, we've got some amazing fighting force in the field."

"Well, we both know I'm the brains. I'm more cut out for the courts, handling negotiations, and building military strategy. The field is all yours. I am going to contact Raymond and tell him we need to have a conversation with the SEC chief. He needs to know about this as well because I hear they were scheduled to investigate Lions Star Capital this year."

"So they are going to turn a blind eye to this one as well?" remarked Gordon

"Well, we have bigger fish to catch, remember? The *Draconists* will look much better on our CVs than Lions Star Capital."

"Couldn't agree more, Walter!"

Walter contacted Andrew and informed him that since the immunity agreements were signed and the internal formalities had been completed, a meeting with the SEC was imminent, and he knew the SEC would ask a lot of questions. They decided there was no need to inform the SEC about the depth of the operation since it could lead to a leak.

Walter called Blake, the Director of the SEC, and said there were direct orders from the President stating Lions Star Capital was not to be investigated over the upcoming five years, as it was a matter of national and international security.

"Five years!" exclaimed Blake. "What nonsense is this? They were scheduled to be investigated this year in December."

"You used the correct tense there. They *were* scheduled to be investigated. Well, now they are not going to be. I don't mean to be so curt and rude, but I cannot offer any more information than I have. I'm merely a messenger," said Walter.

"Messenger, my ass. We go way back to law school when we had each other's backs, but even I have a duty to the country," remarked Blake.

"And you would be fulfilling it by adhering to the orders of the President. And do you remember the rendezvous you had with the Los Angeles Police Department, where I intervened and made it go away?"

Blake's eyebrows pinched together and his jaw tightened as he heard this. He shouted, "You're going to pull that card now! That's as low as you can go, Walter?"

"As I recall, you were entangled with those low lives who were caught smoking crack in your backyard. I never judged you then; why are you judging me now?" remarked Walter.

"Have it your way, Walter. I wish I had not called you that day."

'We both know that's a bunch of bull crap, buddy."

"Yeah, it probably is. Thanks for saving my life then, Walter!"

"I take it we're even now. Thanks for your cooperation."

Had Blake pushed back any further, Walter would have reminded him that he was on the finance task force, and even they could not stop the banks from lending to subprime borrowers who defaulted and pushed the entire economy down the drain. The bailouts the Federal Reserve provided to so many institutions were unimaginable. But then again, he knew it was a delicate matter for now, and he was glad he did not have to pull that card to demean Blake. After all, they were friends outside of work and heavily relied on each other.

Walter informed the lawyers at Roth & Gotham and the General Partners of Lions Star Capital the SEC was off their backs and they would not be investigated for five years. However, an investigation was imminent after five years, but the current events would remain sealed. Mike was relieved he was not going to be banned from the SEC, but he was still worried about how life would be while the *Draconists* were at large, and he was still short of $900 million.

"Let us think of a way to lure this bastard, Victor, out. I think a deficit of $900 million should force him to look for you, and that's when we catch him and fuck him over," said Gordon.

Mike flipped and sounded terrified, "Does this mean I don't pay him now? He's going to kill me. I did not sign up for this. How are you going to protect me? Andrew! Ron! Raymond! Do something!"

Gordon said, "We're currently keeping all options open, and we do need bait."

"I am no bait!" yelled Mike.

Andrew had heard enough. He needed to calm his client down. He intervened and said, "Mike, even we don't know what the plan is. We need to trust Gordon and his judgement. He's seen such cases in the past and has successfully executed them."

Walter, who had been silent up to now, reassured all of them that arrangements had been made to add more professionals like themselves to the team to catch Victor and his gang. Mike felt at ease hearing there were reinforcements, and it was not these two blokes handling his case.

Chapter 11

Snelling started feeling cold around mid-October as temperatures fell to about forty-five degrees Fahrenheit. Mike's racing mind made it hard for him to sleep, and he stayed awake into the early hours. He looked at the clock, which was close to 3:00 am. All he could think about was returning Victor's money and avoiding becoming the bait. He got out of bed, looked outside, but all he felt was the darkness within him. He opened the window and the cool air rushed in. He could see the shadow of the large tree cast across the fence. The moonlight dimly lit the grounds. It was as if nature wanted him to see how the shadows lurked through the night and spread a world of grey to mystify the senses.

As anxiety overtook him, he decided to open a bottle of single malt, his favourite, a twenty-one-year-old Singleton. He inhaled its aroma, which included notes of sweet sherry-soaked peaches, ginger, oranges, and crunchy red apples, giving way to flavours of stewed fruit, treacle toffee, and berries.

The cool Californian air brushed his face as he sipped. He missed his office, the comfort of home, and the thrill of driving his car. He felt an urge to call Victor and admit his mistakes, but he knew it would probably be his undoing. Instead, he called Damien and Gary, and unsurprisingly, they too were wide awake. Slumber was playing hide-and-seek with them. Since none of them could sleep, they decided to have a drink on Mike's patio.

They drank well into the night and watched as the rays of the sun cut through the clouds. Its warmth, coupled with the cool breeze, reminded them of forgotten solace. They realised they were missing out on life's simple pleasures, and Mike once again apologised to them. Both Damien and Gary patted him on the back and said they probably would have done what he did. They began reminiscing about how they met at a bar and started Lions Star Capital. They were hungry for success and wanted to make it big in the world of Wall Street—and they did. Almost every stockbroker wanted to join them, and every company they invested in felt privileged to have them on its board.

Mike realised he had been so engrossed with work it had been three years since he had seen his family. He felt the urge to call home, but wondered how they would react. Damien and Gary urged him to call his parents. Though they advised him not to breathe a word about the fiasco the three of them were in. He agreed it would be a bad idea to tell them this, especially since he had not seen them in three years.

It was 7:00 am on the West Coast, but Mike's family lived in Charlotte, North Carolina, where it was about 10:00 am, and he was sure his parents would be awake. His father woke up every morning at 5:00 am and went for a jog. Once he returned after an hour, he would fix the garden and complete other household chores. His mother would wake up around half past six and prepare for another day in retirement. The two of them would sit in the garden and enjoy their morning coffee and discuss the latest news. His father was the President of the Residents' Association and had his honorary office to go to. He would arrive at a leisurely hour of about 1 pm after lunch and finish his work by about 5 pm Mike was longing to hear his parents' voices and finally decided to call home.

He gathered the strength to say, "Hey Dad, how are you? How's your retirement going? Any updates on your latest run times?"

"Mike, is it you! My god, it's been ages since I heard your voice. I called your office a couple of times last week, and your secretary said you weren't in. Are you on vacation on a remote island?

"No, Dad, just working from another city in California. I have a meeting with some new investors, so I thought I'd take a hotel close to their office."

"Ahh, getting more money into Lions Star Capital. Some people have money to invest in this market?" asked Frazier Sr.

"Yeah, we could be striking a deal with a major investor. They seem to have some spare cash and realised it's a good time to be a contrarian investor," responded Mike.

Frazier Senior was well-versed in the world of investing and finance. He was a CPA by education and had retired as the CFO of a large steel conglomerate. He chose to retire early and cash in on his Roth IRA and 401(k). He responded, "It's great to hear you guys are doing well, even during the choppy times. Also, I invested a couple of million in an Index ETF (Exchange Traded Fund) a few days ago. The valuation is dirt cheap, and I wanted to take advantage of it."

Mike laughed, "I see the trader in you still lives."

"Living and breathing, Mike! Just like the good old days when I made a fortune by investing in Apple in 1985 and selling it just two months before the housing market collapse."

"That was one hell of a trade, Dad. Alright, great catching up with you. I'm happy to know you're doing all right. I'll come and see you and Mom soon, okay!" said Mike.

"We're already looking forward to you visiting. See you soon, son!"

While speaking to his father, Mike felt a weight in his throat. He was getting emotional, and the second he disconnected the phone, tears began to roll down his cheeks. He desperately wanted to ask his father for advice, but couldn't. Even if his father had $900 million, he did not want to drag him into this mess. He felt lighter after hearing his father's voice. Damien and Gary's parents lived in San Francisco and New York, respectively, and they would meet up more often. Mike was always invited to Damien's Christmas dinner when he was away from home. Damien and Gary decided to go back to their temporary residences and sleep through the lazy Sunday.

Meanwhile, Carter landed in San Francisco and was received by Gordon and Walter. Gordon and Carter hugged like two childhood friends. The two of them had performed missions together in the past. They realised there was nothing comparable to the camaraderie of the forces. It's as if you are family for life unless you go rogue or are compromised. That's considered a cardinal sin, and you are either court-martialled or executed.

Within minutes, Asha arrived and joined the three of them at the coffee shop. Carter was sizing her up. He had been briefed by Walter about her prowess and could see why she was nicknamed 'Kill Machine'. After sipping coffee and sharing brief introductions, the four headed straight to the black site for an update on the mission. By then, the integration between Admiral and Poseidon was complete, and Nautilus was operational. They could now access live footage from nearly every camera connected to the internet. The surveillance videos displayed all movements of every citizen across the US and the UK. It had become so advanced, that if if criminals knew about it, they might settle for ordinary jobs and lives. However, Nautilus was never meant for such purposes. It was designed for international security, and once the mission was over, the connection between the two systems would be destroyed but never forgotten.

Vikram, the most renowned ethical hacker from India's Research and Analysis Wing, also joined Sentinel. He had previously worked on international assignments with MI6, the FBI, and the CIA. His accomplishments included protecting the Indian banking system from a threat, catching the hacker within an hour, and recovering two billion dollars stolen from the bank. He once penetrated a multi-layered firewall to help arrest an international drug dealer and sent a Trojan horse that recovered all historical transactions and pinpointed the location of the current drop. Additionally, he had collaborated with various secret task forces and earned a reputation for working magic with computers, earning him the title 'the Wizard' in the world of international cybersecurity.

Walter assembled the team at the black site and said, "Welcome, Team Sentinel! That's what we are calling ourselves. Each of us has been assigned to this secret task force, and we have one mission: catch Victor and his gang, the *Draconists*, and neutralise them. We would love to arrest him alive and have him rot behind bars, but if needed, we can execute him too. We know he has been at large for a while now and is at the top of the most-wanted list across the world. We've established he has been manipulating the results of some Formula One races and has been betting accordingly to earn money on the side. We know he moves the proceeds of crime through an entity called Lions Star Capital, which helps him launder the money."

Asha asked, "Are we going to catch the owners of Lions Star Capital as well?"

Gordon answered, "Actually, they are the ones who came to us. We have granted them immunity and are currently placed under witness protection. They are our confidential informants."

Asha and Vikram looked a little disappointed, but they knew that looking at the bigger picture was always of paramount importance. Gordon and Walter shared with the team the video recording of the time when Mike explained how the transactions flow and how the money is transferred. Vikram looked quite impressed, but said he would have used a Bitcoin transfer for this. Everyone else looked at him, wondering what he was talking about. He then explained that Bitcoin was still not made public, but some people treated it like digital currency, and the same could be transferred from one wallet to another, and for this transfer, all you need is the wallet ID. It was digital currency and in the coming years, could prove to be one of the best investments in the world.

Carter was a little old school and said, "Well, I don't think any of us has ever heard of something like this. It sounds like a highly sophisticated system."

"That's true! It is highly sophisticated, and since it is not regulated, it is virtually impossible to trace the originator and receiver of the transfer. The only way to track the transfer is if you know the wallet IDs," responded Vikram.

"What in God's bloody hell is this system?" inquired Gordon.

Before Vikram could dive deeper into the details, Walter put an end to the digital-currency tangent and steered the conversation back on track, suggesting Bitcoin can be what it wants to be in the future. But right now, they needed to catch Victor and be thankful he did not know how to use Bitcoin, or else arresting him would prove to be extremely problematic.

Over the next three days, they were going to devise a strategy to lure Victor into the open and catch him in the act. They knew he would soon be short by $900 million, which would push anyone to react and possibly even make a mistake. This was his only known weakness, but they were sure there had to be more. Maybe a girlfriend or a partner he regularly visited or lived with from time to time. Both his parents had passed away, so his known family ties were restricted to his brother, Jerome. Within the next hour, Vikram pulled up all the known crimes where the *Draconists* were involved. The case file had almost become a novel—the accusations ranged from drug smuggling, human trafficking, weapons supply, money laundering, murder, and, most recently, manipulating the results of Formula One races.

The five of them knew if they caught him and stopped his gang, it would rid the world of one of the most notorious criminal syndicates and would lead to the arrest of others with whom he was in cahoots. Once they had him in custody for manipulating the results of Formula One races and money laundering, they would be able to uncover all the other crimes and ensure he did not walk another day as a free man.

Chapter 12

Mike, Gary, and Damien were discussing the next order of business. Mike looked concerned. He turned his gaze towards the heavens and sighed.

"It's been five days since Victor threatened me," he said.

"Well, he's received about three billion, so that's shut him up," responded Damien.

"Guys, there is a deficit of $900 million, which we somehow have to make up. I don't know how on earth we're going to do that. Quite honestly, I'm fucking stressed!" said Gary.

They were all tensed and instinctively contacted Raymond, who offered to speak with some of his clients and inquire if they would be interested in buying any of the investments held by the firm. They agreed, and Mike gave the names of the legitimate companies where some of the dirty money was invested.

A few hours later, Raymond contacted Mike with the news: one of his clients was interested in buying one of the investments. The catch, however, was that there would be a loss on the books. The client was prepared to offer $100 million for an investment they had paid about $120 million for. Mike wasn't thrilled, but under advisement from Gary and Damien, the deal was accepted.

Dire times called for dire measures, and taking a twenty-million-dollar loss seemed to be the most practical course of action in the current circumstances.

"In all this chaos, Mike, I think you made one smart move by side-pocketing the investments where you put Victor's money," said Damien.

"Let's thank our stars for that," said Gary in a condescending tone.

In all the turmoil, Mike had learned to take a few punches on the chin. In a subdued voice, Mike said, "Gary, listen, man! I'm sorry, alright! I got greedy. I promise it won't happen again."

Gary lightly patted his back and began monitoring the stock market.

Mike had cooked the books in such a way that any amounts Victor wanted invested were recorded as a return of capital. Mike took special care of these book entries and ensured they were so minuscule that individually they were immaterial and would not catch the auditor's eye.

Raymond pulled out his encrypted phone and contacted Walter. He told him Lions Star Capital had managed to secure another $100 million. Subtly, the call was made to inquire whether his team had formulated a plan to catch Victor.

"We've been able to secure the services of some world-class agents. Once everything is in place, I'll contact you, and we'll need Mike to place a call to Victor so we can track his location."

"That's great news, Walter. I'll look forward to hearing from you," responded Raymond.

Meanwhile, at the black site, Vikram was pulling up all the crimes they could relate to the *Draconists*. Over the past decade, they had killed fifty-nine people, eight of whom were federal agents. They had laundered billions of dollars, manipulated

Formula One races, bribed at least twenty government officials, trafficked about two thousand children and three thousand women, supplied weapons to Al-Qaeda, the Indian Mujahideen, and even smuggled weapons for the Russians.

This much was known because in each of these incidents, the *Draconists* had lost a few people, and while investigating their call history, their conversations with Victor came to light. But somehow, the evidence was always tampered with, and Victor continued to roam free. Those who had been bribed were paid so generously that they vanished. Victor arranged for them to be relocated, given new identities, and allowed to start fresh lives in some hidden corner of the world. In case someone refused to cooperate with Victor, they were executed, and the case file was always closed with a note saying "inconclusive".

Vikram entered Walter's cabin and told him that because of the integration of Admiral and Poseidon, they were able to track crimes in the UK where the *Draconists* were involved. Walter looked up and said, "A long rap sheet is great, but we'd better find a way to catch this son of a bitch so we can pin it on him and make him pay."

Vikram responded, "Right, Sir! Also, the call tracing system is now ready."

"What do you mean by 'now ready?' I thought we already had one in place."

"Well, sir, the one in place was outdated. I have rewritten the code in a manner that the system can even track the last location of the burner phones once they are disposed of. But I'll need the IMEI number for it. While it is switched on, all I need is the number, and even if the signal keeps bouncing off the entire globe, once the call is disconnected, it will provide a radius of five miles within which the signal originated. That should reduce the time taken to find Victor and give us a perimeter to work in."

"Well, they don't call you The Wizard for no reason, right, Vikram!"

"Well, I keep a few aces up my sleeve," responded Vikram.

"I'll let the others know our technical side is in place, and soon we will need our muscle in the streets kicking ass."

Walter gathered the entire team together, and they appreciated the system Vikram had created. It was a state-of-the-art technology, reducing the amount of time to track criminals. Carter looked highly impressed and punched Vikram on the arm to signify his respect.

As the applause died down, Asha said they would need a plan to lure Victor into the open, and the only way was to tell him it would take longer than expected for him to receive the money. They needed to find a way for Victor to go looking for Mike. And they had to catch him in the act.

Vikram looked confused and said, "So we are going to pull Mike out of witness protection and hand him over to the *Draconists*?"

Carter addressed Vikram's concern and told him, "We will be around Mike. We'll be watching him like a hawk. Although Victor will not nab him personally, he'll have an important person from his gang fetch the man responsible for making him lose $800 million."

"It's a risky plan," admitted Gordon, his arms folded across his chest in concern.

"But there is no other way. He might send Hector, his second in command, for this pick-up, and catching him would be a great victory in itself," said Walter.

"Well, I hope he sends Hector. I have a score to settle with him," said Asha.

"So you were a conscious choice MI6 made and not just a random pick," said Gordon.

Asha said nothing, but just smiled in a manner as if she was already unleashing her killer instinct to dismember Hector. Hector was Victor and Jerome's right hand. He was physically lean and mentally sharp. He was fit like a former athlete. He had the skills to get out of every situation. He was street smart and knew how to persuade people. He was six feet tall with well-groomed black hair and a clean moustache. His eyes were dark, shaded, but calculative. His aura oozed seriousness. He had a persuasive and articulate voice. It had a thick Mexican bend to it. His tone could shift gears and turn rough at will.

Indeed, pushing Victor to come out of hiding was the best way to arrest him. Catching Jerome first would alarm Victor, and he would go underground. This was a risk they were not prepared to take. The entire world had pledged enough resources to assemble a formidable team. They realised Mike could end up being collateral damage, and this was a risk the government was prepared to take. After all, he had brought it upon himself.

Walter picked up his phone and realised in a short period, Raymond's number had become one of his most dialled numbers.

Raymond answered the call and said, "Hey, Walter, is there any update on the case? Mike and the company are running out of money."

"That's exactly why I called you, Raymond. We have formulated a plan, and we need the three of them to come in this evening at 7:00 pm. We're going to start Operation Capture," responded Walter.

"Great news, Walter. I'll let them know it's their time to shine."

"See you soon, Raymond. We'll have our vans reach your office around 6:00 pm. As usual, we're going to have four vans—one each for our informants and one for you, Ron and Andrew!"

"Sounds good, Walter. We'll see you at 7:00 pm."

Raymond contacted Andrew and Ron and informed them that everyone had to assemble at the office around 6:00 pm. Both the senior partners were busy with other client meetings and asked Raymond to go ahead without them. They would be available by phone if needed. Raymond reached the building around 5:45 pm and within fifteen minutes, he was on his way to the black site.

Mike, Damien, and Gary were on their way from Snelling. The tradition of being blindfolded was now part of the disguise whenever they were visiting the black site. They entered the same interrogation room they had been in a few days ago. This time, Mike was not as vulnerable as before. Somehow, the air felt lighter. Gordon and Walter greeted them and, without wasting a single moment, Walter said, "We have put together a task force, as you all are aware and can see. We have been in conversation with the Attorney General and have concluded we will not be going after Jerome first; otherwise, Victor will get the hint and go into hiding."

"So, what's the plan?" asked Mike.

"You see, Mike, I'm sure you realise we need to catch Victor in the act. We need you to call him and admit there is a shortfall of about $800 million, and you've somehow managed to put together twenty-five million dollars in cash, which you can hand over to him," said Walter.

Raymond was baffled to hear this and responded, "Is it your policy to mentally torture confidential informants each time they walk in to help you?"

"Well, Raymond, that is not our policy. But in this case, we're left with no other choice. If you have any bright ideas, please enlighten us. Let us describe the plan in detail. We will ensure everyone remains safe and Victor is caught," said Gordon.

While Mike was wondering whether he had put his faith in the right hands, Raymond said he needed to contact Andrew and keep him abreast of the situation. For the first time, Raymond was exasperated that Andrew was not in the meeting. He walked out of the interrogation room and told Andrew what the task force was suggesting. Andrew took a deep breath and said, "Tell them if that's what they want to do, then our security personnel is going to accompany Mike during the drop. He can remain hidden in the trunk of the car, but Mike does not go there alone."

Chapter 13

Raymond walked back into the room and said Mike would need to go for the drop of twenty-five million. Hearing this, Mike went pale and almost fainted. He pinched himself, hoping it was a nightmare he would wake up from.

"However, accompanying him will be one of our bodyguards. He can remain hidden in the trunk of the car and out of sight, but Andrew does not want Mike to go alone for the drop."

Gordon and Walter frowned and tried reasoning with Raymond, but Raymond was adamant.

"See, guys, we've given you all the information you need to catch Victor. If you're going to send my client into the field, then, being his attorney, I need to make sure he remains safe; otherwise, we're all walking out of here," said Raymond.

Gordon and Walter walked out to have a conversation. They had reached an impasse with him for the first time. They decided on their own accord and said they would let one security officer be present with Mike. After all, all eyes would be on Mike when he made the drop. There had been situations in the past when they would team up with private security personnel for various jobs. They entered and informed Raymond of their decision to allow

Mike to be accompanied by one security guard. Mike felt a little at ease, but he was still nervous about being present at the drop site.

Walter said, "Look, we have come up with a plan. Mike needs to call Victor now and tell him the markets have crashed due to the housing crisis. He can use all the fancy finance jargon he wants, but he needs to tell him there is a deficit of $800 million, and he's arranged for twenty-five million dollars in cash, which he wants to drop off. Of course, nothing comes free, so you would need to transfer the amount to the government in due course of time."

Hearing this, the hair stood up on Mike's flesh. He jolted back. "If Victor becomes aware of this, he's going to kill me."

"We don't think he'll kill you, Mike. You owe him over three-quarters of a billion dollars. He would want you alive. But more than that, he would want the twenty-five million dollars in cash now," said Walter.

Raymond agreed and said, "In his line of work, cash is what drives the economy. His resources must also be running dry."

"Exactly!" responded Gordon.

Mike gulped the water kept in front of him and started rehearsing his script. A drop of sweat formed on his brow, and his hands shivered. Damien and Gary had never seen Mike so nervous. He was used to talking to various boards and clients and spitting financial terms and advice as if he were a born orator. But then again, his life was not in danger in those times. Who would have known a cocky bastard like Mike could also piss in his pants? Mike started writing down all the relevant points, and within ten minutes, he was ready for the speech of his life. This may well be the speech that saves him or leads to his demise.

Vikram said the call needed to be at least one minute for them to trace Victor's location. Victor picked up the call on the second ring and started, "What's the status of the money? You have four more days left to complete the four billion."

It was the first time Gordon and Walter had heard Victor's voice. It was cold and calculating. Direct, persuasive, and commanding. There was an intense pitch to it that made him intimidating. They couldn't believe they were so close to him. In another room, Carter and Asha were hearing the conversation as well.

Mike was nervous, and he was sweating from head to toe. In a nervous voice, he stammered, "You see, Victor, the capital markets have crashed and all valuations are in the dumps. You know, we don't hold too much money in cash, so your investments are down by about twenty per cent, and we're short by about $800 million."

Mike felt his stomach push into his spine. He had never thought he would be able to go through this, but here he was fighting for his life. Before he could recover from his own body turning on him, he heard Victor blasting his lungs out. He screamed, "You son of a bitch! How could you lose my money? YOU ARE GOING TO PAY FOR THIS WITH YOUR FUCKING LIFE. I WILL SKIN YOU ALIVE."

Mike grew even more nervous, and his throat felt drier than the Sahara Desert. In a faint voice, he somehow stammered, "Victor, please understand, things were in great shape a few days ago, and none of this is my fault. I have about twenty-five million dollars in cash I can hand over to you."

Mike glanced at Gordon, who received a gesture from Vikram that there were twenty seconds left. Gordon signalled to Mike to continue the call. But Mike didn't need to make an effort. Victor was hurling abuses at the other end, and Mike almost fell as he continued to receive death threats. Victor was breathing fire, and he shouted, "I'll have one of my associates pick up the cash from you. But I am going to keep haunting you till I get all my money back. I am going to be your worst nightmare, and you won't be able to sleep till you've returned all of it and even more."

"I promise, Victor, I'll return all your money."

"Shut the fuck up, you scoundrel. I am going to send you the location and instructions for the drop. And you'd better come alone. If you involve the cops or anyone, I will shoot you myself," bellowed Victor.

Victor finally disconnected the call. There was a deafening silence in the room. Victor was fuming, and Mike was terrified. Vikram informed them that the call went on for over a minute, and as suspected, the location of Victor's phone was bouncing all over the globe. The system was recording all of this, and within a few hours, they would have the radius within which Victor was operating. Mike started crying in fear, and this was the second time in five days that it had happened in the interrogation room. He screamed, "Are you fuckers happy now? Don't you even know what I am going through? That jerk is going to kill me. Didn't you hear him say he wants to skin me alive?"

Although Damien and Gary looked petrified, they comforted Mike. Walter said they would now wait for Mike to receive the instructions for the drop, and once the location is received, they would send their team in advance and have eyes at the location from every direction. Once the guy came to collect the cash, they would all close in on him and capture him. They would then transport Mike to a secure location. The plan sounded great on paper, but Mike was still nervous and shivering in fear.

After about three hours, Mike's phone buzzed. It was Victor with the instructions. The message read, "Bring the twenty-five million dollars in unmarked notes and in a black bag tomorrow at The Golden Gate Park at 8 am. There is a golf course within the park and a dumpster close to the eighteenth hole. Near the seating stand, there is a black trash can. Leave the bag inside and go. Remember, NO FUNNY BUSINESS. We'll be monitoring every movement of yours."

It was almost midnight, and everyone was exhausted. Mike felt as though he was going to walk into the hands of death the next day. Damien and Gary were sent to their respective safehouses, but Mike was going to stay the night in a government dormitory close by. They could not risk sending him around the city in case he decided to make a run for it. Walter told Mike he would need to wear a wire and a camera. Vikram informed them he had prepared a listening device and a camera that were woven into a jacket and could easily be mistaken for the stitching. The device had a battery life of twenty-four hours. Mike looked confused as to why this was required when all he had to do was make the drop and walk away. Walter explained there was a chance the person who came to pick up the money would encounter Mike, and they wanted to be ready just in case. Mike looked like he had seen a ghost. Making the drop seemed like walking through hell, but he understood there was no one else who could do it.

Once Mike was transported to a state dormitory close by, the entire Sentinel team met to decide the plan of action for the next day. Gordon's instinct was telling him something untoward was about to transpire. Since Victor said he would be watching Mike, there was a good chance his people would be there before 8:00 am, and they might capture Mike while he was delivering the cash. He and Walter decided Asha and Carter, along with five other officers, would wait in hiding in Golden Gate Park. They would hold station from night to the early morning, but they would move in slowly only once Mike dropped the cash.

Gordon decided they would have a separate team of five observing Mike to ensure nothing happens to him, while the rest of them would have eyes on the drop site. The team agreed, and the troops were brought in, and Gordon briefed them. They said they would need to make sure the guy gets the cash, and then and only then were they to move in on him; otherwise, Mike's life would be in danger. They would have officers stationed in cars close by so they could follow Victor's accomplice. But they did not have to capture him immediately.

Carter questioned, "Why are we not going to nab him?"

Gordon replied, "We are going to follow him so we know where they are hiding. That's when we raid the place and capture Victor."

"How do we know Victor will be in there?" asked Asha.

"At the moment, we don't. But since Mike will be wearing a camera and there will be a tracker in the black bag, we'll know his location. We'll be able to track him, and if the location of Victor's associates matches that of Mike's, we'll know where their hideout is, and that's where we should find Victor," said Gordon.

"What will happen if the location is different?" asked Walter.

"That's the unknown element here, and it is troubling me. There is some level of uncertainty in the plan. But we'll have one of their hideouts, and we'll keep tabs on it. Plus, probably, Victor is there because the money will be there," said Gordon.

"The good old trick, follow the money!" exclaimed Vikram.

"Probably! Possibly! I don't know! We'll find out tomorrow," remarked Gordon.

Chapter 14

John Parx contacted Walter and informed him that the twenty-five million in cash was ready. It was in unmarked bills, as requested by Victor. Walter said they planned to embed a tracking device within the wheel of the bag. The stage was being set to catch Victor, and everyone felt his days were numbered. It was about midnight, and the team, including Asha and Carter, headed toward Golden Gate Park. Gordon stayed back and watched the mission unfold along with Walter.

On the way, Carter wanted to know why Asha hoped Hector would be there at the drop. Asha recounted an incident from a few years ago at the border of Russia, where she almost caught Hector trying to smuggle drugs into the European Union. A war-like situation ensued, wherein bullets were flying in every direction. However, while transporting him, her partner double-crossed her and let him go.

Although she was able to kill her partner, Hector got away, and on that day, she had sworn she would be the one to either kill or imprison him for life. Before she killed her double-crossing partner, she learnt Hector was also the right-hand man of Victor, who led the *Draconists*. So, there was a possibility the *Draconists* had some stake in Russia as well. Carter was impressed because only an exceptionally skilled agent would be allowed to operate at the Russian border. It was a mercurial and sensitive region, and no one really knew whom to trust and whom not to.

"You look like you've never heard stories of an MI6 agent," said Asha.

"It's an extremely dangerous region, and MI6 only sends its best agents over there. I don't always come across someone who has worked in that region," remarked Carter.

Asha thanked him and asked him to save the compliments for when the mission was complete. She had one goal for today, which was catching Hector, if he was present. As they reached the golf course, they realised two cameras could be connected to Nautilus. Asha called Vikram and informed him of the location of the two cameras on John F Kennedy Drive and 47th Avenue that were overlooking the golf course. Vikram went through the various streams and found the footage. Asha waved through one of them, and they smiled.

"We somehow find fun even in the most serious and dangerous jobs," said Vikram.

"That's one of the reasons I'm with you, Vikram," said Asha.

Carter overheard her and said, "You guys are together? It never appeared so."

"Well, we go back a long way. We were together in college in India. We've been together and away, and through it all, we always found time for each other."

"Wow, that's some story. I'd love to hear it someday," said Carter

"We have a few hours before catching that asshole," said Asha.

Vikram heard this and asked her whether it was wise to let him know they were engaged. Asha reminded him that Walter was already aware, and he was the main reason she had asked to be assigned to this mission. Catching Hector was a bonus. Although she would love to kick his ass, she was happier to have been able to be in the same city as Vikram. She told Carter the two of them had been dating since they were in college. After college, she chose to become an agent, and he chose the field of technology. Although their fields were different, they had the same goal—to rid the world of crime. They both believed doing what's right did not need to have the boundaries of country or religion. They were deeply inspired by the song 'Imagine' by John Lennon, which sparked a fire that could be quenched only by doing good in the world.

As a child, Asha took kung fu lessons and always dreamed of joining the defence forces. After completing her basic training, she was recruited by India's National Defence Academy, while Vikram joined the Indian Air Force as a Cyber Systems Operations Specialist. Although their postings were vastly different, they always found ways to meet at regular intervals. A few years later, Asha was recruited by MI6, while Vikram continued to serve in India. Eventually, he was offered an opportunity to move to London and assist in upgrading the UK's defence systems. That marked the first time they lived in the same city, sharing three years in London.

"What happened then?" asked Carter.

Asha smiled and replied, "Well, what was to happen. Once again, one of us received an opportunity of a lifetime. It was Vikram this time. The FBI contacted him and wanted to hire him as their IT specialist. The job was so top secret that that's all he is allowed to say, even to me."

"Wow, you guys went through a lot."

"I'm sure it's all going to be worth it," responded Asha.

"It will all be worth it if you come back alive," said Vikram.

"You've been listening to our conversation?" joked Asha.

"Well, what am I supposed to do if you leave your mic on and keep talking?" asked Vikram.

Carter, Asha, and Vikram shared a light moment. They couldn't risk being loud and raising an alarm. Asha and Carter began walking around to investigate the drop-off spot. While they were walking, Asha continued her story and said she and Vikram were planning to get married in February next year. So, when she heard about a job in San Francisco, she spoke to her superiors in MI6 and told them the whole story.

Since she was already on loan from the Indian Government, they allowed her to move to the United States. The Indian Government, too, did not mind her moving to the US since she had done her fair bit of service to the country. Plus, helping catch the *Draconists* was something even the Indian Government wanted on their shield. They needed more bargaining power in Geneva, and what better way to do it than by helping annihilate a global criminal syndicate?

"That is my journey, Carter. What's yours?" asked Asha.

"Oh, this will be interesting," said Vikram.

"You have a lot of expectations," said Carter.

"You know I'm right!" said Vikram.

Carter laughed and said, "Guilty as charged."

He told them he had led various missions in the past and graduated from Quantico. He was an expert marksman and recalled an instance while training to be a shooter, where seven out of ten shots almost went through the same spot, and his score had to be calculated by reviewing the camera footage.

After graduating from Quantico, he joined the FBI as a field agent. He was involved in various cases, and when a high-profile case came up, his commanding officer recommended him. Turned out the case required him to make a shot from on top of a hill. He was supposed to shoot the driver of a vehicle manoeuvring its way through the twists in the road. He was required to make a kill shot, and he ensured the bullet penetrated the driver's temple, killing him instantly.

He was then promoted within the FBI and was chosen for SEAL training. Three years after he completed his SEAL training and represented them on countless missions, he joined the United States Army Special Forces, colloquially known as the Green Berets. While he was part of the Green Berets, he was deployed in Iraq for about two years, and upon returning, he was presented with an opportunity to join the CIA. There was a joint task force formed to catch a human trafficking ring, where he met Gordon, and the two of them were partners. "Gordon was actually my commanding officer."

Both Asha and Vikram said, "You have worked with Gordon before?"

"Don't be so surprised, guys. This was a pure coincidence. But yes, he and I have worked together before, and believe it or not, we worked as partners."

"It didn't seem so," said Vikram.

"It didn't seem like the two of you were engaged either," remarked Carter with a smile.

Carter continued to tell them he was also part of the task force that had taken down multiple drug lords, human traffickers, and mass murderers. Although he had served his country on countless missions, he had never worked with Walter. He had only heard stories of how Walter would present cases in the court while he was the District Attorney. Later on, he was picked by the Attorney General to help lead various task forces and formulate plans to thwart any threats to national security.

After walking around the course, Carter found the dumpster close to the eighteenth hole. Right opposite the dumpster was a large tree. Carter climbed up and set up a camera pointed right at the drop-off spot. He turned it on, and Vikram could now see the drop-off spot as clear as daylight. Now they would be able to see who was going to collect the money. Even if there was a chase, they would probably have enough evidence to link Victor and the *Draconists* to money laundering. The stage was being set for one of the biggest arrests of the decade. Who would have thought a crash of the financial markets could throw a wrench in the operations of an international criminal who was at the top of the most wanted list and result in the downfall of the largest crime syndicate in the world?

Meanwhile, Mike was in his dormitory, wide awake. Although he desperately wanted to sleep, he was barely able to get his mind to stop wandering. His mind swung like a pendulum, where he would constantly wonder what would happen if Victor were caught and what would happen if the plan failed. He was at war with himself, and anxiety was preying on him. He took a few deep breaths and was finally visited by slumber before the biggest and worst day of his life.

All he wanted was the comfort of his bed, but all he felt was the pain of regret. How he wished he had not gotten into a situation where he had wagered against Victor. His life would have been so much more peaceful. And right now, peace was one thing that eluded him.

Meanwhile, Vikram watched as Mike tried to fall asleep. He was asked to keep an eye on Mike and ensure he does not try to escape. He pitied Mike's current condition and thought to himself, *no amount of money is worth the life of mental imprisonment.*

Chapter 15

It was not only Sentinel that was formulating their strategy, but also the *Draconists*, who were planning to pick up the twenty-five million dollars in cash. Victor decided to send Hector to the pick-up site personally. He was the only person Victor trusted when it came to moving cash around. He informed Hector that Mike was not supposed to leave from there, but was to be brought to their hideout alive, where he would be taught a lesson.

"Will you be killing him?" asked Hector.

"That bastard owes us almost $800 million. I'm going to beat him within an inch of his life. I want him to see death smiling at him, and then I will demand he pay us something extra just to make up for the delay," said Victor.

"Got it, boss. I believe he needed us to knock at his door."

"More like break down his door," responded Victor.

Victor's phone rang. It was from the Attorney General's office. He was informed there was a team up to something, and Victor needed to be vigilant. Victor was accustomed to being ambushed, and he didn't pay much heed to it. His source said there was a new lethal task force operating to catch him. Victor responded, saying,

"There has always been a task force wanting to catch me. I've been evading the law for years now."

"Victor, this one is serious. They have DOJ, MI6, FBI, and CIA on your ass."

"So what! I've been evading these agencies for almost all my life," responded Victor with a smirk full of overconfidence and pride.

"Victor, I don't have all the information, but please be careful. I don't know who is feeding them information, but they seem serious and determined this time around."

Victor hung up the phone and told Hector to be watchful and cautious the next day, as there could be some heat from various criminal agencies.

"Looks like either our friend has involved the cops, or someone has got wind of what is happening," said Victor.

"Should we cancel the drop then?" asked Hector.

"No, the plan remains. But I will send an additional van with eight people as backup for you. Looks like Mr. Mike is not that smart after all when it comes to cash. Did any of our *hawaladars* inform us of being contacted by Mike?" asked Victor.

"No, boss, Mike has not contacted any of our people," responded Hector.

"Hmm… So, he's either involved with the cops or he's just too careless when it comes to cash. Either way, we need him alive, and I want you to remain cautious during your operation. If you need to drop the cash and catch the guy, do it. But don't kill him now. I want to extract every penny he owns," replied Victor.

"Understood, boss. We'll get him alive along with the cash," said Hector.

Victor knew Mike would be there sharp at 8:00 am, and he planned to take the money and kidnap him. Once he was in custody, his gang would teach Mike a lesson. Hector pulled out his pistol—it was a Beretta 92, one of the most effective semi-automatic pistols. He said, "Boss, I can empty this chamber in his head whenever you want. Nothing will give me more pleasure than killing the man who doesn't pay us what we deserve."

Victor responded, "That day might come, but today is not that day. Today, we need him alive so he can make up for the loss. But that doesn't mean he gets to walk away scot-free."

Hector and three of his associates decided to reach Golden Gate Park the next morning at 7:00 am. They would need to make sure everything was in place. Each of them had a specific role for the drop-off. They would drive in a black Mercedes-Benz Sprinter Cargo Van with black opaque windows. The glass was toughened and bulletproof proof and the body was armoured.

Whilst Carter and Asha, along with ten team members, had already taken their positions in and around Golden Gate Park and the golf course, Gordon, Walter, and Vikram assembled at the black site at 5:00 am. Mike was brought in at 6:00 am, and while Walter and Gordon were preparing Mike, Vikram handed him the brown jacket with a camera and a listening device embedded within the stitching and invisible to the naked eye. Mike's heart was racing, and his nervousness was making him sweat.

The spy system had been activated, and all cameras were pointed towards Golden Gate Park. In addition to the camera installed by Carter in the tree at Golden Gate Park, Vikram was aware of the cameras on John F. Kennedy Drive and 47th Avenue, which were the approach roads to the golf course. He would need to maintain a close surveillance of the surroundings and report any suspicious movement to Gordon and Asha.

It was about 6:00 am, and Mike was transported from the black site to the office of Roth & Gotham. Walter arranged a car for him to drive to the drop-off site. It had a hidden tracking system in case Mike decided to make a run for it. Gabrielle, one of the private security guards hired by Roth & Gotham, took his place in the trunk and ensured his gun was loaded. He was a former CIA field agent who now earned his living in private security. He asked Mike to leave the trunk open and park in reverse so he could quietly move into the park without being noticed. He instructed Mike not to try anything funny or else his life would be in danger.

Mike was now used to being told his life was in danger. The black bag with the twenty-five million dollars was sitting in the front seat. For a normal person, this amount of money would mean financial freedom, but to Mike, it was a noose tied around his neck. He felt like a puppet controlled by the government and the *Draconists*.

He quietly turned around, sat in the driver's seat, and started the car. He revved the engine a little and realised how much he missed driving. He started driving towards the golf course in Golden Gate Park. It was about seven miles away from Mission Street, and it would take him about thirty minutes. He took a right on Seventh Street onto McAllister Street and drove across Hyde, Larkin, and Polk Streets, taking another right on Franklin Street. As he was driving through Turk Boulevard, he crossed the University of San Francisco and started remembering how good the college days were. When he was free from any responsibility and every rash decision could be corrected with a simple "I'm sorry". As he turned the car onto Fulton Street, he realised the drop-off point was just ten minutes away.

Knowing he was about to reach the golf course, his heart started pounding uncontrollably. His hands began shivering. The car automatically slowed down. He wished this were a nightmare and he would wake up one day before the day he lost the bet to

Victor. Out of nowhere, a car pulled up behind him and honked loudly. Alas, reality slapped him in the face. He moved aside to let the car pass and was treated to a loud "Fuck you!" which he conveniently ignored. He took a left onto 47th Avenue and parked his car between Fulton Street and John F. Kennedy Drive.

As he parked his car, Vikram, Gordon and Walter were glued to the screens watching the roads and the body cam. They could hear Mike breathing heavily as the time for drop-off approached.

"Sir, do you think he will chicken out at this moment?" asked Vikram

"I hope not, and I don't think so," said Walter

"He's got twenty-five million in cash. If I were him, I would make a run for it," continued Vikram.

"I'm happy you're not in his shoes then."

"Believe me, sir, so am I."

Both Walter and Vikram continued to monitor the progress and noticed a black van near the edge of John F. Kennedy Drive. They could not see the number plate clearly since there was a tree obscuring their view. Vikram alerted Walter and told him the black van did not look like the van in which their team was transported.

"You're right, Vikram! It's not our van. It seems the *Draconists* have sent in the cavalry. We need to warn our team. We might have a war on our hands," remarked Walter.

Chapter 16

"Asha! Carter! There is a black van at the edge of John F. Kennedy Drive, and it's not ours. Approach with caution. I think it's Victor's men," remarked Gordon.

"Understood! We'll approach with caution," replied Asha.

It was ten minutes to eight, and the situation was getting tense. Vikram and Walter were constantly monitoring the feeds from all cameras. Mike was checking the time and watching it pass by slower than ever. Gabrielle quietly moved into a bush on the outskirts of the golf course. He made sure no one was watching him, and he gave Mike the signal to move in. Mike took the bag and was about to get out of the car.

"Target is about to move," said Asha.

"We have eyes on him. He's still in the car," said Carter.

Gordon called in, "Be careful, guys. Victor's men are somewhere around you."

Vikram spotted the black van moving towards Mike's car and parking right in front of it. Before Mike could move out, another one parked behind his car, sandwiching him. Mike was terrified and thought the devil was giving him an evil smile.

"We're fucked," yelled Vikram. "It's an ambush."

"Son of a bitch," barked Gordon.

Before any of them could respond, Hector exited his vehicle and tried to pull Mike out, but Gabrielle shot at Hector and missed his head by less than an inch. Gabrielle then started firing at the cars blocking Mike to stop them from getting away, but he received a sea of bullets, and one of them went through his chest, killing him instantly. Asha and Carter joined in, but they could not save Gabrielle. Three of the members from Victor's gang were killed in the crossfire, and Asha even managed to get a bullet through Hector's left calf muscle. The bullet was still lodged in, so even though it was a flesh wound, it was more painful than usual. Hector was down, but one of his associates nabbed Mike and put him in their van. Another tried to carry Hector with them, but Carter shot him in the back of the head, executing him. Hector was on the ground and breathing heavily. He tried hopping to the van and tripped. He fell face-first, but his hands saved him. His associates were driving off without him, with Mike and the cash in their custody.

Sentinel was pissed at losing Mike, but glad they caught Hector alive. Asha pushed Hector to the ground, and when he tried to resist, she kicked his injured leg, and he screamed in pain. She unarmed him, cuffed him, and pushed him into the back of the van. His head was covered with a black cloth, and two guns were always pointed at his head. Carter took Hector's phone, turned it off and removed the SIM card. They needed to make sure no one could trace the location of the black site.

Gordon and Vikram were glad there were no casualties from their end, but losing Mike was not part of the plan. But they captured Hector, and one car was already following the vehicles that were carrying Mike and the cash. The system now had two active trackers, one in the bag of money and the other within the jacket worn by Mike. The car used by Mike had bullet holes all over it. It was picked up by the government crane service and sent to the salvage yard. At the black site, Vikram kept tabs on the location of the cars transporting the money and Mike. To his shock, the cars moved in opposite directions. Victor was separating the cash and Mike to ensure he always had leverage, but there was only one car following them. Sentinel had provided their team with two armoured Cadillac Escalades. One of them was carrying Hector and the team to the black site, and the other was chasing Victor's men. One of the vans jumped a red light and went straight on, and the other turned left. The Cadillac was right behind the Mercedes that broke the light, and it followed straight. The tracking device with the money stopped abruptly, and it looked as though the money was being held at a location close to Golden Gate Park. Two agents were immediately dispatched to the scene, but all they found was an empty black bag. It seemed the *Draconists* had come prepared. Vikram asked Walter, "Did they suspect there would be a tracker in there?"

Walter looked pissed at watching half his plan fail and said, "I smell a rat. There is no way Victor would have known of this. Someone tipped him off. We can't trust anyone at this point."

Meanwhile, the other Mercedes carrying Mike sped off and took a left on Park Presidio Boulevard and joined Shoreline Highway. It continued onto the Golden Gate Bridge. The car now picked up speed as it crossed Sausalito and took a right onto Sears Point Road. The Cadillac was being driven by Henry, one of the members recruited by Sentinel. He called in saying he was following them but had fallen behind due to traffic. Vikram said it looked like they were heading towards Napa Valley. Vikram noticed the tracker Mike was wearing had stopped near Madonna Estate, a local wine estate. Vikram informed Henry and asked him to slow down near Madonna Estate, as that could be the place Victor was hiding.

As Henry entered the parking lot, he noticed a bunch of clothes lying on the ground. He contacted Vikram and told him he had found a brown jacket and blue jeans lying on the ground. It looked like they made Mike strip in the car and throw off his clothes.

"Or Mike is involved and has absconded along with the *Draconists*," said Walter.

"You think that is a possibility?" said Vikram.

"At this point, anything is a possibility," responded Walter, as he made his way to his office, uncertain whether he should feel glad Hector was caught or whether Mike was now either a hostage or absconding.

With no other choice, Henry was forced to make his way back to the black site where Hector was now being held. He informed Vikram that the van carrying Mike had escaped. Either it was Victor's modus operandi to strip his victims of their clothes and discard them along the way, or Walter was right; there had to be a snitch. No one else knew the jacket had an internal camera and tracker. Walter and Asha were conducting the interrogation. Asha had specifically requested this as she wanted to be the one to wipe the smirk off Hector's face. She was prepared to play bad cop and lambaste him. After all, she had a score to settle.

Hector recognised her from two years ago. He laughed condescendingly and said, "I remember you! You had tried to capture me two years ago and failed."

"Two years ago was different. Today I shot you and have you cuffed, you rotten piece of shit. Two years ago, you had me double-crossed. Today it seems the tables have turned," said Asha.

"What makes you think you're not double-crossed today?" said Hector.

"Double-crossed or not, you're captured, and in our custody," responded Asha.

Hector looked disgusted and spat on the floor. Asha threw a punch that rattled his jaw. Walter intervened and started questioning him. Hector was proving a hard nut to crack, and the only word he said was "lawyer". Every question had only one answer: "lawyer". Luckily for the group, Asha had requested Vikram perform a full background search on Hector and his family. While the interrogation was being conducted, Vikram completed the search and simultaneously searched for the van that had abducted Mike.

Vikram called Asha out and handed her a file. He said, "This should seal Hector's fate and give us the information we need. Asha glanced through the file and noticed pictures of a lady, a little boy, and two ageing parents. His parents were in Puerto Rico, but his wife and child were in San Francisco. They were living just adjacent to the Tenderloin area. Asha confidently walked back and presented him with the photographs. They knew the school his child went to and where he and his wife lived. Hector hurled abuses at them, but then said he would talk; however, he needed some time by himself.

"We aren't stupid, Hector. You think we'll leave you alone in here so you swallow some pill and commit suicide?" said Walter.

Hector looked at him with eyes full of rage. Walter had him searched from head to toe, and they found two cyanide pills, which they added to the evidence bag.

While Hector was being interrogated, Mike was having the worst day of his life. He had just been kidnapped and stripped to his boxers while being driven around with a black cloth over his head. He was used to being blindfolded amongst the cops, but had absolutely no experience being driven around by ruthless criminals. How a situation played out in reality was often different from one's perception, and Mike was now living proof of this.

The van finally stopped, and he was pushed into a rundown, deserted building. Victor's men had one hand on his neck, and his hands were tied behind his back. He was made to walk up several stairs and was constantly stumbling. He was finally flung into a chair in a dark room. It was chilly, and he felt the tension in the air.

The cloth was removed from his head, and he noticed there was only one spotlight shining on him. He observed there was only one window with an exhaust vent for ventilation. Before he could think of anything, one of Victor's men threw a bucket full of cold water on him. As he began to make peace with being drenched in cold water, he heard heavy footsteps walking up the stairs, and before he could turn around, he heard a voice he recognised. It was Victor.

"Looks like we have a thief and a double-crosser amongst us. I wonder what's going to happen to you now, Mike!" said Victor in a cold and emotionless tone.

Chapter 17

At the black site, Hector was being questioned regarding the role he played in the hierarchy within the *Draconists*. He was screaming in pain, and Walter said he would be treated medically only if he divulged information about Victor and what the plans of the *Draconists* were. Hector said he would give all the information, but needed immunity. Asha asked him to shut the hell up because he was not in a position to bargain. He was, anyway, part of the top ten list of most wanted criminals across the world, so even his capture or execution would count as a victory. The only thing they could guarantee was that he would not be served the death penalty if he cooperated.

Hector agreed to share the information he had and begged for the bullet to be removed. By now, the adrenaline in his body had shot up. He was sweating and profusely bleeding as well. This was the body's natural response to ensure it could maintain homeostasis. His wound was burning, and he felt as if his leg was on fire. He was transported to a makeshift hospital within the black site, where his hands and legs were cuffed to the bed, and he could not move. The on-site doctor removed the bullet and taped the wound up. Hector requested some morphine to ease the pain, but Walter told him to fuck off.

"Don't play these tricks with us, Hector. We know you're trying to buy time to save Victor's ass, but let me tell you one thing—you are going to be prosecuted," said Walter.

He was taken back into the interrogation room, where this time Gordon and Asha were interrogating him as Walter was looking over the footage shown by Nautilus. Because of the body cam Mike had, they had footage till Madonna Estate, but thereafter, there was nothing. However, using Nautilus, they were able to follow the van up to Gravenstein Highway, after which it vanished. They saw it turn right into one of the by-lanes within the forest. Meanwhile, Vikram was working on extracting all the information he could from Hector's phone. It was password-protected, but it took Vikram just about ten minutes to breach its security protocol. All the data was copied, and the phone, SIM card, and battery were destroyed in a microwave. If there was a tracker within it, it was now deactivated.

With the bullet out of Hector's leg, he started being a cocky ass again. Gordon was not as nice as Walter when it came to dealing with criminals. He caught Hector by the back of his neck and pinned his face to the table. Meanwhile, Asha kicked his left calf muscle, which sent a huge sense of pain through Hector's body, and he screamed, "You bastards, I'm going to make sure you both have the most gruesome end to your lives."

Asha responded, "At the moment, it's you who is in a gruesome situation. Half handicapped and arrested." Hector stared at her in disgust and anger.

Meanwhile, Vikram was scanning through the data he had extracted from Hector's phone. There was one number that was frequently called, and it matched Victor's number, which Mike had provided. They had tried tracking it before, and it did lead to an approximate location. Vikram ran the number through the system, but it was switched off.

"Had Victor changed his number?" thought Vikram.

Vikram extracted Hector's banking information and sent this data and call history for scrutiny. The analysis was alarming. The system revealed that Hector was also speaking to someone in Washington, D.C. It was a private number that could not be traced.

Vikram alerted Walter about this and said there was a mole and it was in Washington, D.C. The only people they had spoken to in Washington were the Attorney General and the President, and they, too, were unaware of the entire plan. But it seemed someone had been supplying information to Victor, which was why they converted the money collection into an ambush, or maybe that was his plan from the beginning. They knew he would come back and try and rescue Hector. They could not trade Hector for Mike, as it would completely defeat their purpose. In a war like this, winning small battles was equally important. Walter took a strong stance and ordered the entire team not to report anything to Washington, D.C. without his knowledge. He would filter out the information since Vikram, and he might have identified a leak high up the ladder.

Asha and Gordon started interrogating Hector again. This time, they asked how he knew about the ambush. Hector said they had the means to get their information. Vikram was tired of hearing Hector play hide and seek with them. He barged into the room and slammed some documents on the table. He confronted him about the leak, and he wanted the information immediately. Hector's eyebrows furrowed, and his mouth slightly opened. He couldn't believe how he got that information, but he smiled back, saying, "What happened, sending the IT guy to do something you can't?"

He looked Vikram dead in the eye and said, "You don't know what you're dealing with, techie. Its best you guys let me go; otherwise, all hell will break loose."

Vikram looked back at him and said, "You're the one tied. And you're thinking you have bargaining power?"

The members of Sentinel didn't know whom to trust at this moment. But they needed to know who was Victor's source in the government. Vikram threw out the idea that it was either the Attorney General or the President. Everyone looked concerned. If this were true, then they were probably being double-crossed by someone who sanctioned the formation of the task force and could effortlessly disband it. Carter asked if there was a way they could use the technology they currently have to find out who this person was.

"So you want us to trace phone records of the President, Attorney General, and everyone in their office?" asked Vikram.

"We won't be able to trace their call records because their phones will be highly encrypted," said Gordon.

An idea dawned upon Vikram. He went back to their phone tracking system and asked Walter for his phone. Walter joked about whether Vikram suspected him, but then Vikram said, "We can't trace their phones, but we can check when we were talking to them."

Walter still looked oblivious, but handed Vikram the phone. Vikram plugged it in and extracted the call times when they were communicating with the Attorney General last evening. And the call was placed to Hector from a private number while this call was in progress, so it meant the Attorney General's office was bugged, and someone had been listening in. This person was not John himself but someone who had access to the information. Someone who knew what he was doing and whom he was talking to.

Carter said, "I remember the call. We first reached out to Frank, John's secretary. He had patched us in."

"Could it be Frank? Nobody knows the Attorney General's schedule better than he," said Vikram.

Walter looked at Vikram for a moment and said, "You could be right about this. But first, let's make sure no one has bugged our lines."

"Our lines are not bugged," asserted Vikram.

"How can you be so sure?" asked Gordon.

"Because I have created a program that constantly checks every part of Nautilus and our phone lines for any outside threat. I made it myself, and it is not even on the market yet," responded Vikram.

"So we're sure John's office is bugged, then," said Carter

"Looks like it, and we need a way to communicate this to him without letting anyone find out," said Walter.

Carter looked at Vikram and asked if there was a way they could send a message to the Attorney General without it going through Frank. Vikram was already strategising for this. "Can we use Morse Code?" suggested Vikram.

"But Frank will be able to get it decoded," said Gordon.

"This means we need to involve the President directly," said Walter. "Gordon and I will go to his office and meet him in person. I don't want to have this conversation over the phone."

Once the President was on board, they felt they could finally get the double-crosser, Frank, and continue their mission. Vikram suggested that after the meeting, John should let things go on as usual for a few days so Frank does not pick up a scent. Then they will send the Attorney General's office a confidential letter from an unknown source using the US Postal Service. The envelope will contain a blank page, which will be his cue to confront Frank.

Everyone was on board with this plan and hoped it would yield the expected result.

Walter contacted the President's office, and once the call was patched to him, he requested an in-person meeting where he said he needed to convey some important information that required the two of them to meet and to maintain secrecy. The President knew the stakes were high, and he gave them a time of 6:00 am the next morning. Walter and Gordon would fly to Washington, D.C., meet the President, and return immediately. The President arranged for them to be transported in his private security jet since the situation had escalated to a point where he could not risk them travelling commercially anymore.

Chapter 18

At the abandoned building of Marcelus Roofing and Welding Fabricators on Gravenstein Highway, where Mike was being held hostage, Victor slapped him across the face and pulled him up by his collar. The ropes that tied Mike's hands to the chair were pressing on his wrists. He could feel the coarse rope threatening to cut through his bones. Suddenly, Victor realised Hector was missing, which is when Shane, one of the drivers of the van, said Hector had been shot and captured. He told him that when one of the guys was trying to help Hector back, he was shot in the back of the head execution-style. They were forced to flee the scene since Mike was in custody and the money was collected.

Victor was more furious than ever at not being kept in the loop regarding Hector's capture. He picked up a wooden chair and slammed it on the ground in frustration. He pulled out his gun and shot Shane in the head, saying, "How's that for execution-style!" He then turned to Mike and punched him in the face. He made his associates hold Mike with his hands behind his back and repeatedly punched him three times in the midsection. Mike felt as if he was going to throw up in his stomach. By now, he could feel blood trickling from his nose and the corner of his lips. Victor had so much rage in his eyes. He resembled the devil incarnate.

Hector's capture was a severe blow for the *Draconists*. He turned to Mike and said, "I am asking you nicely, did you call the cops on me? Answer me truthfully, and I might spare your life." Mike knew that if he revealed the truth, he would be killed.

"Victor, I swear, I don't know what happened. I never contacted the cops, I swear. I was scared as hell when I heard bullets. I was prepared to drop the money in the dumpster as you ordered. Please believe me, why would I put myself in danger?" said Mike.

Victor was livid, and in his anger, punched Mike on the temple. Mike fell to the floor and was knocked out, but breathing. He was then tied back to the chair. Victor took Mike's phone and started scrutinising his call history. He saw one contact pop up consistently. It was saved under the name of "Raymond (Roth & Gotham)". A quick internet search revealed Roth & Gotham was one of the most successful law firms. He wondered whether Mike had revealed everything to his lawyer, who had contacted the cops. He had his associates throw ice-cold water on Mike to wake him up. Once Mike was half-conscious, Victor grabbed him by the neck and asked him why he was speaking so much with Raymond.

Mike coughed up while trying to recover, and he was barely able to speak. Victor then got a blowtorch and set it on the flame, and took it close to Mike's head. In fear, Mike's adrenaline shot through the roof. He said they were his legal counsel. Since the financial markets were in turmoil, he needed advice on how to proceed. Victor was not convinced. He took Mike's phone and called Raymond's number.

It had been a couple of days since Raymond, Andrew, and Ron had heard from Mike or Walter. They had been given strict instructions not to call any of them. Raymond and Giovana were enjoying their time at the Ritz-Carlton. They had almost forgotten they were actually in hiding. Seeing Mike's number flash on his screen, Raymond was distracted from his romantic escapade. He stared at the screen for a few seconds that lasted an eternity. He clicked the green button on his phone to answer the call and said, "Hello Mike, how are you? How can I help you?"

The voice at the other end said, "What do you do for Mike?"

Raymond recognised the voice at the other end of the line. He froze for a moment. He didn't want to believe his thoughts. He needed to remain oblivious and asked who it was. He received a response that said, "None of your business. Tell me what you do for Mike." Raymond maintained a composed tone and said he was the general counsel for Mike and helped with finance consultancy.

"Do you work with the cops?" asked the voice.

"No, I do not. I work for Roth & Gotham. We are a law firm. Who is this?" said Raymond in a professional voice. "Can I speak with Mike, please?"

"Mike is not available at the moment, but I will ask him to call you," said the voice, and the phone was disconnected.

Raymond was concerned, and he felt a sense of nervousness take over him. He called Andrew and informed him about the phone call. Andrew contacted Walter and started a conference call with Raymond. They wanted to ask Walter why on earth Raymond was receiving a call from Mike's phone with Victor on the line. Walter was being elusive and said he could not discuss ongoing investigations. He didn't want Andrew and Raymond to know Mike was captured. In a frantic voice, Raymond said he had just received a call from Mike, and the voice on the other end probably belonged to Victor. Walter looked flustered—why would Victor contact Raymond through Mike's phone? He then told Raymond and Andrew the drop had not gone to plan, and Mike had been captured. They were working on a strategy to get Mike back and catch the *Draconists*. Walter, however, confirmed Damien and Gary were safe, and unknown to them, there were local police officers keeping an eye out for them.

Raymond was flabbergasted as to why no one was contacted. Walter informed him that it had just been a few hours, and their protocol was to inform all parties involved within twelve hours. He said currently, he was not able to give out any details, and all he could confirm was that Mike was kidnapped. He said he had sent four undercover agents to guard Damien and Gary, and one of the members of the *Draconists* was in their custody. Although he told Raymond not to mention anything about the arrested gang member to Damien or Gary, as any leak in information could prove fatal for Mike. Although he requested that Raymond inform Damien and Gary about Mike's capture, they should always remain alert.

Raymond and Andrew were perplexed at hearing this, and after speaking with Walter, they immediately contacted Damien and Gary. They were happy to know they were safe and informed them about Mike's kidnapping. They were told not to venture outside, and all their needs would be taken care of. Raymond even asked them not to call or receive any calls from Mike's phone, as it could put Damien and Gary at risk. Damien and Gary were stupefied and, at the same time, livid at being kept in the dark. They decided to continue working from the safehouse. They prayed Mike would return safely.

The news of Mike's capture was not sitting well with his business associates. But for Walter and Gordon, it was time to take the flight to meet the President. They received news from the President himself that two vans would be sent to take them from the black site to a secure airfield. Once they reached the airfield, they were asked to change into what looked like airline staff. As they entered the airline, they were treated to luxury never seen before. Since they were flying the red-eye, they decided not to indulge in any alcohol. They went over the information they would relay to the President and presented their recommendations regarding the communication with the Attorney General. They landed in D.C. at about 5:00 am and were hurried to the White House in armoured vehicles. Dawn was just about to break, and it appeared the rose garden was playing hide and seek through the eyes of the night. They entered the President's office to find him poised in a navy suit, sky-blue shirt, and maroon tie. He was wide awake and active despite working sixteen hours a day on average. In contrast, Walter and Gordon looked like flight attendants. But the President didn't care since it was all part of a decoy.

The President greeted them with a firm handshake and asked them to take a seat. He looked at both of them and said, "It's good to see you both here. What is it you wanted to talk in person that couldn't be communicated over a call?"

"First, sir, Hector was wounded at the drop location, and we were able to capture him."

"Well, that's great news, Walter!"

"But our confidential informant, Mike, was captured. They ambushed us, and although none of our officers were injured, we believe there is a leak in Washington, D.C."

"Do you realise the gravity of your statement? A leak in Capitol Hill! That's a serious allegation. You'd better have the evidence to back it up," shouted the President. He was visibly agitated.

Gordon interjected and said, "There is a leak in the Attorney General's office. We believe his secretary, Frank, has been leaking information to the *Draconists*. He's on Victor's payroll."

"I never liked the guy, but are you sure?" responded the President.

Gordon then went on to explain the time when the President, Attorney General, Walter, and he were connected through video conference, and there was a call made from the Attorney General's office to Hector and Victor. So, there had to be a bug in that office since Frank was the one who patched the call.

The President was impressed with the analysis and said he always suspected Frank was up to something. He also realised why

Walter had to break protocol and bypass the Attorney General. The plan was for the President to call a meeting with the Attorney General and inform him about the bug. After the update was completed, Walter and Gordon headed back to San Francisco.

While Walter and Gordon were on their way back to San Francisco, the President assembled a team and went directly to John's residence at 7:30 am. The President was greeted by John's wife, Sabrina, and she offered him breakfast, but the President politely declined. The President asked John if there was a place they could talk in private, and John took him to his study. As they entered the room, the President handed John a note containing the entire update the President had received from Gordon and Walter. He said, "John, your office is bugged, and Frank is the culprit. He's been leaking news to Victor and Hector. Also, I want to inform you that Hector has been captured and is in the custody of Walter and his team. The bad news is your confidential informant, Mike, has been kidnapped. Don't ask me how I know all this, just understand if the information was communicated to you first, Frank would set off more alarms and the entire task force would be at risk."

John was appalled. He had trusted Frank with everything, and that's how Frank repaid him. He was genuinely hurt, and anger engulfed him. Greed often took over a person's ability to think and act rationally. He realised he would need to confront Frank and have him imprisoned for treason. He wanted to shoot him immediately, but had to wait to receive a blank piece of paper from an unknown source.

As Walter and Gordon landed, they received an encrypted message from the President's office. They didn't need to take any action regarding the blank piece of paper. They looked at each other and thought the President had lost it, but clearly, they had no idea the meeting with the Attorney General had taken place without either office knowing of it. Anyway, an order was an order.

During the entire morning, John was trying to find the bug in his office. He overturned his desk. Pulled out each drawer and still couldn't find it. He stood up, and his gaze fell on the chair on which he was sitting. He flipped it around and finally found a tracker under the seat. By noon, John received a blank sheet of paper from an anonymous person, and he immediately scheduled a meeting with Frank for 1:00 pm. He smiled and put it back where he found it. He would use his ace of spades at the right time and nail this fucker.

Chapter 19

It was 1:00 pm, and Frank walked into John's office. John apprised him that he would be travelling for official business to New York that week and wanted to discuss his schedule and move some things around. While talking to Frank, John slipped in a question, "How's Victor doing?"

Frank's head tilted, and one eye squinted in confusion at hearing this question. "I'm sorry, I don't understand what you're referring to, sir!" responded Frank.

John's sneering lips and flared nostrils caught Frank's gaze. He said, "Don't fuck with me, Frank! Tell me where you have hidden the bug."

"There is no bug, sir. I assure you, and I don't know what you're talking about," replied Frank.

John pounded the bug on the table, which made a loud sound, and Frank's hand went straight to his ear as the sound was unbearable. "You mother fucker, how dare you bug my office?" blasted John.

"You're smarter than I thought, John. But you'll never get away with this," shouted Frank.

John was livid, and he threw a punch at Frank. Frank ducked and retaliated with a punch to John's jaw. John was well built, but this punch still rattled him, and his mouth was full of blood. He picked up the laptop and swung it across Frank's face. Frank was now bleeding as well, and they both began brawling in the middle of John's office. Frank threw John across the desk and said, "You're going to pay for this with your life."

John got up in a fit of rage and pulled out his gun. He had aimed it directly at Frank. Frank involuntarily raised his hands in the air, and sweat formed on his brow.

"If I kill you now, Frank, nothing will happen to me. I have all the evidence I need to incarcerate you, and I'm going to make sure you rot in jail for the rest of your life," said John.

Frank slowly walked towards John and implored him to calm down. He said, "John, you're being naïve. You don't understand how the world works. Victor and his gang are involved in every crime that takes place across the globe. They can make you rich beyond belief. Your family will be happy and comfortable, and your kids won't have to work for a day in their lives."

"I am a patriot, Frank. I love my country beyond anything. I have never and will never touch dirty money in my life."

John now pointed the gun directly at Frank's head and asked him to turn around and walk with him out of the office. He was going to hand Frank over to the guards outside and make sure he was sent to a maximum-security prison, where he would be miserable for the rest of his life. Frank turned, but he knew he would not last a day in prison, and he had no intention of going there either. He felt John pointing his gun at his left scapula, and as he had learnt in military training, he swung around towards his right and used his elbow to land a hit on John's temple. John fell on the ground and was lying on his left side. The gun slipped out of John's hand, and Frank grabbed it. He pointed the gun at John's head. John pretended to beg for his life, but Frank did not heed his request. John slipped his right hand into his pocket and slyly clicked the panic button. Within seconds, the guards outside entered his office and saw John lying on the floor with Frank pointing a gun at him. Frank yelled that John was a traitor and was planning to betray the country. John was grunting in pain and somehow managed to scream, "Liar!" The guards were in two minds, but their duty was to protect the Attorney General. Frank knew he was cornered and started panicking. He fired a bullet, but it just grazed John's ear instead of going through his skull, a lifeline in the midst of total carnage. Immediately, one of the guards shot a round of bullets towards Frank. One of them pierced his stomach, and the other went through his lung. He killed him instantly.

The guards arranged for John to be taken to the hospital for treatment, and his family was informed of the tragedy. The President, realising what had happened, ordered the Attorney General's office to be cleaned up. He spoke with Walter, and they decided they were going to declare Frank and John dead and say the two of them were working on various important cases and were poisoned by a mutual enemy. An investigation would be ordered, and a new temporary Attorney General and Secretary would be appointed. They needed to fake the death of John to ensure Victor did not do anything drastic to Mike. In the midst of adversity, they had managed to kill one major member of Victor's gang. With Hector in custody, things had started grim for the *Draconists*.

The next day's newspaper headline read "Double Murder on Capitol Hill. Attorney General and Secretary Poisoned." The article elaborated on how the Attorney General and his secretary were murdered by poisoning. The President called a press conference and stated they were murdered by someone who may have gained access to the Attorney General's office and poisoned the two of them. The press was all over the President and wanted answers, but the President deflected the questions, saying the investigation was ongoing and he could not divulge any further information at that moment.

Ron was stunned by reading the newspaper. He called Walter and expressed his shock at reading the newspaper. He wanted the truth from Walter. But Walter knew he could not reveal much. He told him many events connected and disconnected occur around the country, and they were doing everything to ensure Mike would be able to return safely. "You're as diplomatic as diplomatic can be," said Ron.

"That's my job, Ron, and that's what I'm paid to do," replied Walter.

Meanwhile, John was recovering in the hospital. He had received stitches to his back from being tossed across the table and even had a hairline fracture in his jaw. His face was bandaged up, but luckily, his limbs were working fine. Nevertheless, he was under observation and was ordered to operate from home. The new Attorney General would take on all other cases, and all information about the task force would be wiped out from the office.

Victor heard the news of the poisoning of John and Frank. He was not happy at losing his contact. He needed to find a new gullible and money-hungry source in Washington, D.C., who was ready to look the other way and even cover up for him whenever required. He began beating Mike. His body turned black and blue from the punches and kicks. Mike pleaded with Victor to stop. His only bargaining power—three-quarters of a billion dollars. He called Victor's greed and said, "If you let me go, I'll be able to transfer some of that money to you and reduce the deficit."

"In all this mayhem, I almost forgot about the shortfall of three-quarters of a billion dollars," said Victor.

His blood boiled, and he lambasted Mike once again, literally within an inch of his life—as he had promised Hector. By this time, Jerome entered the premises and stopped Victor from beating Mike. He grabbed Victor from behind and said, "Easy, brother, we don't want to kill him just yet."

Jerome was sophisticated beyond class. While conducting his business, he was generally accustomed to wearing tailored suits with shiny leather shoes. A well-trimmed beard and coupled with his thick, muscular frame, made him appear like a bouncer. His Rolex Daytona popped out of his sleeve, signalling his ostentatious lifestyle. The automatic handgun was clipped to his belt. It was a signal to his competitors and opponents—cross my path and death will cross yours. Behind his luxurious brute personality was a cunning businessman who knew when to exude force and when to grease palms.

Jerome led Victor into another room and handed him a cigar. As they lit up, the conversation drifted to their troubled childhood—the years that likely forged one of the most notorious criminals the world had ever known. Their father was a violent alcoholic, abusive to their mother and them. He refused to divorce her, yet showed her no kindness. For the brothers, every day felt like a meeting with Satan.

There was a time when their father beat Victor so savagely, he nearly died. The scar across Victor's cheek was a permanent reminder of those brutal days. Their father would bring other women into the house and force his wife to watch as he defiled them. On the rare days he was away, the mother and two sons would finally experience a sliver of peace and have a reason to smile. But that peace was always short-lived.

One morning, when Victor was fifteen, he awoke to the sound of his mother screaming. He rushed downstairs to find his father threatening her with a knife. He swung the knife at her throat, but it was blocked by her hand. She began bleeding and begging for mercy. Finally took the baseball bat and beat her so badly that it split her head, and she died on the spot. The kitchen and hall were full of blood. Their mother lay lifeless in the centre with her mouth open. Motionless and battered.

For a moment, Victor was emotionless and cold. He felt a chill run through his spine. Luckily for him, his father did not see him watch this unfold, and he started cleaning up the body and the blood stains. Their father started digging their backyard, where he planned to bury his now dead wife.

Victor realised that since their mother was dead, in time, their father would probably kill the two of them as well. He took this opportunity to strike back. He stole his father's gun from the toolbox and sneaked up behind him, and shot him in the back. His father was in pain but had enough strength to turn around to watch his teenage son with a gun pointed, and before he could leap across to stop Victor, he fired a second shot that went through his chest, and he fell to the floor. Victor realised he was still breathing, but he wanted the bastard dead. Victor emptied the gun in his chest and put one bullet in his father's head, thus killing the person who had traumatised his entire childhood. Within half an hour, the brothers had become orphans.

He went to Jerome and told him everything. Their neighbours heard the gunshots and called 911. Within minutes, the police arrived at a gruesome crime scene. The hall was full of blood, the mother dead in the middle of the home, and the father lying lifeless in the backyard next to a half-dug grave.

Victor and Jerome were immediately taken into custody, and Victor narrated the entire incident to the police officers. The two brothers described in detail how their father would abuse and beat them and their mother. They noticed multiple bruises on all three of them, and Victor took responsibility for killing his father and said he didn't know what took over him, and everything happened in a flash. He said he didn't realise how and when the gun got into his hands, and when he fired the shots to kill his father. The neighbours corroborated the story about their father being an alcoholic and abusive towards the three of them, but never reported the crime as they feared for their own lives.

A court case was registered, and Victor was found not guilty on the grounds of temporary insanity. The public defender's office was sympathetic towards them, and all the witnesses and evidence pointed to a troubled childhood. He and Jerome were ordered to undergo counselling, and since they were underage, they were put under foster care. However, they never recovered from their childhood trauma, and once they were eighteen, they were on the streets and engaged in almost every vile activity out there. Jerome somehow managed to get a job as an apprentice in a real estate firm where he learned the business, and within five years was an independent realtor. Victor, on the other hand, got entangled in the illegal dealings of the streets. He began playing a part in robberies and soon even ended up murdering someone. Although none of it could be proven, the cops always had an eye out and were looking for evidence against him.

One day, unknowingly, he ended up helping a conman escape the cops. This person was Pedro, who was the erstwhile head of the *Draconists*. He was immediately scouted by Pedro, and soon Victor moved up the ranks and gained Pedro's trust. He assisted Pedro with various shady deals relating to weapons delivery, drug smuggling, human trafficking, and prostitution. Jerome's real estate connections were used to launder money and bribe government officials.

Pedro had a weakness for alcohol and gambling, and every month, he would lose a ton of money while gambling under the influence of alcohol. One night, while he was gambling at a local casino in Las Vegas, he ended up punching the hotel's head of security, and a fight ensued. He pulled out his gun and shot towards the head of security, but the bullet missed him and instead penetrated the leg of another hotel guest. Oblivious to his knowledge, there was an undercover police officer who tried to mellow things down, but Pedro wouldn't have any of it. He pointed the gun at the officer and was about to pull the trigger. But the officer's reactions were lightning fast, and he shot back in self-defence. Pedro was shot in between his eyes and he died on the spot. This was the beginning of the end for Pedro, and the era of Victor had begun.

As Victor was growing through the ranks of the *Draconists*, he became Pedro's right-hand man and soon wanted to run the *Draconists*. Pedro's untimely demise was welcomed by Victor, and he declared himself the new leader of the *Draconists*. Although he was hungry for power and wanted full control of the gang, he respected Pedro and had high regard for him. After taking over the operations, Victor realised there was a certain level of uncertainty in the business model of betting on the results of Formula One. He decided to manipulate one side of the bet by using a portion of the laundered money. He would pay some high-ranking officials in Formula One Teams who would ensure an incident would impact a part of the race. He wanted the overall result manipulated, but there were no gullible individuals in the top teams.

Based on this information, Victor would place his bets. There was news in the air that he played a part in manipulating the results, but his rivals could never prove anything, and the *Draconists* continued to be highly respected in the world of scum.

Chapter 20

The United States government organised the funeral for John and Frank. Victor sent some of his men under disguise to attend the funeral to potentially discover what had transpired and if something was amiss. He was sceptical that the entire truth was not being revealed. His men reported nothing was suspicious. Unknown to them, each member of John's family played their part perfectly. Victor was annoyed about the lack of inside information and began screaming at Mike, who was terrified for his life. He somehow controlled himself and did not spill a word about involving the authorities. But Victor had a hunch. The money Mike owed him kept one of his arms tied behind his back.

Victor took Mike's phone, called Raymond, and told him he needed to drop Mike as a client or else his life would be in danger. Raymond, who was as cool as a cucumber, said he would not be able to fire a client based on a threat from someone he did not know. Raymond's bluff paid off, and Victor revealed himself as the leader of the *Draconists*.

Victor smelled something funny. No one in all these years had not felt threatened by him. And the only plausible reason was that there had to be a piece of the puzzle he was missing. And Frank had taken this piece with him to the grave.

This time, he screamed at Raymond, saying he knows he's a Senior Associate at Roth & Gotham and he knows the office is at 456 Mission Street. He said he would blow up the entire building if they did not drop the case. Raymond began stammering and said they merely provided legal advice to Mike, but Victor had nothing of it. He was used to having things his way, and at this time, he was frustrated that Frank had been killed, and Hector had been captured. He cut the call in a fit of anger. He caught Mike by the collar and said, "If this lawyer of yours does not drop you as a client, I am dropping a bomb on the building of Roth & Gotham."

Mike was helpless and remained silent. He sank back into the chair, battered and bruised and barely able to speak. Raymond instantly contacted Andrew and Ron, and they connected with Walter. Raymond explained to Walter what had just transpired, and the entire staff of Roth & Gotham was under threat. Walter knew arranging for the security of the entire staff would take ages, so he advised that everyone work remotely.

Ron and Andrew suggested that all partners should be provided security, and the rest of the firm could work from wherever they pleased. However, Walter had a gut feeling that Victor was bluffing, and he wanted to call that bluff. He arranged for undercover police officers to walk in and out of the office of Roth & Gotham, disguised as lawyers and keep an eye on the street for anything suspicious.

In the meantime, Hector was in survival mode. Gordon and Carter were trying to mentally exhaust him to make him anxious enough to talk. He was constantly locked up and made to sit in an empty room. His hands were cuffed, and his legs were tied. They did not want to imprison him till Mike was safe, as they could not risk him having access to a telephone and contacting Victor through the prison system. They knew someone as resourceful as Victor would have eyes and ears in every prison. When Vikram went to give him his meal, Hector tried to make conversation, and as

Vikram was distracted, he struck him, and Vikram almost fainted. Hector had somehow broken through the cuffs. He banged the chair on the glass and picked up a shard and managed to catch the door before it closed. He held the sharp edge of the shard against Vikram's jugular vein.

The entire facility was on high alert. Sirens were ringing throughout. How did they not see this coming? They had never had a prisoner escape, and what would be worse was that the location would be exposed once Hector stepped out. While holding Vikram, he yanked Carter's gun and fired bullets across the premises. The analysts ducked for cover. Asha and Gordon could not get a clean shot as Hector held Vikram close. Hector managed to limp out of the facility. Vikram tried to fight back, but Hector punctured his bicep with the glass and even shot a bullet towards Carter. Carter's quick reflexes ensured he was able to take cover. In the meantime, Hector pushed Vikram away and caught a bystander who had just parked his car. He threatened to shoot him and coerced him into handing over his keys. All this while, Hector held the civilian hostage. He shot towards the officers, who took cover behind a pillar. He managed to get into the car and, while leaving, shot the civilian. Sentinel was forced to attend to the civilian and Vikram while Hector started the engine and got away. This was a catastrophic failure for Sentinel, and everyone was startled. The President would be pissed. How they all wished they had imprisoned him, or even better, executed him. But, right now, they had to get Vikram and the civilian medical attention. The civilian unfortunately succumbed to the gunshot wound, but Vikram escaped with a flesh wound to his bicep. Luckily, there was no major damage to the muscle or the bone. Everything happened so fast, and they were caught napping—a rare mistake had punctured Sentinel's armour. Gordon noticed the car was a black BMW Seven Series, and he got a partial number plate. The beginning numbers were 165.

Asha almost started crying out of concern, and Carter and Gordon helped Vikram enter the black site. The on-station doctor treated the wound and stopped the bleeding. Although his right arm was fully functional, he was ordered to rest for a couple of days. But Vikram was a fighter and had a never-give-up attitude. He wanted to get back to work and track down Victor once and for all. The doctor advised him not to move his left arm as it could cause nerve damage.

The atmosphere at the black site was tense. Everyone's morale was down. No one person was responsible for this. It was a collective failure. Walter knew he had to swallow the poison pill. He immediately contacted the President and brought him up to speed. Although he was embarrassed, he knew he had to follow the chain of command and adhere to protocol. The President was annoyed to hear the news. They were surely on the back foot.

"Sir, being the leader of this task force, I take responsibility for it. The first order of business is to change the location. We'll need you to authorise it."

"I agree, Walter! I will get you that approval immediately. I've asked my chief of staff to check for other facilities in San Francisco. What are you going to do next, Walter?" questioned the President.

"We'll use Nautilus to track Hector's movements. This should lead us directly to the hideout of the *Draconists*," responded Walter.

"Sounds like a plan. Go ahead. Sometimes everyone that shits on you isn't your enemy."

Within minutes of his discussion, Walter received an email from the President's chief of staff informing him that the new location of the black site was on Mission Street. Walter ordered their entire site to be cleaned up and moved to the new secure location.

As a result of the phone call between Raymond and Victor, Walter informed them that security had to be tightened up immediately, and the office of Roth & Gotham had to be evacuated. While the other parts of the site were being cleaned and moved, Vikram's technical mind was alerted. He asked Walter to repeat what he had heard, and Walter realised what had happened. Mike's phone was being switched on at odd hours by Victor to contact various people whom Mike was talking to regularly. He was doing this to check if any of the people were government servants. This meant that his phone could be traced when switched on. Vikram put Mike's phone on tracking, but it was unfortunately switched off. This was another mistake that had cost Sentinel, as they would have known the location of Victor's safe house hours before. The new black site was right in the heart of San Francisco's Financial District and close to the office of Roth & Gotham. It was a busy street, and all everyone cared about was getting to their workplace on time. Hector did not have a cell phone, as it was confiscated upon his capture. But Gordon put out a BOLO (Be on the Look Out) for a black BMW 7 Series with a partial number plate of 165.

Within an hour, they got a hit that a car matching the description was parked in one of the by-lanes in Haight Ashbury. A team of police personnel was sent to the scene, but they could not find Hector. He had abandoned the vehicle and probably stolen another one. The officers asked various pedestrians and shop owners where the person driving the car had gone. One of the workers at a shop selling rock and roll merchandise and bongs said he saw a man wearing a black jacket and blue jeans limp straight on Masonic Avenue.

The weather was apt for a leather jacket. Hector blended in well with the surroundings. He took off on foot, but they knew he would not be able to walk too long due to the gunshot wound on his left leg. It was possible he would either contact Victor from a payphone or utilise public transport to go to one of the hiding places. Sentinel had let go of a criminal who was on their top ten list. It was not every day this happened, and Walter was ashamed that the situation had occurred under his leadership. Once the new black site was set up, he informed his team he would be tendering his resignation as he saw it as his failure. Everyone was gutted. They tried to convince him to rethink his decision. Walter and Gordon were good friends, and even Gordon's persuasion was a moot point for Walter.

He contacted the President and informed him about his wish to resign, but the President did not accept it. He reminded him that it was he who helped catch Frank, who was leaking information to Victor. The President recounted all the acts of service he had performed for the country, and one mistake did not tarnish his record. "If you want to make things right, catch those sons of bitches," said the President.

Walter was glad to hear his service to his country had not gone unnoticed. He thought for a moment and decided not to go ahead with his resignation. He responded, saying, "I will make this right! Thank you for your vote of confidence, Mr President."

The entire team was relieved that Walter was staying. Everyone was staring at the screen, looking to see if they could catch a glimpse of Hector getting away. They rewound the footage from Nautilus and found a clip where Hector was getting away. They saw him drive towards Haight Ashbury and then leave the vehicle. He hailed a cab, and they watched as he turned onto Masonic Avenue and saw the cab cross the University of San Francisco. He did not want to leave a trail, so he got off at the Golden Gate Bridge Welcome Centre. He switched out his leather jacket with another person for a GAP hoodie to alter his appearance. He entered another cab, and the cab driver noticed Hector was limping. He offered to help him, and Hector ordered the driver to drive towards Gravenstein Highway. "I'll tell you when to stop," said Hector.

"What happened to your leg, sir? How did you injure yourself?"

"Just keep driving and mind your own business," replied Hector. He was in no mood to talk. All he wanted to do was reach the hideout and report to Victor.

Chapter 21

Hector rolled down the window and felt his first burst of fresh air in a while. Once he reached Marcelus Roofing and Fabricators, he asked the taxi driver to stop. The guards at the gate recognised him, and he asked them to pay the driver $500. The guards paid the taxi driver and asked him to fuck off from there. The taxi driver was perplexed at everyone's rudeness, but didn't care since he was paid more than what was due. Although he found it suspicious that a person who worked at a roofing and fabricating company randomly paid him so much money. What looked stranger was that the guards were carrying sophisticated weapons. He decided not to delve too much into this. He was glad they did not stick a bullet in his head.

Hector made his way up to the room where Mike was held hostage. He met Victor and Jerome. Victor smiled from ear to ear at seeing Hector. He embraced him like a younger brother and said he was glad Hector was alive. Before Hector could divulge his escape, he said there was an old enemy in the form of a former MI6 agent, and other agents from various agencies within the United States had united to form a task force and bring down the *Draconists*.

When Victor asked him whether Mike's name was mentioned, he said he was not sure what role Mike played because he was inside a soundproof room and could not hear anything. "How on earth did you get out of there?" asked Victor.

Hector narrated the whole incident of how he had managed to break through the cuffs and injure one of the members of the task force. He narrated his escape story and said he needed good medical attention since his leg had started bleeding excessively. Victor was amazed that even after taking a bullet to his leg, Hector was just as resourceful.

On his payroll, Victor had a doctor who would regularly treat injured gang members. The doctor was ordered to keep at least five litres of each type of blood available at all times. For this, he would pay the doctor generously, ensuring his family was well taken care of. He even bribed the blood bank to make sure blood was available whenever the doctor demanded. The doctor examined Hector's gunshot wound and said he would need to rest for a couple of weeks before the wound heals fully. He would be out of action for a while and would have to ease into the physical activity. Hector could not believe he was going to be on pseudo-house arrest. Jerome came out and greeted Hector and inquired about his health briefly, but was more interested in knowing what happened while Hector was in the custody of the task force. Hector re-narrated the entire incident, and then Jerome asked, "Do you think you can take us to the place you were held hostage?"

"Yes, I can. I know exactly where it is," said Hector.

Jerome then suggested they should raid the place and kill as many people in the task force as they could. He said, "These people are hell bent on ensuring we run out of business."

Victor agreed, and Jerome said they should formulate the plan in private before delegating each person their role in the operation. The *Draconists* operated in a pyramidal structure where only the people on top knew everything that was happening. There were a few people privy to parts of the plan, but the foot soldiers were only aware of their respective responsibilities. Only Victor and Jerome knew about the entire operation. Next in line was Hector, and the three of them were the pillars of the syndicate. There were things Hector was oblivious to, but he was satisfied with the role assigned to him since the two of them had saved him from dying many years ago. He was happy to operate under their leadership and had no ambition to overpower them.

Jerome and Victor entered a secluded room. Jerome was of the opinion that there were gaps in Hector's story. He thought Hector had become a confidential informant and was a bigger threat than Mike. "How do you think this guy was able to escape when there were members from the CIA, FBI, and MI6 present in those premises?" questioned Jerome.

"I don't know, Jerome. Maybe it was dumb luck. But I don't think he has changed sides," said Victor.

"Listen, Victor, you have always had a soft corner for him, and I hope this is not clouding your judgement," responded Jerome.

"You think I would let my feelings come in the way, Jerome?" responded Victor.

Victor then reminded Jerome about how he had gotten Pedro killed by bribing an undercover police officer. "I loved Pedro and used to respect him. But when we found out he was slipping information to the DOJ and FBI about some of our associates, I made his death look like an accident, remember?" said Victor.

Victor also reminded Jerome that when a question was raised on the survival of the *Draconists*, he would never let anyone destroy the empire they had built. Jerome looked convinced but said, "I remember everything, brother. But let's keep an eye on Hector, and let's give him a new phone to track his whereabouts and calls.

Anything suspicious, and I am personally going to make his head my target."

"If he is compromised, we'll shoot him together and feed his intestines to the dogs," responded Victor.

Jerome then told Victor there was one more thing he wanted to talk about, and that was the location where Hector was held hostage. He said they should take the location from Hector and somehow enter the premises and see if they can find something that would either help clear Hector's name or confirm their doubts. "That place will be guarded like a fortress. And we risk getting caught," said Victor.

"If it is in plain sight, then it will look like any other building. We need to survey it and observe what activities go on around it and try and locate a covert way we can use to get in," responded Jerome.

"And how will we ensure we don't get caught?" asked Victor.

"We need to find someone new who is ready to be our puppet," said Jerome.

"You know, I have been wondering who it can be. You got anyone in mind?"

"Not at the moment. But let me shuffle around in my real estate lobby and see if any senior officials thrive on getting their palms greased."

"Sounds like a plan, brother," said Victor.

Jerome smiled and nodded. They both knew the headquarters of such a task force would have the President's level of security and even his involvement. He was not sure who Jerome would reach out to, but they needed to know Hector's heart was where his mouth was. Jerome was well known in the real estate sector because he always got the work done. Whether it was getting the city's approval or convincing an investor, he had the means to have his way. Over the years, he was involved in many shady deals where he would use various arm-twisting tactics such as bribery, threats, even kidnapping and extortion. None of his vile acts could be proven, and when they could, witnesses were bought, evidence tampered with, and even officials transferred. He was famously called 'The Extraordinary Broker' in the real estate industry because he had a knack for executing and closing some of the toughest deals.

Jerome walked out to his car and took a private jet straight to Florida, where he needed to sort out a real estate deal. Once he boarded his flight, he was informed that the deal he had to broker was between the Mayor of Miami and another real estate developer, Shine Properties. They could not agree on a price, and Jerome was called in to assist with the deal. Instead of brokering the deal, he offered the Mayor a larger and more ostentatious house in one of his projects and convinced him to take it. The house was next to the beach, offering an ocean view on one side and a pool view on the other. It was a five-bedroom bungalow spread across seven thousand square feet. The front of the house had a private beach, along with a backyard and a swimming pool. Although the market price was three million dollars, he offered the Mayor the property for two million dollars. The mayor was salivating at the generous discount and immediately accepted the deal.

"So, Jerome, to what do I owe this act of kindness. It is not random," said the mayor.

"Well, Mr Mayor, nothing in this world is random. I do need a favour from you. There is always some quid-pro-quo involved in our dealings, and you know that."

"What kind of favour?" asked the Mayor. He knew it had to be something illegal or connected to something illegal. He had always been on the good side of Jerome since he and Jerome used to work in a real estate firm together, and that was where they became acquainted with each other. He just so happened to study law in his free time and make his way up. But the two of them remained on good terms.

Jerome said, "Just like old times, I need some information."

"A million dollars for information, Jerome. This one must be serious."

"Yes, it is serious," remarked Jerome.

Jerome explained to the mayor in brief that one of his men was called in for questioning and somehow escaped. He wanted to know if his loyalty was still in the right place.

"Jerome, if the President is involved, I don't think they will let me in on what happened. You know I am not that important at the national level. I'm just the Mayor of Miami."

"I don't care! Find a way. I know you can," said Jerome.

Chapter 22

While the Mayor was tasked with determining whether Hector was trustworthy or not, the next Formula One race weekend was around the corner, which meant another bribery and betting opportunity for the *Draconists*. Given that cash had started drying up in the world economy due to the fall in the markets, high-value betting was one way to bridge the gap. The Prime Minister of the United Kingdom contacted Alain, the head of FIA, and apprised him as to what was happening. He didn't want to give out the names of Victor or the *Draconists* for Alain's safety, but he informed him about the bribery. Alain's eyes dropped at hearing this deplorable news. He knew this time, if Ferrari scored more than fifteen points, they would be constructors' world champions. Although this was almost a virtual certainty for the season, the story of who would be second in the constructors' world championship was wide open.

McLaren, Renault, and Williams were in striking distance of each other, and no doubt all three of them would want to be second. But being third, fourth, fifth, or lower this season would give that team more time in the wind tunnel for the next season when the technical regulations were going to be overhauled. He hoped none of the iconic teams were involved, as it would tarnish the reputation of the sport even more.

Alain said he would be as sly as a fox in the upcoming back-to-back race weekends and personally attend all driver and constructor briefings. He knew bribery could take place at any level. Probably someone having a performance link in their clause could take a bribe this year and let their team lose, but obtain more wind tunnel time for next year and win, or be in contention for the win. They would then use this to cash in on their performance clause. The race was being hosted at the historic Circuit de Spa-Francorchamps in Belgium. The first national race of Belgium was held in 1925 and has always been known for its unpredictable weather. The circuit was built through the Ardennes Mountains, and in the past, there had been situations where it would be rainy and slippery on one part of the circuit, where the cars would be aquaplaning, but be bone dry on the other. It was truly a test for the drivers as well as the teams. One slip in the strategy and the whole race would be overturned on its head.

The Formula One cars had huge amounts of downforce (the force that pushes the car down towards the ground), and the active traction control (an active computer program that prevents the car's wheels from slipping while accelerating) allowed them to take the corner, Eau Rouge, almost flat out without breaking. Eau Rouge was one of the most iconic corners on the Formula One calendar and leads onto the long Kemmel Straight. The top speed of the cars crossed 350 km/h at the end of the straight. This was the perfect place to get a tow from the car ahead and outbreak (when a driver breaks later and harder than his opponent) to make the overtake.

But this weekend was different. Alain was aware that the sport's name was being tarnished. The first practice was scheduled for Thursday, and Alain went to the garages of all the teams to see if he could find something suspicious. He was talking to every team principal on the pit wall and every senior mechanic in the garage. Nothing seemed out of place or out of the ordinary, but he knew he would not find anything in plain sight. If he wanted to find out who was degrading the sport, he would need to set up an investigative commission within the FIA, but not let any of the teams know.

There were ten teams in Formula One, and Alain decided he would appoint ten people from the FIA to be present in the garage and observe the race from there. None of the personnel knew why they were there. It was a private investigation. They were instructed to observe and talk to the team members and find out if there was anything out of place. Alain himself was walking up and down the pit lane, ensuring everyone was aware of his presence. He was a highly respected person in Formula One racing and was well known as the "Shrewd Frenchman". He had won the Le Mans 24-hour race in the past and was a NASCAR champion in his younger days.

After the practice sessions were completed, he held a briefing with his team to inquire if they had observed anything suspicious. None of them reported anything was amiss and said all teams were going about their work normally. They said the teams were busy finding the optimal race strategy and were working on race simulations and even practising qualifying runs. They tried different compounds of tyres with varying fuel loads to understand how the car would behave and what lap time could be generated. Alain knew this was the first day the FIA was personally present in each garage. It was an unexpected move that could probably result in a change in the forthcoming days. At the end of the day, Alain confided in his deputy, Jacques, about what he had learnt. The two of them were disappointed, but they knew mischief was afoot with their conspicuous presence.

The next day, Alain and his FIA team reached the track well before all the teams were scheduled to reach. They were there to search for anything peculiar. They noticed the team personnel from

Ajax Racing were already in the pitlane meeting with someone whom Alain did not recognise. Team personnel were allowed to enter three hours before the commencement of practice, and no one was expected to be there for another two hours. Ajax Racing was ninth in the constructors' world championship, and their Team Principal, Paul Lambert, was always looking to pick a fight either with the FIA or with other Team Principals. There was news of some of the sponsors wanting to pull out of Ajax Racing due to Paul's volatile temperament and shoddy on-track performance. This made Alain wonder whether Paul was involved in corrupting the sport. It made complete sense operationally; the team was in the doldrums. They had reached a point where most of the team members and racers were disgruntled and did not appreciate the tone at the top.

The team was already being sold to Maserati, who were going to be new entrants in the sport for the forthcoming season. It was common knowledge within the paddock that Maserati's board had made a unanimous decision that Paul was not fit for their team. There was a stark difference in management style and mentality. Paul was a mismatch made in hell.

Paul was belligerent. He had a volatile personality. Hot-headed and vengeful. He came from wealth and searched for opportunities to flaunt. He couldn't be trusted, and he was out of a job for the next season. He was pretty much disliked throughout the racing world. He got the job of Team Principal at Ajax Racing since the owner owed him a favour. He had invested in the team when they were in financial trouble.

Alain, along with his FIA team, walked towards Paul and greeted him with the usual, "How are you?" Paul was perplexed at seeing them and inquired why they were at the track so early. Alain was known to be direct and curt when the situation demanded. He responded by saying, "Team personnel are not allowed in the pit lane for another two hours, but the FIA is allowed. So, the real question is, why are you here?"

Paul was caught off guard. He didn't know what to say and blamed it on his watch, which he claimed had stopped working last night. Alain asked him to leave the pit lane and return after two hours once he was permitted to do so. He also said an official investigation would be launched against Ajax Racing, and the team would be fined for this infringement.

Alain knew he had found the rat in his paddock. Now he needed to know how the results were being manipulated and, more importantly, which results. Ajax Racing has been led by Paul for about five years now, and at the end of each year, many team members would leave due to major disagreements with him. Even the drivers who raced for the team were constantly changing.

Paul was looking into Alain's eyes like a hawk watches its prey. Alain knew he had found the perpetrator. But he needed evidence to prove it. Jacques, the Deputy President of the FIA, asked how Alain would make sure Paul was exposed. Alain responded, "Paul was talking to someone in the shadows who disappeared the second we started approaching. We need to find this mystery man. He and Paul hold the key to this scandal."

Alain and his team of investigators decided they would be present in the garage of all teams for the next few races. They did not want to alert Paul anymore. The presence of FIA personnel at the garages triggered a secret meeting at the track. Which meant the person Paul was talking to had pitlane passes and would be present for the race.

"Or maybe he stole the passes from someone to ensure nothing could be traced back to him. Or possibly another team principal or personnel from another team," said Alain.

Alain headed back to his office, contacted the Prime Minister, and informed him of the progress he had made. The Prime

Minister was satisfied with the progress. He requested Alain not to approach Paul or anyone from Ajax Racing again since the situation was delicate and involved various government agencies. Any wrong move could trigger a string of events that could result in uncontrollable warfare.

"What is going on, sir? First, you inform me of possible bribery within Formula One, and after I find out who it could be, you're telling me to nail my heels to the floor and do nothing," said Alain.

"You see, Alain, the world and international trade and relations hold more importance than Formula One. I promise you will have your revenge. We will present Paul in the courtroom and ensure he is put behind bars. But we need to make sure the other people involved remain safe as well."

"Which other people? Who are these people?" asked Alain.

"People who have made this possible are being chased for their lives. I have already told you more than I should have. This conversation never happened, and you know nothing about the bribery in Formula One. Understood, Alain!"

"I understand, sir."

"Oh, and Alain, please disband your investigative team after next race weekend and stop looking immediately."

"Understood, sir."

"You'd better make sure those men don't breathe a word to anyone, or else your life will be in danger. Keep your eyes and ears open and ensure you're aware of your surroundings. You have instigated mischief, and your mystery guy may want to cover his tracks. I suggest you continue to keep the FIA personnel in the team garage, but rotate them. None of them should be in the pitlane more than once," said the Prime Minister.

"Why is that?" asked Alain.

The Prime Minister responded, "Because we want to operate from the shadows and don't want them to be aware we have a sniff of some illegal activities. It will make them think it was a random check and not targeted. Also, keep an eye out to make sure you are not followed. If you see anything suspicious, please let me know. We will make sure you are safe."

"I will, sir! And thank you for your concern," said Alain.

"You're not going to believe what we just uncovered," said the Prime Minister.

"What is it?" asked the President.

"Ask your team to check for Ajax Racing and Paul Lambert. We believe this guy is your link in the Formula One paddock."

"We'll get right down to it. Appreciate the help."

Chapter 23

Walter updated the rest of the team about the conversation between the President and the British Prime Minister. Alain, the FIA President, had deviously discovered that the team principal of Ajax Racing, Paul, was involved in bribery within Formula One. He narrated to the team how the FIA inspected the track and noticed a mystery man who vanished in thin air once Alain approached Paul.

Vikram ran Paul's name through the criminal database to investigate what the system revealed. After a few minutes, the information flashing on the screen had everyone hooked. The system showed an investment management company, Downforce Capital, owned and controlled by Paul Lambert and his father, Pierre Lambert. The two of them were the General Partners of the investment company. This meant investment funds within this entity were probably being used as a pivot in Europe to transfer the laundered money from Lions Star Capital and distribute it amongst the various perpetrators.

Now they needed someone on the inside of Downforce Capital who was willing to provide them with information, investor lists, cash flow patterns, and payment details. Walter contacted Raymond and asked whether he had heard of Downforce Capital.

"Heard of them," laughed Raymond. "Are you joking, Walter? They are one of the biggest fund houses in Europe. I would say they are the equivalent of Lions Star Capital. If Lions Star is the top dog in the United States, then Downforce is the alpha in Europe," remarked Raymond.

"I see our worlds lack correlation. Do you have any other information on them?" asked Walter.

"I assure you, they are not our clients. But I can ask around and check if someone knows something about them. Let me tell you, their lawyers are not going to incriminate their client, and everything will be attorney-client privilege unless they know a crime is being committed. Even if you somehow get the International Court of Justice to subpoena them, they are going to send you everything they have and everything they don't. You and your team will be buried in paperwork for years," clarified Raymond.

"You make it sound like we've hit a wall," said Walter in a disappointed voice.

"Well, not exactly," said Raymond.

"What do you mean by that?" asked Walter.

Raymond said, "You know, half the world is looking for a new job. I'll check their website and press releases to verify if someone important recently resigned. If so, then you can have them interrogated and decide whether there was something unusual about the way they operate. The thing is, their filings will all be on time and contain all the required details. They will be meticulous enough to ensure they do not raise any alarm bells. But accountants hide their mistakes in the footnotes."

"So once we find him, you're saying we'll have to secretly call him for questioning," said Walter.

"I'm sure you guys will think of something. It's your bread and butter, but in the meantime, let me see what I can dig up on Downforce Capital," said Raymond.

After disconnecting the call, Raymond logged onto the website of the UK's Financial Conduct Authority to check if he could download Downforce Capital's latest filings. Since the Investment Manager of Downforce Capital was listed on the London Stock Exchange, there was a plethora of information available. He discovered they had investment funds operating in the USA, and there they would need to file Form ADV with the SEC.

After spending a few hours on the FCA and SEC websites and digging through various public filings, Raymond realised the CFO of Downforce Capital had changed three times in the last three years. Two of the CFOs had passed away under mysterious circumstances. The third one had been reported missing but was later found in Manchester, where he had secured the position of CFO at a family office.

Raymond was working on the balcony of his ostentatious hotel room, and at around 6:00 pm, while he was watching the sun set and sipping a glass of Pinot Grigio, he informed Walter about the information he had gathered regarding Downforce Capital and, more importantly, about the mysteries of the ever-changing CFOs. They now had one former C-Suite executive from Downforce Capital who could be interrogated, but they needed to do so without setting off alarm bells.

Vikram entered the data regarding the CFOs, and what came to light petrified everyone. The case of the two CFOs who had passed away was marked as inconclusive. One of them had died in a car crash. His brakes had failed, and the car went head-on into the water. The second died in a go-karting accident at a company event. Downforce Capital had taken all its executives to a private go-karting event, and while go-karting, the brakes of the go-kart failed, and the CFO was launched across the barrier and landed on the other side of the track. He had damaged his neck and spine, and within five days, he succumbed to his injuries. Both CFOs perished with brakes failing, and both cases were marked as inconclusive. This was enough information for Walter to request international support from MI6 and Scotland Yard, especially when the company they worked with was alleged to be involved in money laundering and bribery.

Raymond emailed his findings, which stated Paul and his father, Pierre, had taken a total compensation of about fifty million pounds in the last three years. That was well above the average of the last five years, and the earnings of the fund house had not increased exponentially but had reported a steady growth rate of about ten to twelve per cent each year. They would need access to the books and probably even have a forensic audit ordered. But for this, they needed to prove money was being laundered, which would not be difficult, as they had the list Mike shared with them.

Once the list was cross-referenced with the information they had just obtained, the name Downforce Capital stood out distinctly. Carter took the flash drive they received from Mike and plugged it into the computer. Vikram started searching the transactions where Lions Star Capital had wired money to Downforce Capital. The total money that had been transferred over the last five years was about four billion dollars. "Looks like we have found Victor's biggest co-conspirator. I am sure this father-son duo has to be involved in more than just investment management and Formula One," said Gordon.

"If we remember what Mike told us, they would invest money in companies and funds that would later declare bankruptcy. Maybe that's what Downforce Capital does as well," said Asha.

Walter could see how far the criminal network had spread. He was satisfied with the progress and said, "Team, this is great work, and I think we do owe Raymond a round of drinks. Also, we would need to recruit an accountant who helps us decipher all this financial information."

Looking at all the information on the screen, Carter said, "We should probably ask Roth & Gotham if they can help us. They're already aware of half the operation and the people involved. Since they would want the sword hanging over their head to disappear, I think they would be more than willing to assist us in our endeavours. More importantly, they are on our side."

"That's a great idea, and I think Raymond is perfect for the job. Hopefully, he agrees, though," replied Walter.

Walter called Raymond and asked how he was enjoying the confines in his luxury suite. Raymond was not pleased to hear that and thought it to be a punch below the belt. He told Walter the confinement was forced and, quite frankly, he was longing to move back into the city and experience the hustle and bustle he was so accustomed to. He missed driving his car and wanted to pull the window down, push the pedal, and feel the wind in his hair. Oblivious to Raymond, Walter was smiling from ear to ear. He had hit the nail on its head and knew Raymond would not disappoint him.

"Since you miss being out in the open, I have a temporary job offer for you," said Walter.

"Job offer! Walter, I am already employed with Roth & Gotham. Are you trying to poach me into public service?" asked Raymond.

"Not exactly, Raymond. Let me explain our ask of you. We would like to employ your firm to help us inspect the books of Downforce Capital. We have found some questionable information we have been able to cross-reference to the data Mike provided."

"So Victor is in bed with Downforce Capital," commented Raymond.

"Exactly! And, we want you to help us solve this financial mystery. I remember Andrew informing me of your affinity for numbers, and I think this will tickle your grey matter exactly the way you like it. Oh, and you might have to travel to the UK for this," said Walter.

"Travelling to the UK. Are you planning to send me to the battlefield?" questioned Raymond.

"We are not going to send you unprepared. We are going to train you how to use guns. If you stick to the script, we know you can pull this off."

"You have a way to persuade people, and no wonder you are called The Closer," remarked Raymond.

"I'll take that as a yes," remarked Walter.

Walter disconnected the phone call and said, "We have our forensic investigator, and he will be joining us tomorrow morning." The atmosphere within Sentinel was once more ecstatic and Walter contacted the President and updated him about what they had uncovered.

The President was delighted to hear the good news and said, "You guys have turned adversity into potential victory. Great job! Keep me posted."

Chapter 24

While Asha and Gordon were making arrangements for Raymond to travel from The Ritz at Half Moon Bay to their new black site, Vikram noticed a temporary position of Legal Head was available at Downforce Capital. Walter and the President updated the British Prime Minister about the information they had uncovered. The Prime Minister said he would have the police investigate the offices immediately. However, Walter presented a different point of view by suggesting they send in Raymond as a Trojan Horse, disguised as an employee in their legal team. "There is a position open at Downforce for a Legal Head, and Raymond fits the role perfectly. They need someone who is involved in the world of asset management from a legal standpoint," said Walter.

The plan was that Vikram would prepare a flash drive that transmits live data to Sentinel. Once Raymond was in, he would insert this flash drive in the main server and within a few days, Raymond would resign, stating personal reasons. Anyway, since he would be on probation, his notice period wouldn't be longer than a week. "Has this lawyer friend of yours agreed to perform this dangerous mission?" asked the Prime Minister.

Walter confidently replied, "Yes, he has! And over the next few days, we are going to train him in basic combat in case he needs to make a run for it."

"I hope you blokes know what you're doing. You know what, I'll assign one of my guys as his personal security officer," said the Prime Minister.

"That would be fantastic," remarked the President.

"We might need your investigators for an interrogation of the former CFO in Manchester. But we want to ensure we can do it without disturbing his life," said Walter.

The Prime Minister agreed with Walter and said, "It will be beneficial to have an ace up our sleeve in case we need someone to be a witness in court."

While Asha and Gordon were on their way to Half Moon Bay, Walter informed Vikram he needed a flash drive with a specific function. Vikram started preparing it immediately. He said he would need a couple of hours, but it would not take too long. The flash drive would act as a portal through which data is transferred to their black site. And if someone catches onto the signal, it would ping all over the globe, so no one would be able to find the location. Walter nodded his head in approval and was impressed with Vikram.

While Vikram was preparing the flash drive, Asha and Gordon walked in with a black cloth over Raymond's head. They removed the black cloth, and Asha announced, "Voila! Presenting Downforce Capital's new Legal Head and soon-to-be weapons expert." Raymond was not amused. He shrugged his shoulders, and the expression on his face was one of disbelief. He began to wonder what a precarious situation he had gotten himself into. When he informed Andrew and Ron about it, they first thought he was hysterical or out of his mind. Amusement turned to shock when they realised he was actually going to do it. They asked him to be vigilant since the situation could turn on its head at any time.

Walter welcomed Raymond and thanked him for showing bravery and agreeing to risk his life. He said Gordon and Asha would be training him over the next few days before he travelled to England. "But I need to interview and apply for the job. I have not got it yet," said Raymond.

Vikram walked over to him and presented him with his offer letter. Even Walter looked shocked and said he was not expecting the process to be so smooth. "How on God's holy earth and more importantly, when did you do that, Vikram?" asked Walter.

Vikram was smiling like a schoolboy who had just topped his class. He said he had been thinking about how to get Raymond in when he realised getting him in as a permanent employee might pose problems since they would need him to resign within a week. Therefore, he got himself a job as a third-party consultant for Downforce Capital. He hacked into their system and created a job opening for a temporary Legal Consultant, and set the duration of the assignment for one week. He wrote a code that took all of Raymond's information from LinkedIn and prepared a résumé he uploaded, and even closed the job opening. He finally created a fake email address for Raymond and mailed the offer letter.

Raymond was flabbergasted. He looked at Walter and stammered, "You guys can do all this?"

Walter smiled and said, "I can't. But this man can."

After completing his training with a pistol, Gordon gave him a brief on guerrilla warfare, hit-and-run strategies, and specialised techniques like smoke screening and camouflage. Within the next day, Raymond received his temporary work permit for the United Kingdom. The President of the United States and the Prime Minister of the UK pulled all their strings to get the work permit within a day. Ron authorised a fake letter of absence for

Raymond on the letterhead of Roth & Gotham since they did not want to raise any suspicion within Downforce Capital or worse, alert Victor.

Raymond spoke to Giovana and informed her about his little foreign assignment. She did not approve of him going on an undercover mission and was shouting and howling at him for agreeing to do it without her permission. Raymond was silent. He knew he had made a mistake, and the more he tried to reason with her, the more she fought back. Finally, she calmed down and told him to be safe.

"I'll be back within a week," said Raymond.

"They are international criminals, Raymond. It's not a normal court hearing. I'm terrified for you," cried Giovana.

"Don't worry, I will be smooth and sleek," he said, smiling. Internally, Raymond was more doubtful about his ability to pull this off, but he needed to maintain a brave face in front of Giovana.

"You'd better come back alive, mister. And this is an order. If not, I am going to kill you," said Giovana.

"It's all for the client, honey. I am only doing my job of safeguarding their interests. I promise I will come back alive."

"I don't know which other lawyer would go to such lengths for their client. I don't believe your ethics code talks about dying for a client. Especially one that is knee deep in criminal activities."

"It's a service to the country, not the client," justified Raymond.

"I don't care! You are coming back ALIVE, you hear me?"

"Yes, ma'am. Loud and clear."

Chapter 25

The next morning, Giovana kissed Raymond goodbye. She reminded him once more that he needed to come back alive, and he promised he would. She was holding back the tears, but as he got into the cab, tears rolled down her face. She prayed he be back home alive in one piece.

Raymond boarded the American Airlines flight from San Francisco. He had packed two bags with three suits and seven sets of clothes. He was flying business class and was welcomed aboard with a glass of champagne. The air hostess introduced herself and offered to help him with his carry-on bag. Raymond was neither in the mood to entertain nor be entertained. He had luckily been allotted the window seat right at the beginning of the section, and there was no cubicle next to his. He quietly settled in, put on his blinders, and tried to fall asleep. He received two meals throughout his flight and drank two glasses of scotch.

He landed in London the next day and was greeted by a friendly immigration officer. She asked his purpose of visit, he said he was coming to perform legal consultancy for Downforce Capital. He presented her with his temporary work visa, offer letter, as well as a copy of his law degree. She then asked for his return flight details, which he shared and upon scrutinising the documents, the officer was satisfied with what she saw. She stamped his passport and said, "Welcome to the United Kingdom. I hope you enjoy your stay in our country."

Raymond walked out of London's Heathrow airport, where he was greeted by his chauffeur, Alex. The Prime Minister had sent a black armoured Range Rover to pick him up, and Alex was his security officer who would be driving him around for the week. Alex greeted him and introduced himself. Once they were in the car, he handed Raymond a pistol with a temporary gun licence. This was the second time in the week that Raymond was handling a firearm, and this time he was nervous since it was attached to his body like a limb.

Raymond would be staying at the Marriott Hotel Kensington, which was about three and a half miles away from the office of Downforce Capital in Chiswick Business Park. He landed on Sunday at about midday and checked into his hotel by 2:00 pm. He wanted to explore the city and went to see the London Bridge and Big Ben. He stopped at a local pub, enjoyed a glass of cold beer, and had a random chat with the bartender and a couple of indigenous Londoners who advised him to always carry an umbrella as the rain is never at bay in the city.

The next morning, Alex was waiting for him outside the hotel at 7:30 am. They reached the office of Downforce Capital, where Raymond was greeted by the receptionist. She had already prepared his temporary access card and an office for him. The office contained a wooden table and an office chair similar to his cabin at Roth & Gotham. He had a view of the central lake within Chiswick Business Park. Within an hour, the General Partner, Pierre, greeted him with a formal "good morning" in a thick English accent.

Pierre was dressed like a typical English businessman. He wore a navy-blue tailored suit. He was well-groomed and wore expensive eyeglasses reflecting seriousness and precision. He was a man of numbers and believed in ever-growing investor wealth and confidence. To him, everything was a competition, and he wanted to win at all costs.

The two men shook hands, and Pierre briefed Raymond about the piling legal work that needed to be completed. Most of it was drafting contracts, and Raymond already knew how that was done. During his days as a paralegal, Raymond was one of the best drafters at Roth & Gotham. He had gained experience with European clients as well, and this was going to be a piece of cake.

He was handed a laptop that was connected to the company intranet. Normally, temporary position workers were not given access to all portals within the intranet, but since the drafting would require access to previous versions of contracts and other company information, Raymond was provided unrestricted access to all files. Once Raymond was alone in his office, he messaged Walter, saying the flash drive was ready. Vikram contacted Raymond and instructed him to insert the flash drive in the laptop. Raymond kept a copy of English Contracts Law next to his laptop, which cleverly hid the flash drive from line of sight. Once the flash drive was inserted, it was activated, and Vikram gained access to Raymond's laptop. He was hoping he could also gain access to the Company's intranet, but he instantly realised that they had installed a multi-layered firewall. Vikram didn't want to send a virus to Raymond's computer and disable the firewall, as it would lead to an internal investigation at Downforce Capital, which they could not afford during Raymond's presence. Vikram realised Raymond needed to permanently penetrate Downforce Capital's system by plugging the flash drive into the main server.

Vikram informed Raymond he could continue working on the contracts as if nothing had happened. He asked him to keep the flash drive hidden from security, and on the last day, he would have to find a way to insert it into the main server. Raymond was granted immunity by the British Prime Minister to do anything that needed to be done. He needn't worry about circumventing the law. The next few days went by smoothly for Raymond, and he was now used to hearing praises from Pierre for his exceptional work. Pierre even offered him the position of Legal Head, but he had to decline since he said his wife was not in favour of moving. Raymond would spend a few hours every day trying to figure out how to gain access to the server room. He noticed that access to the server room required a special access card, and it had its own set of cleaners. This was the opening Raymond needed. It was the last day, and Raymond needed to act fast. That evening, he noticed that while the server maintenance staff were on duty, one of them inadvertently forgot their special access card in the office kitchen. Raymond instinctively grabbed it and walked out of the pantry towards his office. He left his card there in case someone came back to him; he could easily call it an honest mistake, as all ID cards looked similar.

On the last day, the receptionist handed him his check for £2,500. He thanked her and put it in his bag. Raymond informed her he would need to work late as he had received some urgent contracts from Pierre that needed to be completed. She said he could leave his laptop and other company accessories in his cabin, and he would receive his letter of service via email. Once everyone had left the office at 5:00 pm, Raymond went to the washroom and opened the supplies cabinet, where he found a uniform the cleaners would generally wear. He swiftly changed into it and headed towards the server room. Raymond put on a hat and looked down to avoid being caught on camera. He swiped the special access card on the scanner, and the light flashed green. He made sure he was wearing gloves so his fingerprints would not be captured.

Raymond entered Downforce Capital's server room. It was a fortified nerve centre of Downforce Capital's operations. It had multiple air conditioners maintaining a constant temperature of sixty-eight degrees Fahrenheit. There was a silent hum of the cooling fans. The blinking LEDs suggested there was an astronomical amount of data being stored, sent, and received.

Raymond contacted Walter and confirmed the flash drive was inserted. Walter gave Vikram the thumbs-up signifying Raymond had accomplished his mission. Vikram breached the firewall, and the flash drive began transmitting data. Raymond slyly walked towards the washroom to change back into his suit. From the corner of his eye, he saw the cleaner frantically looking for his badge. The temporary badge did not have the name or the picture of the person it was assigned to, and so the cleaner was oblivious as to whom it belonged to. Raymond swiftly entered the washroom and changed back into his suit. He headed towards his cabin, packed his things, and while moving out, he handed the server cleaner his badge and apologised for it getting swapped in the kitchen.

The server cleaner looked confused, but accepted the apology while Raymond darted towards the elevator, explaining he was running late to catch a flight. As of now, he wanted to be light-years away from London. This was the first time he had done something illegal, and he was sweating profusely. He entered his car and instructed Alex to take him to the hotel immediately. He surrendered his weapon to Alex and packed his bag. His flight to San Francisco was at midnight, and he reached the airport by 8:00 pm. He checked in and cleared security. The officer stamped his passport and thanked him for complying with the conditions of his temporary work permit. Raymond gave a friendly nod and walked towards his departure gate.

Once he boarded the flight, he breathed a sigh of relief, and the air hostess noticed he was tense. She asked him what the problem was, and he said he had a headache due to the long week, and all he wanted to do was sleep. She brought him some food to eat along with a medicine pill that would aid with the headache. Raymond thanked her for the service, and when he opened his eyes, the flight was about to land in San Francisco. After spending sleepless nights in London, he finally allowed slumber to take over him. He slept like a baby and was awoken by the airplane's wheels skidding against the tarmac as it landed. He breathed a sigh of relief as he touched American soil. Raymond finally realised how safe he felt at home.

Asha and Gordon were at the airport to greet him and took him straight to the black site. They wanted to hear what he had learnt about Downforce Capital and if there was any information they could use to add to the case file.

Walter and Vikram thanked him for his courageous act and informed him that the President will be considering him as one of the recipients of the Medal of Bravery. Vikram said almost all the data from Downforce would soon be available within a few days. "Now it's your chance to work your magic on the accounting data," said Walter.

Raymond nodded and said, "Can't wait to help you guys catch Victor and, more importantly for me, free Mike."

Asha and Carter dropped Raymond off at The Ritz at Half Moon Bay. They watched as Giovana hugged him, and tears of joy rolled down her eyes. She looked at Asha and Gordon and said, "This was the first and last time Raymond put his life on the line for you. Next time, find someone else."

Chapter 26

The British Prime Minister was informed that the operation was successful. Soon, they would have the information about which investment vehicles and companies Downforce Capital was using to perform bribery and manipulate Formula One results. The Prime Minister thanked the President and called Alain to bring him up to speed, and said they would soon have more information regarding Paul and Ajax Racing.

Whilst the atmosphere within Sentinel was euphoric again, the Mayor of Miami was able to pull some strings within the FBI. One of his former classmates was a lead investigator with the FBI, and through his connections in the President's office, he was able to determine someone had escaped. There was no way to find out who, but the news was confirmed that there was a criminal who was caught but then escaped. And, in the process, even hurt one of the officers and killed a civilian. There was word around the department that he was being mentally and physically tortured to divulge information, but the department could not extract anything from him.

Armed with this solid lead, the Mayor contacted Jerome and relayed the news. "Your guy is clean. He's not told the cops anything. In fact, he was tortured mentally but did not give in. You can trust him."

Jerome was happy to know Hector could be trusted and thanked the Mayor. He immediately turned to Victor and brought him up to speed.

Victor began gloating, "See, brother, I told you Hector is reliable. I trust him with my life. You were unnecessarily concerned," said Victor.

"You were right! We can trust Hector," responded Jerome.

"Brother, we need to find a way to churn more liquidity. We have a shipment of cocaine coming through, and the payment needs to be routed to Downforce Capital. After which, they will send that money in small parts to Colombia," said Victor.

"Yeah, I do have about five million dollars we can send them through our *hawaladar*. How much do we owe them?" asked Jerome.

"We owe about fifty million for this consignment, and we already owed them ten million from our last transaction, so all in all, we're in debt of about sixty million dollars," said Victor.

"How much does that son of a bitch who is tied to the chair owe us?" asked Hector.

"That fucker owes us close to $800 million," replied Victor.

Both Victor and Jerome agreed it was time to threaten Mike and get the money from him. They called Hector and told him they needed to teach Mike another lesson for all the money he owed and the trouble he was causing. By now, Hector was recovering well and immediately offered his help. It had been a few days since he last beat someone, and he was eager for some practice. Mike would be an easy target.

Hector walked into the room where Mike was tied to the chair and started cursing him. Mike was frightened for his life. He had an intuition that some form of physical assault was just around the corner; otherwise, Hector would not walk in with such energy. He no longer felt sorry for these guys, even though they were short by about $800 million. They were goons and thugs, and they deserved to die, but here they were threatening him.

Hector threw a punch across Mike's face, and Mike fell to the ground. He started bleeding from his mouth and was pleading for his life. "You slimy thief. You think you can run away with $800 million of our money?" barked Hector.

Mike pleaded and stuttered, "Trust me, let me go, and I'll find a way to return all your money. The markets will return, and within a year, you will have all of it and possibly more."

Hector picked him up and loosened his legs. He caught Mike by his throat and pushed him against the wall and said, "You called the cops on me and had me arrested."

"I swear I didn't involve anyone."

"You lying bastard," bellowed Hector. And he punched him in the torso, bruising him. "Now, tell me how much money can you return to us right now?"

Mike was still recovering from the sudden bout of torture when Hector screamed at him again. Battered and bruised, Mike was cursing the time he had entered a bet with Victor, and when he went to the cops. He somehow mustered the courage to say he would need to look at the books of his firm to see how much could be transferred. Hearing this, Hector got angrier and threw him across the floor. Mike's elbows scraped the wooden floor, and his skin peeled off. He felt a knot tighten in his stomach, and his wounds burnt, as if someone had set him on fire.

The torture did not stop there. As Victor stepped in and Hector told him what Mike had said, Victor took a piece of lime and squeezed the juice on his wounds. Mike could not believe this was the level Victor was going to. He was howling in pain as his wounds burned like a furnace. Victor finally decided he needed Mike to gain access to his laptop to initiate the transfer. Once they had enough money, they would decide whether Mike was going to live or not.

Victor asked his on-call doctor to heal Mike to the extent possible, as the next day, he would be travelling to another location to conduct business. In the meantime, Victor and Jerome went to the basement of Marcelus Roofing, where they would conduct their betting operation. They had paid off Paul from Ajax racing to crash, and trigger a safety car. This was supposed to happen after the first round of pit stops between laps fifteen to seventeen. On the sixteenth lap, Maurice, one of the racers with Ajax racing, crashed into the barriers, and the broken bits of carbon fibre from his car were spread across the track. There was debris all over the place, and his car was destroyed. Luckily, he was alright and was taken to the FIA medical centre for a routine check-up.

There was utter carnage on the race track, and the race director immediately deployed the safety car and instructed all cars to drive through the pit lane till it was safe to race again. It had been over ten minutes now, and the track marshals were taking time to clear the track. The race director decided to stop the race and reconvene it once conditions were ideal for racing.

Victor and Jerome rejoiced at this. Their bet had paid off. They stood to earn approximately thirty million dollars. They called the bookie, and he said the money would be ready by the end of the race. After the race, Victor and Jerome collected their money from their regular *hawaladar* and contacted the smuggler who was to deliver the drugs. They said they had about thirty million in cash they would be able to transfer through their *hawaladar*. The Colombians were agitated about receiving half of what they were owed. An argument ensued between the Colombians and Victor, but Victor was forced to give in. The Colombians held back half of the consignment. Jerome and Victor were furious, but they were currently operating with one hand tied behind their backs, with all the money held up by Lions Star Capital. They asked their dealers to bump up the prices of the drugs and to expand the collection. There was frustration mounting within the *Draconists* due to squeezed liquidity.

The next day, they grabbed Mike by the back of his neck, covered his head with a black cloth blocking all visibility, and dragged him into the car. They drove him to his house, where he would have access to the accounts of Lions Star Capital. While Mike was on his laptop figuring out how much money he could move, Hector and his associates ransacked his place. They took five Rolex watches valued at about $100,000, and the diamond-studded Audemars Piguet valued at a million dollars. They also stole his BMW M6 Coupe valued at $120,000. At this moment, Mike did not care what they took from him as long as they did not kill him.

On second thought, he was happy his Ferrari and Lamborghini were parked at his other home, and the documents to all his possessions were in a bank locker. He told Hector he would need to contact his associates and the banker to let them know he was going to transfer money out, and Hector reluctantly agreed. Mike took this opportunity to call Raymond and explained to him what was happening. Behind all the sound of ransacking, Hector did not hear a word Mike said. He was busy trying on the Rolex Daytona and Audemars Piguet to see how they suited his wrist.

Mike placed all calls through Skype and not through the phone. He didn't want the *Draconists* to catch on to what he was doing. His next call was to Damien, where he explained to him which investments were side-pocketed for Victor, and he needed help to dispose of them. Last he checked, they were worth $300 million. He informed Damien that he would be transferring about fifty million dollars, which was anyway earmarked to Victor, and if the sale of the investments went through in the next week, he would be able to cut the deficit to about $400 million. He was hoping this would give him bargaining power and the opportunity to negotiate with Victor.

Damien was perplexed at hearing that Mike was being beaten at regular intervals and almost teared up. He did not care whether they lost investor confidence. At this time, all he wanted was for Mike to return safely. He agreed to do everything possible to sell the investments and save Mike's life. He assured Mike they would manage to reallocate the money to the other Limited Partners over the years and somehow make it up by providing management fee rebates. Mike thanked him and said he needed to go.

As Mike walked out into the drawing room, he saw the carnage Victor's men had created. He begged them to stop and said that over the next week, he would be able to transfer fifty million dollars and had instructed his team to sell investments worth $200 million. He purposely quoted a lower amount to the *Draconists*, given that liquidity was constantly drying up in the market. And he wanted some bargaining power in case Victor came calling. He realised through all the torture, his mind had pushed him into survival mode; he wanted to get out alive.

Once Hector reached the headquarters, he informed Victor that they had taken all of Mike's expensive watches valued at over a million dollars and the BMW M6 Coupe as well. He said Mike had initiated a transfer of fifty million dollars, which would reach the accounts over the next week, and had instructed his team to sell investments with a value of about $200 million. Victor once again grabbed Mike by his neck and said, "If this $250 million does not make its way to me in the next week, I will start selling parts of you on the black market, and the first to go will be one of your kidneys."

Chapter 27

Immediately after Damien disconnected the call with Mike, he discussed Mike's situation with Gary, who also agreed it was time to do whatever was necessary to help release Mike from Victor's clutches. They both put out an offer for sale of the investments from the private equity book. Although the valuation suggested they might get about $300 million, they quoted $400 million to give them room for negotiation in case a high-risk-taking venture capitalist comes along.

The two of them then contacted Raymond and informed him about what had just transpired. Raymond understood the gravity of the situation and said he would talk to Walter and his associates. He asked them not to make any rash decisions and only focus on disposing of the investments. As of now, Victor had not threatened them, and it was better if the status-quo of the situation remained as is.

After talking to Raymond, Walter and his crew realised what was happening with the *Draconists*. "Looks like Victor is desperate since the flow of money is drying up for him," remarked Carter.

"He is going to be making some mistakes. Let's be prepared to pounce," said Asha.

"That's what happens when you are not patient. You end up making rash decisions and reacting on impulses," said Gordon.

"We have Mike's residential address and IP address. I will hack into his internet connection and see if we can get access to the cameras at his home. That should provide us with the registration number of the car used by the *Draconists*," said Vikram.

Everyone realised they were one step closer to discovering the hideout of the *Draconists*. Once they had the registration number of their car, they could follow it using the city's camera system to track its movement and hopefully find the hideout. Once Vikram gained access to the internet connection at Mike's residence and the camera application, they rewound the feed and saw that the *Draconists* had used a black Jeep Compass. They also noticed they had stolen Mike's BMW, probably treating it as part payment or a *gift*. They observed a partial plate on the BMW, but there was no plate on the Jeep, so there was no way of tracing it. The Jeep was probably stolen, or it was a custom-assembled vehicle.

Walter worked with the intelligence services and put out a BOLO for a blue BMW with Mike's partial registration number and for a black Jeep with no number plate. In case anyone came across this, they were to inform the police immediately.

Vikram said he would begin rewinding the camera footage to trace the location of the cars. The time stamp on the camera footage from Mike's home indicated they had left from there around 12:34 pm. It was two hours past that time, and unfortunately, the street camera next to Mike's home was malfunctioning. However, they saw the Jeep and the BMW on the next camera and started following the trail. Using Mike's home camera, they could see the cars leaving from Presidio Heights, where Mike lived.

Asha remarked, "Presidio Heights is the most sophisticated and ostentatious residential neighbourhood in San Francisco. Man, this guy is loaded."

"He's loaded because he works in asset management, and we work with the government."

As they were monitoring the footage, they noticed the BMW and the Jeep travelling in opposite directions. Gordon, Asha, and Carter were following the BMW while Walter and Vikram were following the Jeep. "These guys seem to have already found a way to dispose of the car. They are going to take it to their regular guy," said Gordon.

Vikram and Walter noticed the Jeep took a right on Park Presidio Boulevard and joined the Golden Gate Bridge. They were hoping the cameras were working by now as they had registered a complaint with the city's Public Works Department, but to their dismay, the department continued to twiddle their thumbs, and there was no progress made. If only the Public Works Department had known how important this system was, they would have burned the midnight oil to get it fixed. The cameras started working again right after Marin City, while the road merged with the Richardson Bay Freeway Bridge after Manzanita. The speed limit on the Golden Gate Bridge was forty-five miles an hour, and the distance to Richardson Bay Freeway was about six miles. Therefore, the time taken would be close to eight minutes. Vikram and Walter had their eyes glued to the screen in search of the black Jeep, but they were not able to trace it anymore.

"Sir, do you think they will follow the speed limit on the Bridge?" asked Vikram.

"If I were carrying a hostage, I would drive as fast as possible to ensure I don't get caught. But not fast enough to raise an alarm either," responded Walter.

"Let me check the footage from six minutes, assuming they were travelling at sixty miles an hour. I'll put in the permutations, and we can watch that footage like hawks," said Vikram.

While Vikram was having to compute the various permutations of speed-distance and time to locate the Jeep, Gordon, Asha, and Carter found the garage where the BMW was taken. They decided to go undercover and check what information they could extract about the *Draconists* and the whereabouts of the stolen BMW.

The next day, the three of them draped themselves in blue jeans, white t-shirts, and black leather jackets with metal buttons. They looked like they belonged to a gang, which was exactly the look they were going for. They needed to blend in with their surroundings, which they had executed perfectly. The three of them drove down to Auto Magicians at 2940 Geary Boulevard. They inquired about the various services being offered. The sales executives gloated about how they offered the best prices on all luxury car brands. After being walked around the showroom, Carter asked to see the workshop, which Romero, the manager, refused. Romero had a thick Mexican accent and was well built. He wore a custom T-shirt reading 'Auto magicians'. He said they had heavy equipment and could not risk any of them getting hurt. Carter and Gordon said they had experience working with cars and were aware of the risks, but he refused. He continued to lure them away from the workshop and towards the showroom.

Asha noticed Romero and a few of the workers had a holster, and she quietly whispered that to her colleagues. Asha changed the topic, saying she was looking for a BMW M6 Coupe, to which Romero said they didn't have one but could arrange for it in a couple of weeks. Gordon asked who the owner of the establishment was, as they wanted to meet him or her before purchasing the vehicle, as it helped in building relations, and if they liked the service, they would refer some friends as well. Romero said, "The boss is busy, but you can talk to me."

"What is your boss's name?" asked Carter.

"Why do you want to know the boss's name? Do you want to buy a car or not?" asked Romero in an agitated tone.

"We want to buy a car, but we like to get to know the people we are dealing with because we believe in loyalty. If we like your service, we'll refer our friends to you as well," said Asha.

"The boss is busy. Tell me, from the current display, which car do you like?" asked Romero.

"Like the lady requested, we want a BMW M6 Coupe," said Carter.

"Come back in two weeks. I will show you a BMW M6 Coupe," responded Romero.

"Okay, we'll come back in a couple of weeks. Do you need a deposit for it?" asked Gordon.

Romero was now visibly irritated, and it looked like he was holding in his anger. He said, "No deposit is required. If you don't like it, you don't buy it. Understand?"

"But how will you obtain it for us without taking a deposit? Won't you have to pay your supplier?" inquired Carter.

"Listen, man, you either buy the car or don't. How I get the car is my business, not yours," blurted Romero.

Asha realised Romero was on the edge. He had twice put his hand on his holster but not pulled out his gun. He was distracted by the constant ringing of his phone. Unfortunately, she could not read the name of the caller due to the angle of the screen. She said, "Thank you, Romero! We'll come back in to see if the M6 is available, and if we like it, we'll buy it."

Romero looked at them and waved them out of the showroom, but it felt more like he was throwing them out and forcing them to leave. As they were driving back, they discussed how shady the business model was. "The only way they can run such a show is if all the vehicles they are selling are stolen," said Gordon.

"Their men must be rubbing the Vehicle Identification Numbers (VIN) off the car chassis and engine bay, which is why he did not allow us access to the showroom," said Carter.

"Did you notice how evasive he got the second we mentioned a BMW M6 Coupe?" asked Asha.

"Yeah, and he kept deflecting us even when we asked the name of the owner," said Gordon.

"Did you get a chance to place the listening device Vikram gave you?" asked Carter

"Yes, I did! I placed it on the underside of the table. The only way they will be able to find it is if they overturn the table," said Asha.

As the three of them entered the black site, they ran Vikram and Walter through what they had just witnessed and how Romero, the manager of Auto Magicians, behaved. Gordon agreed that that place was probably a front for selling stolen vehicles and possibly even more. Their prices were unbelievably low, and they were selling legitimate vehicles. Gordon also said it could be a place where some vehicles are dismantled and sold for parts on the black market, so no one would know where a part has been. Walter looked at the three of them dead in the eye and said, "What if Victor and Jerome own that place?"

Everyone began thinking and realised it was not impossible. "We should ask Raymond to help us track the company filings of Auto Magicians and see if it reveals any names that can be cross-referenced to the list Mike gave us," said Vikram.

"That's a brilliant idea, Vikram!" responded Gordon.

The list of questionable companies convoluting was increasing by the day, and they had still not fully gone through all the entities provided by Mike. Their main focus was Victor, and whoever got caught in the net along with him was a bonus. They would use the entire list Mike gave them once Victor gets caught. They didn't want Victor to sound any of his associates and miss the opportunity to catch another international criminal. At this point, they had enough information to convict Victor. All they needed was to catch him, and the fact that Hector had escaped from their facility was proving to be an ineluctable loss.

Chapter 28

Vikram announced in an euphoric yet concerning voice, "I have spotted the black Jeep Compass, and I think it is the one we were chasing since it has no plates." The team dropped what they were doing and focused on the clip Vikram was showing. They noticed the black Jeep entering the Richardson Way Freeway Bridge. The Jeep was travelling at eighty miles per hour and soon made its way onto Redwood Highway. The Redwood Highway had portions of the famous US Route 101, a major north—south highway that traverses the states of California, Oregon, and Washington on the West Coast of the United States. The Redwood Highway was about 213 miles long, and as of now, they did not know where the Jeep was headed.

The Jeep was driving relentlessly and didn't seem like it would stop anytime soon. However, as it crossed Novato Valley, it pulled into a gas station. Through the highway camera, they saw the driver get out and fill the tank. Vikram zoomed in, and Asha, Gordon, and Carter immediately identified the man as one of the workers at Auto Magicians. Their suspicions were confirmed. The *Draconists* were somehow connected to Auto Magicians. Vikram said he would scrutinise the details provided by Mike once they finished chasing the Jeep.

After a quick fuel stop, the Jeep made its way back onto Redwood Highway, and after about thirty minutes, it exited US Highway 101 and took a left onto Luther Burbank Memorial Highway. Soon after, the Jeep took another left onto Occidental Road. This road led them through the vineyards of California, and once it reached Molino, it took a right onto Gravenstein Highway. Everyone at the black site was hoping the vehicle would stop at a point so they could find out where Victor had kept Mike hostage. The Jeep continued on Gravenstein Highway, and once it crossed Paul Hobbs Winery, the cameras stopped providing any footage.

Vikram rewound the footage, but it did not yield any result. The next camera operating on Gravenstein Highway was after Mays Canyon Road, which was about eight and a half miles away from Paul Hobbs Winery. Vikram openly cursed the Public Works Department as he would have to engage in another speed-distance and time puzzle to decipher where the Jeep emerged and what its final destination was.

To everyone's dismay, they could not trace the Jeep anymore, and it looked like the Public Works Department's lethargy was working in favour of the *Draconists*. Vikram watched the camera reels for about two hours but was not able to trace the black Jeep again. "This only means one thing!" he said.

Asha finished his sentence by adding, "The *Draconists* have their hideout somewhere between Paul Hobbs Winery and Mays Canyon Road."

This seemed like the most logical and palpable explanation, and although the distance was less than nine miles, the area to be covered was huge. The presence of various wineries on either side of the highway made it even more difficult to zero in on the hideout. Victor might be the owner of some of the wineries, hiding a back-door operation. But there was no way to prove it. And, no judge would authorise a search warrant without evidence.

"Either that, or there must be some abandoned and ransacked-looking building no one would enter and was being used as a hideout by the *Draconists*," remarked Gordon.

"We need to deploy our teams to survey the area and keep an eye out for anything looking extremely amiss and out of place," said Carter.

"Looks like we are going to go wine tasting, and since that's a field job, Vikram is not included," joked Walter. Walter's joking was a rare occurrence.

Vikram ignored the unnecessary banter. His brain was tired of mathematical puzzles, but he knew it was all in jest, so he laughed along and continued working. When he was in the zone and engrossed in his work, Vikram would operate like a machine. He immediately began the process of cross-referencing Auto Magicians to the list provided by Mike. He noticed over the years, there was a total of $200 million transferred from Lions Star Capital to their accounts, and that investment was written off in the records of Lions Star Capital. It was also accounted for as a distribution in the name of Victor—similar to the accounting that Mike had described to them. It was one of the entities that had dirty money converted into clean, and the investment was made on behalf of Victor. Therefore, Victor was the owner and operator of Auto Magicians. "No wonder Romero didn't want to give out the name of his boss," said Carter.

Walter phoned Raymond and said, "I have some confidential work for you."

"Where do I need to travel to now?" asked Raymond.

"You're funny, Raymond. Andrew was right, you are always out and about with your wits. You don't need to travel. I have a name for you—Auto magicians," said Walter.

"Why do I feel I have heard of this name?" remarked Raymond.

"Maybe because it is one of the companies mentioned in Mike's list," said Walter.

Walter now considered Raymond a close ally, and this was one of the times he would have to tell him what Sentinel had discovered about Auto Magicians. He left out the details about chasing the Jeep and needing to find out the location where Mike was held hostage. Knowing how Victor was, Raymond was not appalled to learn he ran a garage selling stolen cars. Raymond asked whether they had been able to trace where Mike was held hostage and if there was any demand from Victor. Walter said he could not reveal any information concerning an ongoing investigation. Although Raymond was not pleased with the response, he respected Walter and his team and understood the high pressure they were operating under. He said he would revert with the information he uncovers. After all, this was the only case he was working, and had not had this much free time to himself.

After a few hours of research and talking to his source in the IRS, Raymond discovered Auto Magicians had neither filed their last year's income tax return nor applied for an extension. He immediately contacted Walter and told him about what had come to light. He informed Walter that they could probably utilise this information and perform a raid by the IRS and gain access to the premises. Walter acknowledged the information and said he would consider this option when the time was right.

Walter apprised the team of what he had learned from Raymond. Everyone sensed it; Victor was operating with a sword dangling over his head. The pressure caused by the cash crunch had engulfed him. He had started making errors, and his judgement corroded under pressure. They decided the IRS would be informed that a raid may be needed shortly. But right now, they were not supposed to move a muscle, as it might alert the *Draconists*, and they might behave rashly. Even worse, they might harm or kill Mike. With their resources, they might go underground and disappear, and if that happened, it would be impossible to track them. Walter said, "We need to hit all their known places of business simultaneously so they don't know which fire to set out first."

"We should involve our UK counterparts as well and ensure they raid the offices of Downforce Capital and Ajax Racing simultaneously. We need to launch a global attack on the *Draconists* and their known associates," said Gordon.

This seemed like the most optimal strategy, and if it were executed appropriately, they would bring down one of the most notorious criminal syndicates of all time.

With John healing in his apartment, the President took control of the task force. Walter scheduled an appointment with the President and updated him as to what they had learnt. The President was happy to know they had zeroed in on one more illegal business operated by the *Draconists*, and also the radius within which they were holding Mike hostage. The President suggested they send undercover officers between Paul Hobbs Winery and Mays Canyon Road. He asked them to use regular road cars so they would not tip off Victor or any of his associates. "I have just the team that likes a day trip filled with investigative work," said Walter.

"That sounds great, Walter," replied the President.

Walter also informed the President about their idea to hit all known locations of the *Draconists* and their associates globally at the same time. This way, they would not know which adversity to thwart first and might end up making multiple blunders. This would get them caught for good. He also told him the flash drive inserted in the office of Downforce Capital was extracting massive amounts of information, which they would match against the information provided by their confidential informant when they are preparing the case file. "Sounds like you have a good plan in place, Walter," said the President proudly.

"It is all thanks to your leadership and guidance. Thank you for being there with us at our darkest hour," replied Walter.

"I am glad you were convinced to stick around. Look, mistakes happen, but the important thing is that we learn from them and move forward with the experience. Just make sure this is not repeated," said the President.

"You've spoken like a true leader, and I am glad to serve under you. The plan ebbs and flows like the tide. And we need to keep it that way because the puzzle keeps getting bigger by the day. The team is burning the midnight oil without taking a single day off. Once this is done, I think they have earned at least two months of paid vacation," responded Walter.

The President smiled and said, "I'll see what I can do for your team. We'll talk about what you all deserve—much more, of course. And please keep this conversation between us."

"Of course, sir! How is our Attorney General, John Parx, doing?" questioned Walter.

"He is recovering, Walter. I don't believe he will be in action for a few months from now. But he has been helping me with some other confidential projects. Trust me, he is proud of the way you and your team are handling this situation," said the President.

"Thank you, sir, I'll get on with the investigation and keep you updated."

"Alright, Walter! Let's get them."

Chapter 29

It had been a few days since Mike's home was ransacked. Mike initiated the transfer of fifty million dollars in small amounts to the accounts Victor ordered. The money reached them and was consolidated at Downforce Capital. From the accounts of Downforce Capital, a part of it went to Ajax Racing, and the other part to the Colombian drug lord. A total of thirty million dollars reached the Colombian drug lord through *hawala* transactions, and he released the remainder of the consignment. In all the chaos taking place in Victor's world, he finally found a moment where he could breathe lightly.

Victor and Jerome were sitting on the balcony, sipping a single malt scotch and smoking a Cuban cigar. They were discussing how the increase in drug prices had left the demand unfazed, and although the customers were not happy about it, they continued to buy from them as the quality of cocaine they supplied was unmatched. "You think we can make more use of this Mike guy if we release him for a few hours a week and let him trade on the stock market?" asked Jerome.

"If we let him loose, he might contact the cops," said Victor.

"We'll get him his work computer here, and we'll have someone sitting on his head every minute of the day. He won't be able to bat an eyelid without us knowing. Of course, this money is going to be in addition to what he still owes us," said Jerome.

"We also need him to get us the other $200 million his associates were to help with. Haven't seen a dime of that money," said Victor.

"Well, it will take some time, but all that money is already clean, so I will be able to push that into the new real estate project. I am going to gift one home to the fucking Colombian so he never holds up our consignment again," barked Jerome.

"Probably bug it so we can hear his conversations. We need to ensure he is not low-balling us by selling at higher prices," remarked Victor.

"That's not a bad idea, brother. Let's see how it goes," said Jerome.

"I think we should let Mike access his laptop; he needs to understand we mean business," said Victor.

Jerome agreed and said, "Let's ask Hector to get Mike's laptop from his house. He will need that to transfer the money."

"We also need to decide what we need to do about Mike once we have all our money. I wonder whether keeping him alive makes sense," said Victor.

Jerome looked up towards the ceiling, almost as if tapping into his lifelong experience, and said, "Once we find someone who can do what Lions Star Capital does, we can either stop working with him or, if we feel he knows too much, we can silence him and his associates. I still feel he has convoluted with the cops. We should probably send him down the highway to hell. But not right now."

While Victor and Jerome were having a moment of tranquillity, under Raymond's advice, Damien shared all the transaction details of the fifty million dollars with Walter and his team. Now Vikram needed to cross-reference these details from the data being extracted from Downforce Capital to investigate what course the money takes.

Damien and Gary informed Raymond regarding their success in selling some of the investments held in the private equity funds for close to $300 million. They now required wire instructions from Mike, who in turn needed those from Victor. Raymond contacted Walter again and gave him the news about the $300 million. With no way of letting Mike know a major part of the deficit had been recouped, they all feared whether Victor had executed Mike, as he may have lost patience.

Meanwhile, Hector and two of his associates left for Mike's residence to collect his laptop. Vikram had kept Mike's house under continuous surveillance in case the *Draconists* decided to revisit. He noticed Hector entering Mike's home in real time, and within a few minutes, he returned with a laptop in hand. He appeared to be using the same black Jeep they were previously attempting to follow. Everyone was looking at what was transpiring and wondered why Victor needed Mike's laptop.

"If he needs his laptop, Mike is probably alive," said Carter.

"Why would they want his laptop, though?" questioned Asha.

Everyone was scratching their heads when Walter said, "Maybe they know about the $300 million or want him to inquire about it. I cannot think of any other reason."

"But why not let him use his phone?" asked Gordon.

"Because they know the cops are looking for them. They probably don't want to take a risk right now," said Vikram.

"I hope Mike can give us some clue if and when he gains access to his laptop," said Asha.

For now, they were following the Jeep on their screens as Walter instructed them not to put out a BOLO this time, otherwise Victor would know someone was watching Mike's residence, and this would endanger Mike's life even further. They could not risk letting anyone know about Nautilus, or else, criminals would make it their sole goal to steal it and take over the world. "We need to look at the bigger picture, guys. In this charade, we need to catch Victor and ensure our systems remain safe as well. I would love to get Mike alive, but if his life is the price we end up paying to catch the *Draconists*, then it is what it is," said Walter.

They watched as the black Jeep made its way onto the Golden Gate Bridge and then disappeared for about six to seven minutes due to the malfunctioning cameras. They followed it and watched it take a left on Gravenstein Highway and then disappear once again after Paul Hobbs Winery. Again, nothing appeared on the camera set up on Mays Canyon Road. It seemed Sentinel had conclusive evidence that the *Draconists* had their hideout somewhere between these two spots. The next order of business was to go undercover to survey the area. They realised they could not make any dangerous moves until they knew the exact location of the hideout.

The next day, the entire team dressed as civilians and drove towards Paul Hobbs Winery. They decided to make it a well-deserved picnic out of it. The team had not had a single day off in a few weeks, and thought of being on the road, soaking in the cool Californian air, and driving along the wineries was exhilarating and refreshing. The fresh air was invigorating and set a sense of calm within the team. After days of serious work, they were finally able to share a few light moments. Walter said he had a surprise for the team after they had completed their work for the day. "Did you book a private wine tasting tour for us?" asked Vikram.

"You'll know when it's time. Don't try to ruin the surprise for yourself and everyone else," said Walter.

Asha grinned at Vikram being chided, and Vikram gave a look that meant "Don't test my patience."

They crossed over the Golden Gate Bridge, and within an hour, they reached Paul Hobbs Winery. Vikram was more accustomed to working behind a computer and at a desk. The field work was alien to him, but he enjoyed being outdoors for a change. Carter slowed down the car, and everyone in the team was looking for a building or structure that looked out of place.

The team got off at various places and explored them as tourists. They stopped to look around at Dutton Estate Winery, where Walter talked to the manager and inquired about the price of a wine tasting session for a group of ten. After negotiating a price, the manager wanted to serve them wine, but Walter declined and said he would like the wine tasting to be a surprise. After a brief stop at the winery, they shared two pies from Mom's Apple Pie, a local bakery famous for its apple pie. It was owned by a family, and this was the third generation running the business. They then crossed the VCA Forestville Animal Hospital, behind which there was a chicken hatchery named Alchemist Farm. They continued driving along Gravenstein Highway and crossed multiple wineries, and nothing looked as if it was out of the ordinary.

They took a left after Forestville Animal Hospital onto Pocket Canyon Highway, which is when all their nerves stood up. They were more than halfway there and had not seen anything out of place. They stopped for brunch at Sonoma Pizza Co. and enjoyed a spread of pepperoni pizza, *quattro formaggi* pizza, and two calzones. They were quietly looking around when Asha and Gordon recognised Romero. They whispered that Romero was the manager at Auto Magicians. Everyone was alerted, and the pace at which they ate was reduced. The pizza momentarily lost taste as they were staring right at the man who could lead them to Victor. Carter said they might need to follow him out, so they should probably finish their meal and settle the bill so they were ready to go at any minute.

To their surprise, Romero also recognised them and approached Asha. He inquired if she still wanted the BMW M6 Coupe and when she planned to visit for a look. Asha confirmed her interest and said she would come to the showroom soon to test drive the car. She asked what he was doing there. He explained he wanted a day off and was driving through the wineries when he decided to stop for lunch. Asha mentioned it was a family outing, and the conversation ended. "This guy seems friendly," Walter remarked. "You should have seen him a few days ago at the shop. He was in such a foul mood," Carter added. "Fortunately, or unfortunately, Hector isn't here. Otherwise, he would have recognised all of us, and there could have been a full-blown fight right away," Gordon said. "A fight! There would have been chaos and a bloodbath. We need to be careful," Walter warned.

As Romero and his associates got up to leave, Walter and everyone settled their bill swiftly. They quietly followed him outside and watched him enter his car and drive up towards Mays Canyon Road. While following them, they crossed a couple more wineries and a run-down establishment named Marcelus Roofing and Welding Fabricators. "That place looks out of place," remarked Vikram.

"Why do you say so?" asked Asha.

"Out of all the establishments on this highway, that is probably the only one not relating to wine or food," said Vikram.

"I would agree," said Gordon.

"I just saw someone from their car half-wave to the guard at that place. This has to be their hideout," said Walter.

"And damn, it is heavily guarded. Look at the security personnel, they are well-built and look like they have undergone commando training. They are also carrying sophisticated guns, and the fence is covered with barbed wire," said Carter.

"This place also has its camera surveillance. It must be off the grid, which is why nothing comes up on Nautilus," said Vikram.

They believed they had found the hideout of the *Draconists*. But what confused them was that Romero and his friends continued driving. Romero finally stopped his car at Pee Golf Arcade. They were forced to stop there and try a hand at golf. This time, they maintained their distance and did not talk to Romero. They discussed the baseball game, the NFL league, Formula One, and NASCAR. All this time, they were observing Romero and his associates. There was nothing outside the ordinary, and it looked like Romero was indeed taking the day off.

His day out turned out to be one of the most productive days for Sentinel, and Walter requested Raymond to help in digging out information about Marcelus Roofing and Welding Fabricators. Raymond was more than delighted to do so. After all, each detail helped uncover more information about the *Draconists* and got him closer to freeing his client. As promised, Walter took the team for a surprise private wine tasting session at Dutton Estate. They all ensured they tasted the wine but didn't drink much as they had to drive back. "Imagine getting stopped for a DUI, and you turn out to be part of a task force trusted to catch the most notorious criminal," said Gordon.

"That's one way of getting a reprimand or maybe even getting fired," joked Asha.

After reaching the black site, Vikram checked the list of entities Mike had provided them, but to his dismay, there was nothing mentioned about Marcelus Roofing and Welding Fabricators. "It was worth a try, but I didn't think you would find anything. After all, they would not want anyone to know the location of their hideout," said Gordon.

"Let's show some patience and give Raymond some time," remarked Walter.

Chapter 30

Walter's phone rang. "It's Raymond! Looks like he found something," said Walter. Everyone had their gaze fixated on Walter as he answered his phone. He put it on speaker and said the entire team was listening. They greeted each other, and Raymond got straight to the point. "Listen, guys, that company sounds suspicious. The company was officially shut down five years ago, so it is quite odd that they have their display board still up."

"That's good information, Raymond. Can you check if the government has ceased the land, or is it in someone's name? Since the company is defunct, someone would own that land, right?" said Walter.

"I will run a check on that while I have you on the call," said Raymond.

While Raymond was conducting his search, the few minutes seemed to last like an eternity, and Walter was getting anxious. He wanted to tell Raymond to work faster, but he knew it would be fruitless to trouble someone who was helping them.

Raymond finally found the information on the land records. He said right before the company shut down, it sold the land to two people who currently have joint ownership. The current owners were someone named Hector and Romero. "Does that ring a bell? Do you all happen to know anyone named Hector and Romero?" asked Raymond.

Walter was smiling from ear to ear. They had figured out the hideout of the *Draconists* without them knowing about it. There was a pause, and no one said anything. Raymond broke the silence and said, "Are you all there? Can you hear me?"

Walter immediately responded, "I am indebted to you, Raymond. This is great information, and unfortunately, I won't be able to answer your question directly, but I believe you understand what I am trying not to tell you."

"I understand, Walter. I will keep it to myself," said Raymond.

Raymond updated Andrew and Ron about his conversation with Walter, and they were both pleased to know they were one step closer to rescuing Mike. To them, their client was of prime importance, irrespective of what Walter thought. "Raymond, it's been a while, and we've made good progress. I think I am going to send our first invoice to Damien and Gary," said Andrew.

"Won't they be pissed off? I mean, these are trying times for them," said Raymond.

"See, Raymond, people who come to lawyers are always going to be in trying times. But we must set the emotion aside and conduct ourselves professionally," responded Andrew.

"I understand, but it just sounds a little inhuman and wrong," said Raymond.

"If you think it is wrong, it will feel so. Mike didn't think it was wrong when he started betting, and worse, laundering money. Quite honestly, he has laundered dirty money, and I believe he should be imprisoned for it. But then again, he's helping catch a bigger fish, so everyone has agreed to turn their heads the other way and rescue him."

"I understand what you mean, Andrew. How much are we billing them?" asked Raymond.

"I am yet to decide the final amount, but nothing less than four million dollars. I'll still check with Ron to see what he thinks. Nonetheless, I'll send them the first invoice of $500,000," said Andrew.

Raymond could not believe what he had heard. He began feeling a little jealous of Ron and Andrew because he was the one who was at risk and wasn't sure how much he would get out of it. But once he made Partner, he would have skin in the game, and a direct portion of this case would hit his bank account. He stammered while speaking, knowing the amount was a windfall for the firm, and said, "Wow, that's a substantial amount. I guess it must be the highest bill ever."

"It's close, Raymond. It might be the highest invoice ever. Anyway, you are going to get a good portion of it. After all, you're the one doing all the hard work and taking all the risk," responded Andrew.

"Thank you, Andrew! I won't disappoint you," said Raymond.

"I trust you, Raymond. Continue the good work. Speak to you soon."

In the meantime, everyone at the black site was elated as well. They now knew the premises of Marcelus Roofing and Welding Fabricators were the hideout of the *Draconists*. Raymond had sent them the details of the land records, which indicated the size of the plot was about half an acre, and the constructed portion was about 20,000 square feet spread evenly across a basement and two floors. "Looks like we have a lot of ground to cover, and the three of us will not be enough for the raid," said Gordon.

"Are we raiding them now?" asked Carter.

"No, not right away. We need to know what we are dealing with. We need to understand how much firepower they have," responded Walter.

"I think we should get eyes in there, but the only question is how," said Gordon.

"We can use drone technology. I know where we can get one with an attached camera. It will fly above them and give us an aerial view of their premises," said Vikram.

"That is a wonderful idea," said Asha.

"There is a catch, guys. I cannot operate it from here. The one I can source can fly at an altitude of up to 5,000 feet, and I need to be within a five-mile radius to operate it," responded Vikram.

The team's out-of-the-box thinking impressed Walter. They could have eyes above them even while the raid was being conducted. He said he would arrange for Vikram to be within five miles of the area.

"It is time the President speaks with the Prime Minister and informs him that the raid will happen within a week. We still need to strategise how to get Mike out of there. I don't want him to be used as bait," said Walter.

"I thought you didn't care about what happened to Mike," said Gordon.

"I said it's a sacrifice I am prepared to live with. I never said I don't care," responded Walter as he walked towards his office to connect with the President and update him.

The President was thrilled to learn they had zeroed in on the hideout of the *Draconists*. He was pushing Walter to conduct the raid immediately and use the element of surprise. But Walter wanted all bases covered and told him they would need to raid Auto Magicians simultaneously because Romero was part of the inner circle. He also informed the President that they would need the offices of Downforce Capital and Ajax Racing to be raided, too. The President said, "Those two entities don't belong on American soil. I am concerned about catching the *Draconists* immediately."

Walter neither liked the tone of the President nor the fact that he was backtracking on his own words, and reminded him about the agreement they had with the British Prime Minister. He also said Asha was allowed to transfer from the UK and was an integral part of the team. Her working and living in the United States were contingent on the President honouring his side of the deal. "Walter, are you going to fight me for one member of your team?" asked the President.

"I'd fight anyone for one member of my team. And if we do not abide by the agreement, I will call off the raid, and you can fire me," said Walter.

"You know I can. Don't forget how you fucked up by letting Hector slip through your fingers. I still have that file," threatened the President.

Walter's pulse rate increased, and his blood pressure shot through the roof. He somehow composed himself and, in a neutral tone, said, "Sir, I tendered my resignation, which you chose to reject. You have trusted my team thus far, and we have been successful in finding the location of the *Draconists* and even the four important men close to Victor. If you still think I should resign, please let me know."

"I don't want you to resign, Walter. And I'm sorry if my tone is insinuating this. I merely want those guys caught soon so I can include it in my election manifesto. When do you think you will be able to raid the premises?" asked the President.

Walter was agitated that the only thing that concerned the President was the upcoming election. He responded to the President in a calm voice, saying, "Sir, if you don't want me to resign, I respectfully request you not to hold this incident to my head like an albatross. I am deeply embarrassed, and there are nights I wish we had just shot him. Coming to when we can raid the premises, I believe we need a week to prepare a plan to get Mike out and deliver the *Draconists* for you."

The President let out a big sigh and said, "Alright, Walter! I'll give you a week. But I want the *Draconists* dead or alive."

"Sir, that's exactly what we are working towards, and I'll personally make sure this victory forms part of your election campaign. We also need time to go through the data we're receiving from the servers of Downforce Capital. That might reveal more accomplices and companies connected to the *Draconists*," said Walter.

"Thank you, Walter! And I am sorry for the threat. I assure you, you will not be asked to resign, and I will never bring this up again. I'll let the Prime Minister know we're ready to go all in within a week," said the President.

Walter thanked the President for heeding his request and for the vote of confidence. He hated the President had something on him. Whether he got a day off or not, Walter decided once the *Draconists* were caught, he would pull some strings and request to have the file on Hector's escape be destroyed, mutilated, and forgotten.

The President contacted the Prime Minister and informed him of the update. The Prime Minister was elated and said he would have his team ready to raid the offices of Downforce Capital and Ajax Racing. "I believe it is time I send my investigators to talk to the former CFO of Downforce Capital. The information he provides should help you while scrutinising the data," said the Prime Minister.

"That sounds like a great plan," responded the President.

The two heads of state disconnected the call, and the Prime Minister ordered the Director of the National Crime Agency to assign the case to two of the most trusted and decorated officers. The Director was filled in to the extent needed, and he assigned the case to Rose and Clive. The Prime Minister ordered that they were to report to him directly on this case and not to breathe a word to anyone, including the Director of the National Crime Agency.

Rose and Clive made an exceptional team. Both were highly skilled in financial crime investigations and expert interrogators, but they also knew how to handle themselves when situations turned physical. Having worked together on multiple high-stakes cases, they had built a reputation for efficiency, with a success rate exceeding ninety-five per cent. The idea of dismantling a company involved in money laundering and bribery wasn't just another assignment to them; it was the kind of mission they thrived on.

The Prime Minister kept his word to Alain regarding Ajax Racing. He informed Alain to begin forming a team of FIA delegates since Paul's arrest could be authorised within a week. Additionally, there would be a team of police personnel present at the site to ensure they remained safe.

Chapter 31

The next day, Rose and Clive made their way from London to Manchester. They boarded the train at London Euston, disembarked at Manchester Piccadilly, and took a taxi to Winchester Park, where the former CFO of Downforce Capital, Wayne, lived with his wife. He was now the CFO of a family office, and his wife was the Vice President of one of the UK's leading broadband, TV, and Mobile service providers.

It was a Sunday, so Rose and Clive scheduled a meeting with Wayne in advance to ensure he was at home. They requested that Wayne keep the meeting a secret and not talk to anyone about it except his wife. They rang the doorbell around 11:00 am, and Wayne ushered them in swiftly. As they entered the residence, they were astonished to see how tastefully it was built. It presented the opulence of old money as the entire house was well-decked with polished teak wood and a contrasting light fawn and dark brown upholstery. The console table had a darker shade and was designed in an old English manner, reminiscent of Victorian style.

Wayne's wife, Ruby, had a concerning look on her face. It had been about eight months since anyone had bothered the couple regarding Downforce Capital. She offered them tea and biscuits as a courtesy, but she was displeased that their past had come back to haunt them. She told the officers that they had been lucky she received a lucrative job in Manchester, otherwise Wayne could have probably been dead as well. She explained their old neighbour had reported them missing after they abruptly packed up and vanished from London overnight. Wayne added they had chosen to keep the details of their departure private after he uncovered suspicious transactions in Downforce Capital's records, along with whispers about the deaths of two former CFOs. Faced with this, they chose life over loyalty, and Wayne quietly handed in his resignation.

Rose got straight to the point: "Why didn't you ever approach the police yourself?"

"I wanted to, but I feared for my life. I did not want to end up like the two previous CFOs," said Wayne.

"So you don't think it was an accident?" asked Clive.

"I don't know whether it was an accident or not. I learned that both the prior CFOs had flagged some questionable transactions they had noticed. The only difference was they made it official by reporting it directly to the whistleblower hotline," said Wayne.

"And what did you do?" asked Rose.

"I went with the information unofficially to Pierre. I voiced my concerns to him and said I had linked the multiple small deposits to capital withdrawals. I saw the expression on his face change, and he asked me if I had spoken to anyone about it. When I told him he was the only person I approached, he asked me to nip it and leave. He said he would call me back to his office in a short while," responded Wayne.

"What happened next?" asked Rose.

"Within an hour, he called the IT Head, Joe, and had my computer inspected and my intranet account checked thoroughly. I think he also inspected the whistleblower hotline as he had access to it," said Wayne.

In an alarmed tone, Clive asked, "All this happened within an hour of you telling Pierre you want to talk about some deposits?"

"Yes, and I for one found it bizarre. But I had read about the *accidents* in which the former CFOs had passed away and decided to keep shut about what I had uncovered," responded Wayne.

Wayne's hands began to tremble, and a bead of sweat formed on his brow as he began recounting his traumatic experience at Downforce Capital. Ruby, noticing his distress, gently clenched his fist in hers and urged him, "You need to tell them everything."

Rose and Clive assured the couple that their identity would be kept confidential and no one would hear a word of what they said to the police. They asked Wayne if he could detail the transactions, as it would help in capturing Pierre. Wayne looked at Ruby with concern, almost asking her whether this was the right thing to do. She kept holding his hand and nodded in approval.

Wayne informed the officers about the wire transfers that would enter the bank account of the funds and be credited to the capital accounts of a few limited partners, and Pierre and Paul.

Finally, during the year, these individuals would either withdraw the money or make certain investments in their name, which would subsequently be written off as bad investments.

"How do you know these partners were not the ones pumping in the money?" asked Rose.

"Nobody puts in small amounts in private equity funds. My suspicions were raised because when I checked the agreements those partners signed, I found side agreements allowing them to deposit and withdraw money as and when they pleased. This was unusual since no one is allowed such terms in the private equity partnerships," said Wayne.

Rose and Clive looked at each other and agreed this was unusual. They questioned Wayne if he knew where the deposits came from, and he said he had once called the bank to inquire about this, and the banker said it was being deposited from all over the United States and even the Cayman Islands. "The banker did not question you about this?" asked Clive.

"Downforce Capital was one of the biggest customers at the bank, and the bankers never asked us any questions," said Wayne.

By now, it was clear the money being deposited was probably dirty, which had been cleaned through the books of Downforce Capital. It was a classic trick money launderers would use to wash and transfer money. Wayne also told them there were no Caymanian investors in the fund, so money flowing from there was what caught his eye. "Do you happen to remember or have any information to support your claims?" asked Clive.

"I never copied any information from there. But I do remember a few names," said Wayne.

"We would need you to give us those names?" said Rose.

Both Ruby and Wayne agreed that Wayne would not be signing anything that would imply he cooperated with the authorities, but he would be able to provide the names he remembered, as well as the details they needed to look for if they got access to the records of Downforce Capital. Rose and Clive had no option but to accept the offer since all they were told to do was interrogate him and not arrest him. Wayne provided the names of some of the entities he remembered and asked them to look for the limited partner accounts where the transactions in the year netted to zero and the accounts of the General Partners, Paul and Pierre.

After a fruitful conversation with Wayne, the investigators made their way back to London and reported their findings to the Prime Minister. The list contained the names of Ajax Racing, which the Prime Minister expected, but it also had another team's name, Trinity Racing, which had constantly finished last for the past three Formula One seasons. The Prime Minister conveyed the information to the President and informed Alain, along with Ajax Racing, that he also needed to keep Trinity Racing within the ambit of his investigation.

Alain was instructed by the Prime Minister not to make any moves and quietly gather all information he could on the two teams. He was told these were incidental hits, and the main goal was catching someone else. Alain started feeling agitated that, under his governance of the FIA, there was bribery and results were being manipulated. The information obtained while catching the main criminal would aid in building the case against Ajax Racing and Trinity Racing in the Motor Sports Council.

Meanwhile, the President elucidated what he had learnt from the Prime Minister. Walter asked Vikram to run a search based on the information they received from Wayne within the data their flash drive had been transmitting from the office of Downforce Capital. Vikram also ran a cross-check of the entities within the list Mike provided, and there was a direct match for Ajax Racing and Trinity Racing.

The team began discussing the next steps they needed to take once the *Draconists* were caught. The entire data gathered from numerous sources would need to be synchronised and linked. They would need to work endlessly at detailing out the various provisions of the law that were broken with utter disgrace, and list out the plethora of violations that were committed with impetuousness over the years. Every person and entity involved would need to be sent notices and subpoenaed. Many of them would offer to become confidential informants and help provide secret information, which would implicate far more dangerous criminals. The public prosecutor's office and the President's office would end up working overtime, but all would be for the good of mankind.

For now, all the members of Sentinel had to formulate a plan to enter the premises of Marcelus Roofing and Welding Fabricators, rescue Mike, and catch the *Draconists*. It was a daunting task, but the pieces of the puzzle were slowly falling into place. Vikram had ordered the military level drone, which was going to arrive in the morning. He would need to test it, and once they had assembled more team members, identified the time and day, they would execute the plan they had so meticulously formulated. Their timing needed to be on target, for which they needed to ensure they had surveillance over Auto Magicians, Downforce Capital, Ajax Racing, and Trinity Racing.

They knew nothing of Trinity Racing except that their drivers were crashing regularly during the season and the team was going to pull out of Formula One at the end of the year. It did not have a buyer, and overall, their operation was a loss. Their factories and everything they owned were going to be auctioned by the bailiff at the end of the year, and possibilities looked bleak for the owners and operators. The staff were being paid a fraction of their salaries, and tension was mounting in the Trinity Racing camp. Vikram did a quick search on Trinity Racing but could not uncover anything other than what they already knew. Walter and the team decided they would focus on the *Draconists* and Auto Magicians and leave Downforce Capital, Ajax Racing, and Trinity Racing to their counterparts in the United Kingdom.

Now, if one of the miscreants were caught, there would be numerous case files to be presented to the public prosecutors, and Walter would himself help in representing the State and dig into all the legal experience he had accumulated over the years. Additionally, they would even seek the help of the resources of Roth & Gotham, who had been a cornerstone for Sentinel in this case. With Raymond risking his life by infiltrating the offices of Downforce Capital, he had proven to be the unseen joker in this game of poker. Walter almost felt obliged to constantly update Raymond. But he knew his professional duties well enough not to violate the code of conduct, which was not to discuss ongoing cases with anyone unless necessary. Gordon was salivating at the thought of watching Walter take charge in court. The two of them had been working together for years, but Gordon never got to see *The Closer* in live action.

Chapter 32

Hector picked up a study desk and slammed it in front of Mike. Mike was startled and thought torture would take a scarier turn this time around. His entire body ached from every bruise, cut, and scar he had received from Victor and his men. Victor then placed Mike's laptop in front of him, grabbed him by his hair, and said, "Now listen, scumbag, we got this laptop of yours so you can get us the $200 million you promised."

Mike was glaring right into Victor's eyes and knew they had ransacked his place again. He wondered what else they stole this time around. He saw Victor wearing his prized diamond-studded Audemars Piguet, and if he had the strength and the mettle, he would probably chop his hand off and take back his watch. He may be short-tempered, but he wasn't violent. And now, half his spirit was broken at the hands of the *Draconists*, and the other half was barely hanging on. Victor had an evil smile on his face and said, "Ahh, someone recognises their watch. I think it looks better on me, though. Don't worry, I will take good care of it. It's mine now."

Victor sensed dissent in the eyes of Mike and caught him by the back of his neck, and pushed him against the laptop. "Don't look at me like you own me. Remember, you are my bitch until you return all my money and even more. Now, do whatever you need to do to get me back my money. You're going to be here for a while," said Victor and slapped the back of his head.

As Mike was starting his laptop, his mind was racing. Multiple thoughts were running through his head, and they were all related to freedom. He longed for a breath of fresh air, the sip of neat scotch on a cold evening, the aroma of morning coffee, and pushing his car to the limit. He was disgraced by his actions. He wondered what his parents would think of him if they ever found out he was helping criminals like Victor launder money and commit more crimes in the world. He wished he were able to escape from this hell and go back to his normal life. If he could turn back time, he would have never made the twenty-five-million-dollar bet with Victor, which entangled him in a web of crime.

As he entered his login ID and password, he immediately messaged Damien and Gary. He said he did not have a lot of time, and all he wanted to know was whether they had been successful in selling some of the investments. He was delighted to know they were able to sell about $300 million worth of investments. He stated he would need them to transfer about $200 million once he gave the account details. He requested them to keep $100 million safe and ready to be transferred whenever he requested. He asked them to invest it in a money market fund and earn some interest, which could be used to pay the *Draconists*. Although it wouldn't be a big dent in the debt. At this moment, every drop counted, and every dollar he repaid probably meant a lesser beating.

Gary and Damien were taken aback, unsure why Mike would want them to hold $100 million. But for Mike, it was clear—he needed an insurance policy. He couldn't afford to be caught empty-handed if Victor came calling for cash. His mind had shifted into pure survival mode, and he often moved through the day in a daze. He knew he had to maintain his sanity, for his thoughts were his only refuge. He'd never spent so much time pondering life.

Captivity had broken him in ways he hadn't fully grasped yet. The constant physical and psychological torment had left him half-delusional. At times, he would have done anything just to make the beatings stop. Yet, strangely, he began to understand Victor's motivations. A chilling thought crept into his mind: was he developing Stockholm syndrome? He immediately shut it down. He couldn't allow himself to feel empathy for his captors. In a world filled with grey, Mike knew he had to see things in black and white, especially when it came to his safety and survival.

In a calm yet frightened voice, Mike said his partners were able to sell investments worth $200 million and would transfer the money once they received the account details from Victor.

Victor somehow looked pleased, and even Mike was glad he would now cut the deficit to $500 million. Victor provided the transfer details to Mike. It was just one account, that of Auto Magicians. Mike looked confused and glanced at Victor, and said, "You want all the money to be transferred to one account? The bank will end up reporting this to the IRS. Till today, the only reason your accounts have not been inspected is because the amount transferred is less than $10,000 per account. That's the limit beyond which every bank's system automatically flags the transaction to the IRS."

Victor couldn't risk the IRS knocking at his door, so he gave about 20,000 bank account details and said he needed the money immediately. Mike knew he could not ask Damien and Gary to make so many transactions at once, and he could not even authorise the bank to make this transfer because Lions Star Capital would come under the money laundering scanner. He told Victor the transfer would take a week, and although he was displeased, he had no choice but to agree with Mike. However, he made sure he displayed his disgust by grabbing the back of his neck and pinching him so hard that pain shot up to his head. Mike's head pulled backwards, and he grunted in pain. He then asked him, "When do you think you can transfer more?"

Mike said his associates were already trying to sell further investments, but it would take time. These deals are not easy to crack, and Victor was now infuriated and bellowed, "Don't teach me about time. The world runs around like a carousel on my command."

Victor's demeanour changed. He walked around Mike and was now face-to-face with him. He placed his hands on the table and leaned until he was towering over him. His voice was calm, almost eerily composed, but carried a deadly undertone.

"Remember, Mike!" he said coldly. "The clock that ticks for you runs on my will. I can help you cross over to the other side. You've heard the stories people say they see a white light when they're near death. Tell me… do you want that light to dawn upon you?"

Mike froze. Fear flashed in his eyes. He had never seen this passive-aggressive side of Victor. He knew he had to find a way to escape. After all the physical and mental torture, he was sure he would need therapy to overcome the trauma.

The only way the deficit of $500 million can be repaid would be once the economy recovers and market sentiments change. He knew he had about $100 million earning interest and another $200 million earmarked in investments for Victor. There was a shortfall of $200 million. He could convince Victor that the deficit would be made up if given a chance.

For now, he stayed silent, jaw clenched, and looking down. Speaking out of turn could prove fatal.

Damien and Gary brought Raymond up to speed, who reminded them to not only use the secure internet connection but also not to step out without a disguise.

A conversation between Walter, Vikram, and Raymond ensued. Vikram said he could not track the location unless the laptop was on, but if Victor had a secure line, it would be difficult to hack his laptop. "So, it's only Mike who can reach out to us," exclaimed Raymond.

"Not necessarily," said Vikram.

Walter looked confused and had his eyes fixed on Vikram. In a somewhat enlightening tone, Walter asked, "What is on your mind, Vikram?"

"We can request Gary and Damien to check with Mike and tell us how many people are in there with him, and if he can describe to us the kind of artillery they have, we can go in better prepared," said Vikram.

Walter updated everyone on what he and Vikram had learnt from their conversation with Raymond. They realised there was only one way they could obtain inside iinformation—Mike needed to access his laptop. Asha suggested that Gary and Damien should not transfer money for a couple of days. Since Victor had still not received the entire $200 million, it would push him to ask Mike to check for any issues. That's when he would gain access to his laptop and gain inside information.

"It's a dangerous bet, but worth the risk," said Walter.

"I learn a thing or two about the technical stuff from Vikram," joked Asha.

Walter discussed the plan with Raymond, who found the suggestion reprehensible, but he had no say. Damien and Gary were now confidential informants and, in a way, had pledged they would do all they could to help the authorities during this case.

While the transfer of money was stopped, Vikram tested the drone he had received from the US military. It had a built-in camera and could fly at a height of five thousand feet. The camera attached was a high-resolution one built at NASA, and the clarity of the image, even from a distance, was stunning.

Everyone heard a familiar voice from the speaker. It was the voice of Romero from Auto Magicians. It sounded like he was talking to someone at the shop, probably instructing them. He was asking them to clear the garage as they needed to store some customised armoured Jeeps for two days, which would be delivered to the Middle East. They heard him say the consignment would also contain hidden weapons, and the paperwork would make it look like it contained aircraft ancillaries. He then made a phone call and said there was a consignment needing special attention. He fixed the payout at $75,000. This was the break Sentinel needed to throw Victor's strategy off and force him to improvise, which would push him to act recklessly and could potentially cause the *Draconists* to slip up.

"They're bribing someone," said Gordon.

"It's probably someone from Customs and Border Protection (CBP). Couldn't be anyone else," said Walter. He marched to his cabin when Carter called out from behind, "What are you doing now?"

"Ensuring that consignment doesn't leave our borders."

Walter jumped on this opportunity and connected with the Head of CBP, Martin. He said he had inside information that an illegal shipment disguised as aircraft ancillaries containing armoured Jeeps with hidden weapons was being sent to the Middle East in two days. Martin said he and his team would cooperate with Walter, and in exchange, he would want some credit for the seizure. Walter knew better than to argue with someone whose help he needed. He agreed Martin's team would get the recognition they deserved, but the people who get caught would be taken to a location of Walter's will and be further interrogated by Walter and his team. Reluctantly, Martin agreed, for it had been a while since the CBP had caught something that big. And he needed a new badge of honour.

Chapter 33

While the President was kept abreast regarding the findings about the armoured Jeeps and weapons being transported to the Middle East, he agreed they needed to conduct the raid to throw the *Draconists* off and distract them.

While Victor was oblivious to the CBP and Sentinel assembling a team to raid his consignment, he was contacted by one of his partners, informing him that the flow of money had stopped. This infuriated him, and he grabbed Mike with both hands and demanded an explanation as to why the money had stopped coming in. Mike looked confused as well. He said he would need to contact his team and needed access to his laptop. Victor slammed the laptop in front of him, asked him to log in, and inquire why there had been no movement in the money for the past day.

As Mike entered his credentials, he was hoping Damien and Gary had a damn good reason for this. His hands were shaking. His mind started playing tricks on him. He began to wonder whether they had given up on him and had started a new life and a new investment firm without him. The thought of them cutting a deal with the SEC and beginning something new with a clean slate crossed his mind. This sent a shiver down his spine. He thought they had left him to die at the lowest point in his life. His heart became heavy, and he teared up. He was feeling desolate and alone.

But then, he regained his composure, realising he was probably overthinking and hyper-analysing the situation. As his laptop connected to the internet, he received a message from Gary saying he should ping him when safe. In the meantime, Victor received a call from Romero, and this was the window Mike needed. He looked around and realised no one was paying attention to him. They were now accustomed to him being around, stuffed in a corner—voiceless and broken. He told Gary he only had a few moments and asked why the transfer was stopped.

Gary said the transfer would resume the next day, and he should say technical difficulties had crept up at the bank, as the amount being transferred was huge. He then asked Mike how many people were with him.

Mike glanced around and said there were five people around him, and at least three were outside because they kept coming in and out to speak with each other. He said he was unsure of how many were outside and on the other floors, but there were at least three. He said he was held hostage on the top floor, and there were times he was tortured like a prisoner of war. He was given insipid food just once a day, and it was now impacting his health, coupled with the physical and mental torture, he was becoming delusional.

Gary sympathised with him and said he would re-initiate the transfers from the next day, and everything would be okay. By this time, Victor's phone call ended, and he kicked the table in front of Mike, demanding an explanation. Mike was startled and looked at Victor with fear. He informed him that since the amount of the money being transferred was huge, there was a complication at the bank which his team had sorted, and the transfers would be reinitiated from the next day. Before shutting his laptop, Mike deleted the chat with Gary to ensure Victor did not read it accidentally. Victor warned him that if there were any more holdups, he would begin cutting Mike's fingers and feed those to the dogs.

"You don't know what I am capable of, Mike. I have done such vile deeds in my life that this would not even make me flinch a muscle," said Victor.

Mike was horrified and assured Victor that the transfers would resume within less than twenty-four hours.

Meanwhile, Gary informed Raymond that there were at least eight people in there with Mike, and he was held hostage on the top floor. He also requested that Walter and his team do something immediately since Mike was being tortured and could not take it anymore. "His spirit is broken, Raymond! We didn't sign up for this," said Gary.

"I understand, Gary. This world is merciless. I assure you, Walter and his team are doing everything to get Mike back."

"I really hope so," responded Gary.

Raymond understood Gary was going through unprecedented trying times and had never been tested in this manner before. Raymond realised the perils of the physical world were unparalleled by those of sitting behind a computer. He decided not to let Gary in on his two cents. The last thing he wanted was the client firing them because of an insensitive remark.

A brief conversation between Raymond and Walter revealed to the team that there were five people around Mike and at least three guarding the premises. Vikram said he would use the drone to get clarity on the number of people guarding outside, but they would not know how many people were present on the first floor. Gordon realised he would be leading a team that would be going in half blind. He had led countless missions such as this in the past, but going up against the *Draconists* would be a different ball game altogether. He knew capturing or killing them would be an accolade for the entire team, and it would boost their careers unimaginably.

Walter decided that Asha and he would be present with the CBP officers as they searched the containers, while Carter and Gordon would begin formulating a plan on how they would raid the headquarters of the *Draconists*.

The day had arrived when the consignment was set to be sent off to the Middle East. Walter contacted Martin and said he and one of his agents would be present while the raid was being conducted. Martin outrightly declined and said it was his area of operation, and no one other than his officers would be present.

In a calm and convincing voice, Walter said, "Look, Martin, there is a snitch on your team. And, you don't know who that person is. What would you do if he turns on you? We can't afford this operation to turn on its head because of your low-hanging ego. It's a matter of national security. Your best bet is to have us on your side, looking out for you."

Martin took in a deep breath and said, "Remember, I get the credit for this part of the operation. And your officer needs to dress up like my team and maintain the disguise till you both leave the premises."

Walter responded, saying, "I agree. But remember, we're walking away with all the evidence and interrogating anyone we catch. That's the deal."

Martin had a frown on his face, and he hated being pushed against the wall. However, it was Walter who delivered the tip to him, and the CBP needed something to show for. He reluctantly agreed.

As Asha and Walter were making their way to the San Francisco port from where the consignment would be sent to the Middle East, Martin ordered his security team to seal down the premises and not let anyone leave. He informed them that a special agent would be joining them only for this raid, and they were supposed to operate as a team. His agents were confused on hearing this, but over the years, they had stopped questioning Martin's decisions, since he was always spot on with his judgement.

In his career, Martin was known to be a nightmare for those exporting or importing questionable goods. He oversaw operations related to what went in and out of the United States. His work had exposed countless shipments—some laden with drugs and others that carried something far darker: women and children being trafficked. His scepticism and relentless efforts in keeping the US border safe had helped convict various drug cartels, smugglers, and human traffickers. And now, he wanted another medal on his chest, seizing a consignment containing illegal weapons.

Asha asked Walter why he was entering the field since he generally operated from behind the scenes. Walter assured her he would not get in the way but would observe the operations on camera from Martin's office. Although Asha knew there was something brewing, she could not point a finger at it, and Walter ensured it remained a mystery.

Walter, on the other hand, knew exactly why he was going into the field. Asha was an excellent agent, and Martin was known to poach officers into joining the CBP and dishonour the promises he made. He had friends at important places. And many times, even a hold on agents high up in the CIA and FBI. And at this time, Walter neither had the bandwidth nor the energy to deal with inter-department politics. He thought it best to let Asha know of this after the consignment was ceased.

Once Walter and Asha reached the port, they were greeted by Martin. Martin stood at five feet eleven inches. His job many times required him to be a brute, and he ensured he was in top physical shape. He was well-built and worked out regularly. Lifting heavy gave him the physical stature that made him tower over others.

He was known to be uncompromising in his dealings—a friend to patriots and an enemy to traitors.

Martin wanted more information about the consignment and who it pertained to, but Walter had obtained a letter from the President ordering the CBP to turn over everything that was seized and everyone who was caught. The letter also mentioned Walter had the liberty to divulge as much information as he deemed necessary. Martin looked disgusted at this, but he had no option but to honour the President's letter. "What information do you have on the President that he's given you so much power?" questioned Martin.

"I am exercising my liberty of not divulging any information that is not relevant," replied Walter in an authoritative tone.

Martin bit his lip and remained silent. He and Walter knew each other from before, as they had crossed paths at various government conferences. They had similar ideologies when it came to upholding the law, but differed on how to ensure the law was abided by. Martin was ready to step over as many people as necessary to get his way, but Walter was more conservative. He preferred the roads of diplomacy and building allies along the way. But this time, Walter did not care for differing ideologies. Walter also knew the raid would add feathers to Martin's hat, and thus, he was forced to cooperate. The thought of ceasing illegal weapons being exported would make him salivate even in his dreams. He needed to be tactful and discreet.

Martin gathered the team and introduced Asha to everyone. Walter stuck to his word and observed the operations from Martin's office. It was a team of five CBP personnel led by Martin, plus Asha. Martin began briefing the team and said, "We're looking for a container with the Middle East as the destination. The export documents will list out the contents as aircraft ancillaries. However, its contents are extremely dangerous. The container is housing armoured Jeeps, which contain hidden weapons. Our friend

Walter has a special order from the President—once the operation is complete, we need to hand over the seized contents to them."

Walter knew Martin was trying to throw unnecessary jabs at him, but he ignored them and wished the entire team luck. Martin pulled out the list of containers being sent to the Middle East and found there were five. Three of which had aircraft ancillaries listed in the description. As they opened the three containers, they saw each of them containing two Jeeps. Along with seizing six armoured Jeeps, they seized a plethora of weapons. The consignment contained thirty automatic pistols, fifteen AK-47s, ten shotguns, and ammunition. The list was prepared, and Martin signed and stamped it. Walter and Asha ensured the items were transported to the official warehouse, and only Walter or anyone authorised by the President was allowed access to it.

Martin looked pleased with what they had seized, and Walter assured him he would get the credit for it. Walter observed that one of the officers, Blake, was constantly on his phone after the consignment was seized. He alerted Martin, who went ahead and snatched Blake's phone. "You know phones are prohibited in this area, Blake," barked Martin. He then noticed Blake had sent a text to an unknown number saying, "Your consignment has been seized. Act immediately"

Martin looked at Blake and screamed, "You're a fucking snitch. I am going to ensure you rot in prison for a long time. I swear I will pull every string I can to guarantee you are imprisoned in maximum security. You're a traitor to your country. You bastard!" Before anyone could react, Asha pulled out her gun and pushed it against Blake's head. The other officers were dismissed while Martin continued to bellow abuses at Blake. Asha cuffed him, threw him into the chair, and pointed a gun at him. Meanwhile, Martin ordered him to be searched and confiscated his phone. The search on Blake revealed he was carrying a pocket knife for protection, which was allowed as per CBP rules.

Martin was about to enter the phone into evidence when Walter reminded him of the President's order, and he reluctantly handed over the phone to Walter. Martin was already annoyed at learning Blake was a snitch, and handing over everything to Walter was like rubbing salt on his wounds.

Walter called Gordon and updated him on the happenings at the San Francisco Port. He and Carter were asked to make their way over immediately as they had captured one of Victor's accomplices in the CBP. "That's great news, Walter. We can now interrogate him and extract all the information he has," said Gordon.

"That's the plan, Gordon. We're going to get all the details from him on how he has assisted the *Draconists* in the past and how many times his palms itched and were greased while he turned a blind eye to crime," replied Walter.

Martin overheard the conversation and blurted, "You guys are catching the *Draconists*? You mean to say Blake was working for them all this time?"

"We are in the process of catching them, and don't worry, we will give you and your team the credit you deserve," said Walter.

Gordon and Carter arrived, and the four of them took Blake to the black site. A hard day's work had finally yielded some reward.

Gordon commented, "The fact Victor knows his consignment is seized might push us on the back foot."

"I disagree," said Walter. "If we play it right, he might be forced to act irrationally, which would impair his judgement and provide us the opportunity we need."

"So what's the plan?" questioned Asha.

"For now, do nothing. Let time play the odds in our favour. If we go all-in now, we might jump the gun."

Chapter 34

Reading the text message from Blake, Victor had his balls in his mouth. He immediately tried to contact Blake, but his phone was switched off. He informed Jerome about what had happened, and even Jerome looked concerned. This was a major setback for the *Draconists* since they had already received half the money from the buyer and rolled most of it into their next drug consignment and part of it into their next gamble. Cash was a scarce commodity.

It would take a few weeks to make that back, and more importantly, their buyer in Iraq would be challenging to deal with. He did not have the resolve to call the buyer and inform him about the interception of the package at the US Border, even though he had an agent in his pocket. "There has to be some leak within the *Draconists*," said Jerome.

"Who could it be?" asked Victor.

"There is only one person within our team who has recently been captured and able to escape," responded Jerome.

"You think Hector is not clean and has been double-crossing us?" asked Victor.

"Think about it! He gets captured, somehow limps across the city, and makes his way back. Right after his return, something or other has been going wrong."

Victor was infuriated and wanted to believe Hector was clean, but the points made by Jerome could not be ignored. Hector's loyalty was always a point of discussion, and even though the Mayor of Miami confirmed Hector's loyalty, the truth could always be different.

"You think we should just kill him or talk to him once?" asked Victor.

"You're emotional, but I am not. I would just empty the chamber in his mouth and make sure he dies instantly. I want to shoot him so many times he can't exercise his vocal cords in his next life," responded Jerome.

"After everything he has done for us, I still want to give him a chance," said Victor.

Jerome responded by saying, "He's not been much of a use after the bullet went through his leg. He costs us more than he brings in at this moment."

"Yes, but in the past, he has been instrumental in securing drug deals and even brokering higher prices with the human traffickers. We are still benefiting from his connections. We can't write him off," said Victor.

"Yes, and he has been compensated for his services. I don't think we'll lose those connections. You think he is loyal, right? Then let's test him," suggested Jerome.

"What kind of test are you suggesting?"

"Our weapons buyer in Iraq runs a terrorist operation. We should send him to appease the leader of the terrorist group. Let's see how he fares. If he can convince and appease them, then he's ours," said Jerome.

"And what happens if he is not able to deliver?" asked Victor.

In a cold and methodical tone, Jerome said, "We get him executed outside the country."

Victor took in a deep, slow breath. He didn't want to believe Hector had betrayed him after all they had been through together. But Jerome was his brother, and more importantly, he might be right. It did not sound plausible that Hector limped across the city to reach them, and since he was back, the only fruitful things he had done were to negotiate a higher price for their drugs and heckle Mike occasionally. Hector had been sent in the past to negotiate on behalf of the *Draconists*. But a disaster as damaging as this warranted his and Jerome's intervention. However, testing Hector was important as well. Victor summoned Hector and informed him their weapons consignment had been intercepted by the CBP, and since they did not have all the money to return to the buyer, they needed him to travel to Iraq, appease and guarantee them the *Draconists* would make it up. He said the reputation of the *Draconists* rested in his hands. Hector was honoured to have been chosen for this mission and started preparing for his travel to Iraq.

In the meantime, Jerome and Victor contacted their buyer and informed him that the consignment had been intercepted and they were able to return about twenty-five per cent of the money. The buyer started berating them, "You fucking Americans cannot be trusted. I am going to make sure you pay for this."

In a calm and controlled voice, Victor said they would be sending one of their men to Iraq, and he was ingenious and resourceful in the field. He told them they could utilise his skills, and he would be with them in Iraq until either all the money was returned or a fresh consignment was prepared and delivered. The buyer was not happy but accepted the offer. The thought of having one of the *Draconists* as part of their operation was invigorating.

Victor was hoping Hector would be able to appease the Iraqis and come back safely. As Hector made his way to the San Francisco Airport, he was not sure what Victor expected of him. All he was told to do was assist the terrorist group in Iraq with their operations.

Before Hector could enter the airport, he was nabbed and put in the back of a van. His eyes were covered by a black cloth, and as he tried to fight back, one of the kidnappers stunned him using a stun gun. He was then injected with a sedative, which put him to sleep for the next couple of hours. As he opened his eyes, he felt dazed and realised his hands and feet were tied. Eight men were standing around him with AK-47s in their hands, and their faces were covered with a black cloth.

All he could see were their eyes and foreheads, and by the look of it, he concluded they did not look American, and since they spoke Arabic, he figured they were representatives of the Iraqi terrorist group.

The local leader was furious that the weapons and armoured cars did not reach Iraq. He started walking towards Hector with his assault rifle pointed between Hector's eyes. The leader punched Hector across the face, pulled his hair and stretched his head back, and blasted at him, saying, "You think we will trust you people after you steal from us?"

Hector was appalled as to what had just happened. He was under the impression that the deal was made wherein he would fly to Baghdad and assist the group until a new consignment of weapons was delivered. What he was not aware of was that Jerome had made other arrangements for him. Hector was made to kneel on the ground, and one member of the gang stood behind him with a large knife at his throat. "You see, for us Iraqis, there are two possibilities: You are either with us, or we kill you. There is no in between. And you are not with us. We cannot trust you."

Hector was terrified and tried to clarify what had happened. He was fumbling for words and somehow gained the strength to say, "Please let me expl…"

But before he could complete his sentence, he was beheaded with one clean cut. Hector did not feel a thing except fear. There was no pain but only shock in his eyes. A picture of his severed head was sent to Victor and Jerome. Victor was gaping at the sight of this, but Jerome looked unfazed. "Jerome, we need to find a way to avenge Hector's death," said Victor.

"No, Victor, they avenged us for his betrayal."

"You mean to say you knew this was going to happen? You arranged for this? Why didn't you tell me you had signed Hector's death warrant?"

"I told you we would test him, and it looks like he failed. He failed to convince the terrorist gang we would deliver on our promise, and this is the price he paid. It is time to return half the amount to them before they send someone to behead us. Regarding the other portion, I have decided to give them two mansions from my real estate project for free. It will act as an insurance policy till we are able to compensate them," responded Jerome.

Victor was still shivering from what he had just watched. This was the first time Jerome had ignored the structure of the *Draconists* and acted on his own accord. Victor wondered whether he had become so soft and blind that he couldn't see Hector was compromised. Or was Jerome so heartless that he would do anything to maybe become the sole leader of the *Draconists*?

Victor's head started aching, and when his vision landed on Mike, he saw an easy target to release his anger. He started beating Mike endlessly. Pain rushed through his body. He felt as if someone had run a truck over him. Romero had to restrain Victor or else he would have killed Mike. "Boss, what are you doing?

Why are you beating him so much? We still have a lot of money to recover from him," said Romero.

Victor now had tears running down his face. He was in two minds. His heart said something else, and his mind believed something completely different. He didn't know whether he should mourn Hector the traitor or Hector the fallen friend. "No amount of money can get Hector back. He has been executed, and I don't even know if he was on our side or not," shouted Victor.

Jerome left the premises and went to take care of transferring two mansions in the name of the Trust controlled by the Iraqi terrorist gang. Once he got into his car, Jerome contacted the leader and thanked him for taking care of Hector. He paid the local leader $50,000 in cash for killing Hector and said the registered documents of two mansions would be delivered within a day, which would more than cover the amount paid to them.

Through the grapevine, Sentinel heard of a beheading that occurred in San Francisco, but there was no news on who the person was. Rumour had it that there was a rivalry between two criminal organisations, and one of them decided to push matters down a dark alley. Soon, the police found a severed head near the waterfront at Pier 39, and the press had the picture of the head circulating across news channels.

"Holy son of a bitch," said Vikram in a slow and alarming tone.

'What is it?" asked Walter.

"Look at the screen, sir! That's Hector's head. He was the one who was beheaded. Who do you think did this?" said Vikram.

"It is not easy to get a hold of someone as crafty and strong as Hector," said Carter.

"Looks like he was delivered to them," said Asha.

"I think the *Draconists* are caving in," suggested Walter.

"They might have thought he was somehow passing information to us since we captured him, and then he escaped from our clutches and somehow managed to reach the hideout," said Vikram.

None of them were happy at the sight of the beheading, but they were glad to know their plan of pushing the *Draconists* to do something out of character and drastic was working. Victor was in a tight spot, and Sentinel wanted to take advantage of this situation, but they could not ignore the beheading. They knew the *Draconists* were connected to the Iraqi terrorists locally and internationally, and they had been on the most-wanted list as well.

"Catching them along with the *Draconists* will be the icing on the cake. But let's focus on the *Draconists* for now. We'll get information about the Iraqis once we've captured Victor," remarked Walter.

Chapter 35

The interception of the weapons consignment and the beheading of Hector were not the only two big blows to the *Draconists*. The fact that Jerome had gotten Hector killed without discussing it with Victor was irking him. He was not sure how to react or what to think. In his mind, Victor felt the balance of power shifting. But according to Jerome, he did what he had to do to ensure the *Draconists* remained uncompromised.

Walter decided it was time to give the news to the President that their raid on the export consignment was a success. The President laughed in delight and imagined informing the voters of his success. He said, "That should stop them in their tracks, at least momentarily."

"Yes, sir, and I have other news as well," said Walter.

"What's that? Why do you sound concerned?" asked the President.

Walter said, "Well, sir, you remember Hector, the guy we had captured and who escaped?"

"Yes, of course I do! What about him?"

"The head that popped up at Pier 39 was his. It looks like he was beheaded by the local Iraqi terrorist group. Seems the Iraqis are short of some weapons, and they might use alternate methods to obtain them," said Walter.

"You mean they won't use the *Draconists*, or do you mean they won't be using the San Francisco port?" asked the President.

"We're not sure, sir, but we do have the voice transmitter hidden at Auto Magicians, which we are constantly tracking. It has not yielded any further information yet. Maybe they are having their meetings at their hideout and discussing their future actions over there."

The President was pushing Walter to initiate the raid on the *Draconists'* hideout, but Walter was adamant that they needed more time to prepare. He knew any misfire at this point would push the *Draconists* into hiding. He explained to the President that any brash move at this point would make their antennas rise straight up, and they would start to lay low, which was not something he and his team could afford. Walter suggested the US and UK governments work together and activate their sources in Iraq to see if any weapons supplies were expected by the terrorist organisation.

Walter said, "If we can raise some tension in Iraq, the *Draconists* may loosen up a little in the US and focus over there. They might even send some of their people to help the Iraqis, which would allow us to hit them while they are at their lowest."

"You make a great point, Walter. But you must understand my position. I need to show the citizens something. They need to know I am the right choice. And, stopping an organisation like the *Draconists* is exactly what will secure my win, and I will be re-elected for my second term," responded the President.

Walter understood the President's predicament, and therefore, he suggested, "Sir, our team needs a few more days to prepare.

Thanks to the military drone we acquired, we are going to survey the area without being detected. I know our original plan was to attack Auto Magicians and the hideout simultaneously. But I suggest we start working in Iraq and raid Auto Magicians first."

"Why the change in plan, Walter?"

"Sir, are you fond of chess?"

"I have dabbled with it in my early years, and I was quite fond of it. I do play it when the opportunity arises. But why do you ask?" questioned the President.

"Chess originated in India in the 6th century, and the idea of the game was to capture the opponent's king. Let's think of our strategy to capture the *Draconists* as a game of chess. We know Victor is the king and Jerome, the queen. While sending Mike with twenty-five million dollars in cash, we found that Hector was one of their knights, and while following them out of Mike's house, we discovered that their other knight is Romero. Now, the two next important players in the game are the bishops and the rooks," explained Walter.

"Okay, I see where you are going with this. So, we know the knights, and one of them is dead. Who are the bishops and the rooks?" questioned the President.

"Right! One knight is dead, and the other one, Romero, manages Auto Magicians. The bishops are the people who provide the *Draconists* with inside information and are probably Blake, the CBP officer whom we arrested, and Frank, the former secretary to the Attorney General, who has been killed," explained Walter.

Walter went on to tell the President the important pieces in the structure of the *Draconists* were being knocked down one by one. He said their next order of business should be to capture the other knight and rook.

"Rook! You mean rooks, right! And who are the rooks?" asked the President.

"Well, let's see, their money launderers, Lions Star Capital and Downforce Capital. They have already shot themselves in the leg by keeping Mike hostage, so Lions Star Capital is not operating as they need, and Downforce Capital is linked to their bribing and betting business of Formula One," said Walter.

"I see you've thought of something. Where are you going with this, and how do we capture the other rook and knight?" asked the President.

"Although we need to try and neutralise the rook and knight together, we still want them to play the game our way and not overturn the board. So, we first take out the knight and let the rook move around freely for a while. There is a Formula One race coming up, so the accounts of Downforce Capital would generally show more than usual activity. Once we have captured the other knight over here, with the help of our friends in the UK, Downforce Capital will be neutralised while we ambush their local hideout," suggested Walter.

"Your idea does have merit. How do you suggest we capture Romero?" asked the President.

"Raymond informed us that Auto Magicians failed to file their tax return, which remains pending. Here is where we need your help. We need you to speak to the head of the Department of Treasury and ask him to perform a search and seizure operation on Auto Magicians. Since they work on selling stolen cars, they should have a pile of unreported cash lying around. The IRS officers would need to overturn the premises and seize everything, including the vehicles and the cash. They would then proceed to arrest Romero and freeze the bank accounts. This should knock out the remaining knight, leaving the sole surviving rook, the king and the queen, whom we will be attacking simultaneously."

The President was impressed with Walter's strategic thinking and said, "You truly are a genius, Walter. I knew of your prowess in the courtroom, and now I can see your expertise in battle and strategy as well. Alright, I'll speak with Cory, the head of the Department of Treasury and have them immobilise Auto Magicians along with Romero."

Walter was relieved that the President agreed with his proposal. His analogy of using chess had worked in the past and continued to pay its benefits. He had learnt this from his father, who was once talking to him about the art of war. He knew the drug operation would have its network, and the only way to bring that down was to arrest Victor and Jerome. He agreed that Cory and his team would need to intervene immediately. In the meantime, they would continue interrogating Blake and commence surveying the area around Marcelus Roofing and Fabricators.

The President contacted Cory and gave him a directive to gather all information he could find in the IRS database about Auto Magicians registered in San Francisco. He said it was a matter of national security and mentioned they had not filed the previous year's tax return. He informed him that Auto Magicians was a front for illegal activities, and any cash they discovered during their search was likely dirty money. He added that during the operation, they should seize everything they could get their hands on. For the safety of the IRS officers, the President said he would send three highly decorated and experienced SEALs to assist in keeping the Auto Magicians workers in place.

Cory was surprised that an order of search and seizure was coming from the President himself. He dropped everything he was doing and assembled a team to raid Auto Magicians. He and his team began preparing the documents required while conducting their internal search, and they noticed the owner of Auto Magicians on paper was Romero, who himself was currently under scrutiny for tax evasion. Cory noted Auto Magicians were always late in filing their return by a couple of months. But this time, they were delayed by over a year and had still not requested an extension. Cory assembled his four most honest and capable officers, and within an hour, they were to leave for the premises of Auto Magicians.

While Cory was plotting on how to raid Auto Magicians, Asha and Walter were interrogating Blake. During their interrogation, they learned Victor had threatened Blake and his family with dire consequences if he failed to cooperate. He said that although Victor paid him a handsome amount, each time a member of the *Draconists* came to pay him, he would threaten him and his family. He told them he was ready to testify against Victor and his associates when the time was right. Blake further said he and his family had not touched a dime of the dirty money paid to him. He said Victor had reached out to him about two years ago when a stolen vehicle had to be transported. Over the years, he was asked to turn a blind eye to numerous crimes. Troubled by the constant threats, he was ready to give his statement in writing, provided he received immunity, and he and his family were put in protective custody.

Walter agreed to arrange for this, provided the information checked out. Blake said he had maintained copies of all the documents where he was asked to turn a blind eye to crime, and the same could be cross-checked to the database of exports maintained by the CBP. Walter spoke with Raymond, who agreed to represent Blake as well, and, in his presence, Asha took Blake's written statement, and Walter said he would arrange for the immunity agreement and the protective custody within an hour.

During the team briefing, Walter updated everyone about the progress and how there was a change in plan where they would first arrest Romero and simultaneously work with their informants in Iraq to understand if the terrorist group was to receive a consignment of weapons and armoured vehicles. The entire team was feeling ecstatic that their plan was finally taking the form they wanted and coming to fruition. Vikram said he was going to test the drone, and based on the layout of the hideout being used by the *Draconists*, their strategy could be formulated. Walter said he would work with the CIA and MI6 and plan the logistics for their operation in Iraq. It looked as though the days of the *Draconists* were finally numbered. In a euphoric yet controlled voice, Walter said, "It is important we hit them while they are at their weakest and make our country proud. Let's get them!"

Chapter 36

While searching the IRS database, Cory's team noticed that, in addition to the latest income tax return not being filed, there were a few mistakes and inconsistencies in the two previous returns as well. Armed with this information and the President's directive, they prepared a preliminary case file to conduct the raid on Auto Magicians. Walter contacted Cory and informed him he had been given Cory's contact information by the President, and he would be arranging for three highly trained SEALs to travel along with Cory's team while they knocked on the doors of Auto Magicians.

At about 8:30 am, the three SEALs reached the IRS building on Golden Gate Avenue. They were greeted by Cory, who thanked them in advance for their help. Ahead of the raid, Cory had contacted Auto Magicians posing as a customer to inquire about their hours of operation. He was informed they were open from 8:00 am to 6:00 pm from Monday through Saturday. Cory, along with four officers and three SEALs, made their way to Auto Magicians.

The SEALs parked their car behind a Korean restaurant and away from the line of sight. They didn't want to alert Romero or any of his employees.

As Cory and his team entered Auto Magicians, they were greeted with a formal "Hello, I am Romero, the manager of Auto Magicians."

In response, Cory handed him a letter of a tax search and seizure notice from the IRS. Romero was stunned to read it and demanded identification with one of his hands reaching back to hold his gun in case he needed to kill or injure the officers. But to his disbelief, three SEALs walked in with their HK416 assault rifles, pointing at Romero and the other employees. The SEALs announced that if anyone moved a muscle, they would be shot. The rifle had a range of about three hundred and thirty metres, and Romero knew more than not to try any antics here, otherwise everyone would lose their life.

He tried to negotiate with them, offering them $50,000 each, and Cory said he had now caught Romero on camera bribing IRS professionals and SEALs. One of the SEALs walked up to Romero and pointed his rifle directly at his head. The other SEALs rounded up three other employees, and the four of them were put in a corner and strip-searched. The body search revealed each of them was carrying a fully loaded semi-automatic pistol and two knives. In addition to the weapons, their phones were seized, and the wire of the landline was cut. They looked scared, and Romero was not even able to contact Victor otherwise; he would have requested reinforcements and overpowered the agents and SEALs.

Once the four of them were captured and cornered, two SEALs were constantly standing above them with their rifles pointing at their heads. All four of them looked terrified at being caught off guard. While they were trying to recover from this sudden assault, Cory's team was overturning their showroom and garage. In the basement, they found the area where engines were inspected. One of the officers climbed down and switched on his flashlight. The rays of light revealed piles of money in low denominations wrapped in plastic, the type one would find at a place involved in illegal activities. The other officers discovered the machine used to erase the VINs of the car, and Cory discovered a cupboard containing weapons with the serial numbers scratched off. There was no doubt this was a front for selling stolen cars and delivering illegal weapons.

The third SEAL was constantly moving around the officers, ensuring there was no imminent danger that needed to be addressed. He was impressed looking at the artillery as it contained assault rifles, pistols, and even five handguns. "That's a lot of firepower for a place selling cars," he thought to himself. And although he was tempted to test it, he was in the line of duty and knew full well any mistake during a mission could lead him to be suspended.

Cory contacted his office and requested two vans and a car trailer to be sent to 2940 Geary Boulevard. The IRS had decided they would seize all the cash, vehicles, artillery, and loose machinery, then seal down the premises. While the raid was in progress, one of the officers was creating an inventory list of all the items they were seizing. The cash was counted, and it amounted to about half a million dollars. Once the list was ready, Romero was forced to sign it. The vans and the car trailer arrived, and all the seized cash and goods were loaded and transported. Once their value was appraised, the goods would be auctioned, and the cash would be considered as income on which tax would be levied. He would be arrested for tax evasion, bribery, possession of illegal weapons, car theft, and selling stolen goods. Additionally, his employees would be arrested for being accomplices, and as per the order of the President, none of them would be offered any deals on behalf of the government.

While the four of them were being cuffed and loaded into the back of a police car, one of them managed to run. One of the SEALs tried to take a shot, but the street was too busy, and he could not risk hurting a civilian. The undertaking was a success, barring one employee's escape. But the arrest of Romero meant the mission was accomplished. Once they were arrested, the SEALs delivered Romero and two of his associates to Gordon, Carter, and Asha, and informed them that one of the employees had managed to escape. They were put in separate rooms, cuffed, and tied tightly to their chairs.

Gordon informed Walter what the raid yielded and handed over a copy of the inventory list prepared by the IRS officers. He further elucidated that one of the employees had gotten away. Walter was not happy to hear that, but the good thing was that they had captured Victor's second knight. This had created a huge dent in Victor's operations. His illegal weapons supply business had been shut down, and another important gang member was captured.

Vikram decided he would tune into the history of the camera that was active around 2940 Geary Boulevard. He noticed, around fifteen minutes past twelve, while the arrests were in process, one of the employees at Auto Magicians was able to escape. He boarded a random bus and disembarked after two stops. From there, he hired a cab, and not to Vikram's surprise, the cab took him to Gravenstein Highway and then vanished. Marcelus Roofing and Fabricators had to be the hideout, and today was the day Vikram and the rest would be surveying the premises and hopefully confirm their suspicions.

While Asha and Gordon entered the room to interrogate Romero, he recognised them and said, "So you guys were not customers. You knew the BMW was stolen. You came to check out our operations. I had a hunch you guys were cops by the way you moved around and asked questions."

Gordon smirked at him and said, "Well, next time you give in to your hunch, you will be looking at prison bars. And don't worry, your rap sheet is so long you won't see a day of freedom in this life."

"You think our boss will just sit around and do nothing? You all will get fucked," shouted Romero.

"Shut the fuck up, Romero! You're cornered. And the guy that escaped, we know where he went. And we're going to go after him and arrest your boss. Maybe even kill him," said Gordon with an evil smile.

Romero's eyebrows drew together, and he thought to himself, *How the fuck do these guys know where Charlie went. Maybe they are bluffing and will try and get the address of our base.* Romero decided he would remain silent and keep asking for a lawyer, which was his right. Walter called all of them in the centre and decided not to interrogate them just yet. One, he wanted to plan the attack on the *Draconists'* hideout, and two, he did not want to allow them to ask for a lawyer. Also, they could not afford another breakout at this moment.

Vikram updated them as to what Nautilus had revealed regarding the whereabouts of the employee who escaped. They were now going to aerially survey the premises of Marcelus Roofing and Fabricators to put to rest any doubts they had as to whether that was the *Draconists'* hideout. Walter decided Vikram and Asha would go ahead and conduct their survey while he, Gordon, and Carter would work towards mobilising a team and firepower.

Vikram and Asha made their way from the black site to Gravenstein Highway. Ever since the drone arrived, Vikram seemed enthusiastic and eager to test it. He was waiting for the time when he would be in the field surveying the hideout of the *Draconists*. Asha could feel his child-like energy, and the smile on his face was immaculate when the drone was launched into the air and reached a height of two thousand feet.

The best altitude for drone photography and imagery was between one to three thousand feet. The drone took off, and the screen on the controller was activated. The angle of the camera was adjustable to three hundred and sixty degrees and could provide laser-sharp images, and the top speed of the drone was about a hundred and fifty miles an hour. Within a few minutes, it reached right above Marcelus Roofing and Fabricators.

They noticed the compound had only one entrance. The walls were covered by barbed wire, and there were four guards—two outside and two inside. Each of the guards was carrying an assault rifle. Asha pointed out they looked like automatic rifles. There was a fifty-foot-wide car park where they saw three black armoured Jeeps. Vikram circled the drone around the backyard of the premises, where he noticed a crevice in the walls leading to the forest area. There was no official back entrance, but it looked wide enough for the tactical team to slip through.

Vikram then turned the drone to the front, where there was one window on the ground floor and another on the top floor where Mike was held hostage. He wanted to get close enough to understand who was inside. For this, the camera angle was adjusted to provide the image horizontally, and the drone was lowered and pulled back to avoid being noticed. The last thing they wanted was someone spotting the drone and shooting it down.

As the drone stabilised, they caught some movement within the premises. They noticed one person was tied to a chair, and it looked like Mike. But there was a curtain partially blocking the view, so they could not exactly identify who it was. They noticed shadows of three people around him with guns in their hands, resembling rifles. "I wish the curtain were not half drawn. It would have been easier to positively identify Mike," said Vikram.

"Let's give it some time. Hopefully, we get better images," responded Asha.

As they were patiently waiting, a figure walked up to the window and started peeking out, surveying the grounds of the premises as if to ensure there were no intruders. He slid the curtain, and Vikram and Asha could see his face. It was Victor. His clenched jaw and narrowed eyes depicted how troubled he was. This was the first time they had seen him in close-up. Across the hall, they could see Mike sitting in the chair. He looked weary, and they could see dried blood on his face, which signified that he was being tortured at regular intervals. The first mission was to positively identify the hideout of the *Draconists*. The second was a little more challenging—to identify how many people were in there and what kind of weaponry was at their disposal.

Vikram kept the drone steady, and they were looking straight at Victor, who seemed to be in a pensive mood. He needed to hatch a plan to determine his next course of action. He looked anxious and tensed, and why wouldn't he be; he had just lost Hector to a beheading, and Romero was arrested. Two of the most important people in his operations were neutralised. The *Draconists* looked all but invincible. However, Victor could not be underestimated. He was resourceful, and his ties to other gangs gave him access to multiple men whom he could recruit at will.

The lack of movement within the building pushed Vikram to increase the altitude of the drone, and once again, he got a birds-eye view from the top. They noticed another armoured Jeep entering the premises, and once it came to a halt, Jerome exited and made his way to the building. The door was open from the inside, which meant there were more people on the ground floor. Vikram once again moved the drone to be at the same level as the window. They noticed the two brothers hugging and walking inside, where there was probably another room. Vikram manoeuvred the drone to move around the building, but unfortunately, he could not notice any other windows.

Further, they would need to get a closer look into the window of the ground floor, and for that, the drone would need to be within the premises. The premises were surrounded by trees on three sides, and there was no way of getting a clear image through the forest. Surprisingly, there were no windows on the first floor, which meant the team would be going in half blind. Although this was not ideal, they would have to work with what they had.

Asha and Vikram decided it was time to head back to the headquarters and report their findings. Based on their information and the video recording, they would formulate the plan to ambush the *Draconists*. No one had come this close in history to the *Draconists*.

Chapter 37

While Asha and Vikram were returning from their successful escapade, Walter was contacted by the President and informed that their contact in Iraq had news to the extent that there was a shipment of armoured vehicles and weapons expected to arrive within a day. "This means that the *Draconists* figured out a way to send a consignment after all," said Walter.

The President sighed and said, "I am not entirely sure, Walter!"

"What do you mean, sir?"

"Well, this consignment seems to have its source from Russia, so either the Iraqis are involved with the Russian mob or the *Draconists* have contacts in Russia who are helping them," said the President.

"Asha, one of our team members, conducted an assignment with MI6 in Russia a while ago, where she almost caught Hector, but her partner double-crossed her, and he escaped," responded Walter.

"Well, looks like their contact in Russia is still active. I don't think we'll be able to get that information in its entirety since it is not on US soil. We also believe our contact in Russia got entangled with the KGB and has gone rogue," explained the President.

"That is deplorable. It would have been great to add one more criminal organisation to our list. But it's okay, once we have captured Victor, we will get him to reveal everything," said Walter.

"Capture or kill, whatever the situation demands. If a crime is not happening on US soil, at the moment, quite frankly, I couldn't give a rat's ass about it. Keep me posted, Walter and good work," replied the President.

As the conversation between Walter and the President ended, Asha and Vikram walked in and announced they had visuals of Victor, Jerome, and Mike. Vikram attached the camera feed of the drone to the big screen for everyone to see. They all watched the aerial view, and Vikram pointed out the crevice they noticed around the back.

"The front is secured by four men—two on the outside and two on the inside. So, we'll have to take the four of them out together, or else one of them will raise an alarm. We can't afford to lose the element of surprise," said Gordon.

As the footage continued playing, they noticed Mike, Victor and Jerome. That was all the evidence they needed to begin assembling resources. Asha reminded them there were three shadows with guns on the floor where Mike was held hostage, plus Victor and Jerome and the man who opened the door for Jerome. "So that makes at least ten people, including the four guards," said Walter.

"And we don't know how many people are on the ground and first floors as we couldn't get a visual there," said Vikram.

"Let's assume there are five people on each floor. I don't think that place requires more than five. But what they are guarding is another question," remarked Gordon.

"They've held Mike hostage, and he's not strong enough to take on ten people. There must be something in there of value," said Carter

"It could be a combination of drugs and weapons they are planning to deliver," said Vikram.

"There is a lot of merit in what you all are suggesting. Let's start planning our attack. Interrogating Romero and others can wait. We have enough evidence to keep them locked up for a while," remarked Walter.

Romero and the others were transferred to the city jail and kept in isolation. The black site was the busiest it had ever been. Walter informed the President that the *Draconists*' hideout had been discovered. Asha, Gordon, and Carter were assessing the attack strategy. Once that was finalised, they would know how many people they needed for the ambush. Using satellite navigation, Vikram was trying to assess the spot from where he would control the drone and have eyes on the entire operation. He found an open car park near a Starbucks, which was about one and a half miles away from the *Draconists*' hideout. He could potentially park a van and operate from there.

They needed to get their foot in the door as slyly as possible. They knew if they entered from the front gate, they would not be welcomed with flowers but rather showered with bullets. There were two entry points; one was the front gate, and the other was the crevice they noticed in the boundary wall at the back of the compound, leading to the forest.

Carter suggested they involve Henry, as he had worked with them in the past. Since Gordon and Carter were expert marksmen, Asha suggested she and Henry could take on the guards at the front, but they would need to kill them silently without guns. "So, we're going to get to see some kung fu in action," laughed Gordon.

"Maybe, and I am not ruling it out. It's been a while since I used my kill shot, and I think it's up for some use," said Asha with a straight face, meaning she had probably decided her plan of attack.

"While you and Henry take out the guards on the outside, Gordon and I will relive our good old sniper days and take out the ones inside," said Carter.

"Using the drone, I will have visuals of the entire operation so you all can perform a coordinated attack," said Vikram.

"That's great. You can let us know in case the *Draconists* call for reinforcements," said Gordon.

"Once the guards on the outside are neutralised, you and Henry will have to find a way to enter without the gates being opened, or else Victor and the rest would realise something is happening and we wouldn't be as inconspicuous as we need to," suggested Gordon.

Vikram replayed the footage taken from the drone and noticed a small, unmarked muddy patch that Asha and Henry could use to make their way behind the premises and enter. "Great, so it's settled. You guys should join us within a few minutes," said Gordon.

"We would need around eight SEALs with us to ensure we are not overpowered," suggested Gordon.

"Now let's talk firepower because we're going to need the best artillery the US Government has to offer," said Carter.

"You're right. We see they have automatic rifles, so we're going in with all automatic weapons," said Gordon.

"I'll also be carrying my *kunai* knives, which can kill and injure instantly and the enemy won't even know what hit them," said Asha.

"Once this operation is complete, I would like to learn how to throw a *kunai* as well. It's quite a useful tool," said Carter.

"For sure!" remarked Asha.

"We don't know the kind of firepower the *Draconists* have in there, so we would carry at least four ammunition cartridges each, along with two fully loaded automatic pistols and a knife," suggested Gordon.

"Looks like we're going all out on this one," said Carter.

"We definitely should use the best machinery available to us when the opportunity presents itself," remarked Gordon.

Walter emphatically said, "The best machinery and the best people. I have talked to the President, and we are going to get fifteen SEALs, seven of whom are part of a backup team in case reinforcements are needed. I've requested Henry, and there is no doubt we will get his services."

Optimism was brewing in the Sentinel camp. They had come a long way from witnessing Hector escape to catching Romero. They realised once they were in, there would be two main points on the agenda—one catching Victor and Jerome and the other rescuing Mike. They knew the *Draconists* would use Mike to their advantage as much as possible and probably even use him as a human shield. There was no planning that could help them predict how the *Draconists* would react, and they had already established that rescuing Mike was important, but sacrificing him was a possibility they were not uncomfortable with.

Walter contacted the President and informed him that the plan of attack was in place, and it was time to speak with the British Prime Minister and raid the offices of Downforce Capital, Ajax Racing and Trinity Racing. The President wanted Walter to proceed with their planned ambush on the *Draconists,* but Walter reminded him that the reason they had come this far was the laundered money, which was used to pay off the people in the world of Formula One. It was their moral obligation to keep their word. Reluctantly, the President agreed to update his counterpart in England and have the attacks planned simultaneously. He was tired of waiting, but he knew he needed to trust Walter.

While the President contacted the Prime Minister, Victor's anxiety had hit the sky with the news of Romero's arrest and the sealing of Auto Magicians. He had a feeling the *Draconists* were no longer as secure as they used to be. There had been arrests and attempted ambushes in the past, but they had always emerged victorious. However, this time, the attacks seemed more planned. It appeared the government agencies had inside information. He realised the task force put together was doing a fair bit of damage. The only person who had seen the officers in the task force was beheaded, thanks to Jerome's scepticism and recklessness.

As he walked into the room, his gaze fell upon Mike. His blood boiled, and a fit of rage took over him. He caught Mike by the collar and pushed him against the wall. He wanted to treat him like a sandbag and beat him like never before, but all he finally did was punch him in the mid-section, and Mike went short of breath and coughed in pain. In an aggressive tone, Victor said, "You sleazeball! I want my money back. How much more time do you need?"

Mike was still recovering from the first punch when another one hit him in the arm, and the pain was so much that he could feel a pulse in his bicep. With all his might, Mike said, "Victor, the deficit is just $150 million. If you let me speak with my colleagues, I'll arrange for more. But honestly, Victor, I need time for the entire $150 million. I have more than made up for the deficit of nine hundred I initially owed you."

"You will not be dictating terms. And you said just $150 million, right? Well, you have caused my brother and me a ton of trouble. We lost one of our main guys, and we had to gift a low-life drug dealer a mansion worth three million dollars. In addition to all this, the mental angst of watching your sorry ass has upped your bill to $200 million," said Victor.

Mike looked perplexed, and normally, he would have screamed and shouted at the person he was dealing with. He was not used to being treated in this manner, but when the situation was life-threatening, even he had to give in. In his head, he was cursing Walter and his team for the shoddy job he thought they had done while sending him to deliver the money. He nodded his head in reluctance and was thrown into the chair. While Mike was logging into his laptop, Victor pushed his head into the screen to show Mike he would always remain his bitch.

Mike was chatting with Damien, with Victor standing right above his head. He straightaway typed a message, "I don't have a lot of time, so please tell me how much you can transfer."

Damien read in between the lines and said a $100 million could be arranged, and all that was required were the wire details."

Victor read the message, and the wire details were sent. Mike finally mustered the courage to request Victor to let him go instead of a meagre $100 million, which he would make up as the markets made an upturn.

Victor looked at him dead in the eye, pointed a pistol at the middle of his head, and said, "You'll go when we want you to go. It's no more a free-for-all where you get to roam about the world at your will. I own you now."

Victor still believed Mike was intermingled with the cops, and once the money was recovered, he planned to kill him.

Chapter 38

Raymond was informed about the deficit being cut to fifty million dollars, and no one was aware Victor had demanded an extra fifty, but the news was good. The wire details of the transfer were shared with Walter. But now, Raymond was getting anxious about what the exact plan was to rescue Mike.

He bluntly asked Walter how much more time it would take. It had been a little over two weeks since Mike was held hostage. He feared that with this entire ordeal, Victor was probably being pushed to a point where he was inclined to kill Mike because of all the trouble that had ensued since his capture.

Walter empathised with Raymond and assured him that the wheels were in motion and a plan was being formalised to rescue Mike. He requested some more patience as there were various moving pieces to contend with. "Raymond, you understand this is going to be a joint operation between us and the UK government, right! These formalities take their own course. I assure you we will have good news for you within a few days. Please bear with us, and you should know we are glad to have you on our side."

Raymond appreciated the update and replied, "Thank you for understanding. I know these are trying times for you and your team as well. Is there something I can do in the meantime to help?"

"Nothing at the moment, Raymond. All we need from you is your patience and understanding. But in due time, we will require your inputs in preparing the case docket against the *Draconists* and their accomplices," responded Walter.

"I'll look forward to that. But let me tell you, it is not going to be free. We bill by the hour, and our time is not cheap, so you'll need to get a good budget from Washington, D.C. However, given the close ties we now have, I will give you a special discount," said Raymond.

Walter smiled and said, "I see the businessman in you is always active. We'll figure out a price that works for both of us."

Raymond felt the case against the *Draconists* was going to plan. In his thoughts, he had already been made a partner at Roth & Gotham. Bringing in a government assignment as his first undertaking after making Partner would help him cement his position in the firm. He wondered what Gregory's reaction would be when he would learn that, although Raymond was on mandatory leave, he still managed to make partner and bring in a client as well. This would rub the smile off his face, and it would be the perfect revenge for his snide remarks.

The President informed Walter that, based on his conversation with the Prime Minister, the British investigative agencies would be mobilised within two days. Since they didn't require a lot of firepower, it was not going to be as arduous as their mission. Walter said their team was ready, and the SEALs had already reached the black site.

Now, they were being briefed about the operation and the overall details regarding the location. The weapons had been received, and Sentinel was ready to launch an attack on the *Draconists* and become their worst nightmare. This was probably the first time the *Draconists* were in such a precarious situation with their backs against the wall and their feet nailed to the ground.

Vikram was continuously sharing all the transaction details and information involving Downforce Capital with the UK government and their Financial Conduct Authority. This would aid them in preparing their case and arresting Pierre and Paul for a plethora of infringements, including money laundering, bribing, aiding and abetting crime, defrauding investors and of course, manipulating the results of Formula One. This was one case that would be heard across various courts, including the High Court for all the financial crimes and the FIA Court in Paris for manipulating Formula One race results. Everyone would want the largest piece of the pie; however, they would need to table their egos and find common ground while prosecuting these criminals. Financial crime and money laundering were more serious offences than attempting to manipulate Formula One results. Therefore, the FCA would get the first bite, but the FIA under Alain would not let the offence slide under the table. Alain had a cordial relationship with the Prime Minister, and he would utilise all his connections to bring Ajax Racing and Trinity Racing to justice. He would ensure they were banned for life and even fined a hefty amount.

At the headquarters of Sentinel, all resources were in place for an ambush of a lifetime. They were motivated and fired up to catch the *Draconists* and ready to use all the brute force required to accomplish their mission. Walter reminded them they need to make an utmost effort to rescue Mike; then his death, if it happens, would be treated as a civilian casualty. There would be no repercussions for anyone on the team if Mike were to be caught in the middle of a crossfire. He did not want his team to soften up if the *Draconists* decided to threaten Mike's life. The intent was clear—there would be no negotiations.

The President and Walter were adamant that there was not going to be a trade-off where they would hand over Romero for Mike. But they would use that as leverage to try and get Mike back safely. They would need to play tactical and mind games with the *Draconists* to arrest them and ensure they do not escape.

Asha questioned Walter, "Sir, why do you keep reminding us not to worry about Mike's death?"

Walter took a deep breath and said, "Because when I was dealing with the Attorney General, we agreed to use Mike as bait. He was not happy about the way Mike conducted his business and it was detrimental to investor confidence if an organisation with the stature of Lions Star Capital assists criminals such as *Draconists*."

None of this was a surprise to anyone on the team, and they were all on the same page when it came to Mike's questionable actions and his utter disregard for morality. He had obliterated investor confidence, and even though his life was in danger, he never attempted to contact the authorities or provide an anonymous tip.

"He happily pocketed the earnings and came to us only when he realised Victor would fuck him over," remarked Walter.

Now that the UK government, FCA, and the FIA had assembled their teams, the Prime Minister sent a message saying they were ready for take down. Walter finally received the most-awaited call from the President, and he gave him the go-ahead. His team had sharpened their knives long enough. They were glad judgement day for the *Draconists* had arrived. Three vans disguised as US mail carriers made their way across the Golden Gate Bridge and Gravenstein Highway close to Marcelus Roofing and Fabricators. The vans were stopped away from the line of sight and into a non-operational lane leading into the forest.

Vikram and Walter parked their van a little away from where the rest had parked. He let out the drone into the air to survey the area around the *Draconists*' headquarters one last time before the attack commenced. As the drone was airborne, it soon reached an altitude of two thousand feet.

The live footage revealed four black armoured Jeeps stationed outside the compound—confirmation that everyone was inside, including Jerome. He lowered the drone's altitude to get a better visual inside the building. As the drone hovered near a window, the camera caught Victor and Jerome, with their backs to the glass, and Mike tied to a chair, motionless and restrained.

Once Vikram gave Walter the clearance, he radioed in and informed Gordon he could move in at his convenience. Gordon signalled Asha and Henry to stay within the van till he and the remaining team made their way through the forest to reach the back side of the building, where they had noticed a break in the wall surrounding the premises. Once they reached the crevice that would be used to enter the premises, Gordon and Carter began to set up their sniper rifles on a tripod stand.

Gordon radioed in and said, "Asha and Henry, take your positions."

They ensured they were close enough to take down the guards outside, yet remain hidden from plain sight so as not to be detected. They knew the element of surprise was all they had, and each of them would get one chance to neutralise the guards. Once that was done, they would be able to enter the premises. Asha and Henry opened the door of the van and slowly made their way close to the gate.

All this time, Vikram and Gordon's heart rates were nowhere close to normal. None of them said a word to each other as their gaze was fixed on the screen. They had spent the last few weeks spinning their wheels and preparing for this exact moment. Even though Vikram had rehearsed this scene in his head a million times, he didn't know this is what it would feel like. Watching Asha make her way towards the entrance, his anxiety was visible as his foot kept tapping. Walter noticed this and put an arm on his shoulder in support of his dear friend and colleague.

Asha and Henry hid within a bush close to the guards and were out of sight. Their eyes fixated on the guards. Their predatory instinct was at its highest. They ensured not to make any sudden movements that would alert the guards. Gordon and Carter took their positions, and the rifles were aimed directly at the heads of the guards inside the compound. Asha and Henry did not have the luxury of killing from a distance. The attack on all four guards needed to be coordinated. They could not risk even one of them alerting Victor. A small mistake here could lead to a catastrophe, and all their hard work over the past few weeks would be rendered futile. Such opportunities came once in a blue moon, and they wanted to capitalise on it. Vikram waited for Victor and Jerome to turn away from the window. Only then could he give the signal to commence the attack. A few moments were lasting an eternity.

While the members of Sentinel were in the process of executing their strategy and ready to go all guns blazing, everything was going to plan in the United Kingdom. There was one team assembled in London to raid Downforce Capital, and two teams near the town of Silverstone were mobilised to take down the operations of Ajax Racing and Trinity Racing. Five officers from the FCA, along with three police officers, entered the lobby of Downforce Capital and announced they had an order from the FCA and the Prime Minister to perform a raid on Downforce Capital. The receptionist tried to contact Pierre, but one of the police officers pulled the phone wire, and the other confiscated her cell phone. She was cuffed and moved out of harm's way. They then proceeded to take a visitor pass and enter the access gates. They spread across the premises and made their way to Pierre's cabin. Without warning, they swung his door open and served him with a notice saying he was under arrest for money laundering. Pierre's face turned pale, and before his security officers could react, the police officers aimed their guns at their heads and ushered them outside the cabin.

While placing Pierre under arrest, the officers informed him of his basic rights. However, he ignored their words. He was shouting and screaming at the officers and threatening them with dire consequences. None of them budged, and they proceeded to arrest everyone in the office. The courts would determine who was guilty and who wasn't. The premises of Downforce Capital were sealed until further notice, and Pierre was dragged to the police station for questioning.

Oblivious to his father's arrest and the plan to ambush Victor and his gang, Paul continued working on his tactic for the next race. He had internally bribed his Head of Design to create faulty designs, ensuring the cars crashed out, causing a safety car, which would aid in altering the results of the race.

Four police officers, three FIA delegates, and three FCA officers, including Alain, knocked on the doors of Ajax Racing and presented a document for Paul's arrest, which included charges of money laundering, bribery, and unsporting conduct. He and the Head of Design were arrested and taken into custody. After completing their task at Ajax Racing, they moved on to the facilities of Trinity Racing and arrested the owner, team principal and two racers who had been accepting bribes for the past few months.

While things had gone to plan in London and Silverstone, Asha, Henry, Gordon and Carter were on standby, waiting for Walter and Vikram to give them permission to begin their ambush. They needed to wait and be patient. They could not take the risk of him witnessing the coordinated attack and implementing his exit strategy.

Vikram watched Victor and Jerome slowly walk away from the window. He was hoping and praying they wouldn't turn around, and to his delight, heaven had his back. He looked at Walter and gave him the thumbs up. Walter radioed in, "Move in team."

Chapter 39

Henry slowly moved in, caught one of the guards' necks from behind and slit his throat, cutting the jugular vein on both sides. Simultaneously, Asha threw a *kunai* with all her might, and it penetrated the other guard's neck and throat, killing him instantly. While the guards on the outside were neutralised, Gordon and Carter fired shots, such that one of the bullets went through a guard's temple and the other went right in between the eyes. Within a few minutes, the entrance of the *Draconists*' headquarters was compromised without Victor's knowledge.

Now Asha and Henry had to make their way all around the back to enter the premises through the gap in the barricade, along with the others. The coast was clear to enter the premises, and Victor was unaware that his fortress was under attack. The first part of the plan was executed to perfection.

Asha and Henry would take a few minutes to join the rest of the team. Meanwhile, Carter noticed a trap door covered with some twigs and dry leaves within the forest. It was well camouflaged and remained hidden in plain sight. Only a trained eye would be able to notice it. No one knew where it headed, and an attempt to open it was futile since it was locked and could be opened only from the inside. Gordon wired in to inform Walter that phase one of the plan was complete, and they had found a trapdoor, which was probably an underground escape route built in case the premises came under attack.

Gordon asked Walter to send in four backup SEALs, two of whom are dressed like the guards on the inside. They would be stationed as decoy guards to ensure none of the *Draconists* notice anything out of the ordinary. The two decoy guards made their way through the crevice and walked around the back of the building. Once they reached the entrance gate, they pulled the bodies of the dead guards out of sight and stationed themselves in their place.

Once the decoys were in place, they signalled to Gordon that phase two of the mission was complete. This meant the rest of the members could make their way into the premises and implement phase three, which was breaking through the front door. Gordon decided the other two SEALs would stay back and keep an eye on the trapdoor in case someone from the inside attempted an escape through an underground tunnel.

The team of eight entered the premises of Marcelus Roofing and Fabricators through the crevice, and the first thing they did was to puncture the tyres of all the cars. They needed to ensure all exit strategies at the disposal of the *Draconists* were not compromised. The stage was set to capture one of the most notorious criminal groups in American history.

One of the officers bent down on one knee and placed explosive charges around the door lock and set the timer for ten seconds. Meanwhile, Vikram and Walter were getting an aerial view of the action unfolding in front of them. It took an eternity for ten seconds to pass, but once they did, the explosive device went off, and the door was open. The blast took the *Draconists* by surprise, and before two of them on the ground floor could react, Gordon and Carter shot them in the chest, and they were killed instantly. Before dying, one of them screamed his last words, "Police," and succumbed to his injuries.

Asha, Henry, and four others followed Gordon and Carter's lead. They had successfully taken over the ground floor. Meanwhile, Victor, Jerome, and the remaining *Draconists* equipped themselves with firepower and took their positions, hiding behind all the furniture they could. Mike was tied to the chair and was left exposed, with Victor using him as a human shield. "How the fuck did these guys get in?" barked Victor.

"I have no idea," screamed Jerome.

"We have to defend ourselves and make sure we kill these bastards," shouted Victor.

"There are six of us on the first floor. Hopefully, they can cause some damage to the intruders," said Jerome.

"You think we can escape to fight another day?" asked Victor.

"Are you crazy. That will ruin our reputation. It has already taken a hit in the recent past. A victory right now will surmount our position once again in the world of crime," asserted Jerome.

Victor knew Jerome's ego was getting the best of him, but he also understood the street reputation of the *Draconists* needed to be upheld. All this time, the eight officers began to slowly make their way up to the first floor. They were greeted with bullets, which barely missed them.

Asha and Carter threw a smoke bomb each to distract the *Draconists* while Gordon and Henry neutralised two of them with a kill shot. There was radio silence back in the van. Vikram and Walter watched the screen and noticed no movement.

Vikram reduced the elevation of the drone and aligned it directly in front of the window. He noticed Jerome, Victor, four of their accomplices, and Mike. Walter called in and reported that Mike was being used as a human shield, and the second floor had seven people, including Mike. Gordon confirmed the message while one of the *Draconists* shot a SEAL in the foot, and he was down to one knee.

Angered by this, the seven remaining officers shot bullets in every direction, killing two of them and gravely injuring the other two. Gordon walked over and asked them how many people were upstairs, what weapons they had, and what the available escape routes were. One of them showed him the middle finger, which Gordon grabbed and broke, while Asha removed her pistol and shot him in the head.

The injured gang member was frightened by watching the brutality of the officers. In a bid to live, he spilt the beans. He informed them about the weapons hidden on the first and second floors. Carter cuffed him, and they hoped he lived, as he could provide details during questioning that could lead to further arrests. Gordon instantaneously informed Walter that the first floor had been captured, and one SEAL was down but not seriously injured. The injured SEAL dragged himself across the room on the first floor and positioned himself facing the staircase. In case someone tried to escape, he would rain down bullets on them.

As the silence compounded, Victor and Jerome's heartbeats hit the heavens, and they were in two minds as to what to do. If they went downstairs, they would lose the high ground and expose themselves to capture, and if they stayed up, they would lose the chance to escape through the underground tunnel. Remaining on the first floor would provide them with a fighting chance, but with limited ammunition. Jerome looked at Victor, pointed to Mike, and said, "It's time to use this motherfucker as our ticket out of here."

"You're damn right, brother, screw him over. Since we have most of the money back, he's more valuable as a human shield," said Victor.

"Where are our grenades?" asked Jerome.

"They're on the lower floor. We have guns, pistols, and rifles here," said Victor.

"Fuck!" shouted Jerome.

Before Jerome could react, this time Gordon and Henry tossed the smoke bombs, which reduced vision and allowed them to move up. But before they could, Victor began firing in the direction of the stairs. Jerome and Victor made their way near the window, which Walter reported to Gordon. The other gang members joined Jerome in showering bullets near the stairs. Carter slowly moved up and angled his gun, and shot a few rounds that hit the chandelier. It fell on one of the *Draconists'* heads, and he was knocked unconscious. He had to retreat as one bullet grazed his bicep, but it did not harm him.

Gordon ordered one of the guards from each side to move in close to the window, and said that if they got a clear shot, they were free to take it. Logan and Ross moved in and positioned themselves at a forty-five-degree angle, looking up directly at the window. Walter, in the meantime, sent in reinforcements to replace the guards on either side of the premises.

Two of the *Draconists* were changing positions to be able to get a clearer shot, and while doing so, they were shot in the head by Logan and Ross. Victor and Jerome's eyes widened, and they let out a sigh as they watched their fortress crumble right in front of their eyes. They realised they were cornered and had nowhere to go. But none of them wanted to surrender. They were outnumbered. The only escape route was through the underground tunnel, but to access that, they would need to get to the basement. Their only exit route appeared to be miles away.

Jerome screamed, "You fuckers think you can capture us? You make one move, and we're going to kill Mike."

Gordon responded, "You're cornered. Give yourself up, and maybe you'll have a chance to live, even if in prison."

"You will never capture me. I have evaded the law all my life, and I don't intend on changing that statistic," screamed Jerome.

"You leave us with no option," shouted Carter.

Mike was terrified at what was happening. He wondered whether he was going to be rescued or killed in the crossfire. He was currently being used as a human shield and could not do anything to escape. Victor and Jerome had only one gang member, Marco, left with them.

Marco was promoted once Hector was beheaded, and currently, he was their ticket out of there. Marco realised Victor and Jerome would do anything to save themselves, and he decided to surrender. He screamed, "I surrender! I am coming down, please don't shoot."

"You traitor!" yelled Victor. He knew better than to harbour traitors. He shot Marco in the back of his head and executed him.

"Jerome and Victor, give up! This is your last chance!" yelled Carter.

"No fucking way!" shouted Victor.

"It's just the two of you. Surrender or prepare to die!" screamed Asha.

Jerome went into a frenzy and started shooting bullets down the stairway in an attempt to thwart being captured. A bullet ricocheted off the staircase, and a shrapnel pierced Gordon's calf muscle, and he groaned in pain. But this was not enough to push him out of commission. Gordon had seen worse and continued to stand his ground. "How do you like that?" shouted Jerome.

"You've got to do better than that, bitch," screamed Gordon.

The thought of jumping out of the window occurred to Victor, but he noticed there were guards stationed there as well. His entire life's worth of work was crumbling right in front of his eyes, and he felt helpless. The verbal spat between Gordon and Jerome continued for a few minutes. Asha and Carter tried to peek and see how they could make their way up, capture Victor, and Jerome. They hoped to rescue Mike, who was still right in the middle of the line of fire as Victor was using him as a shield.

Involuntarily, Asha threw a *kunai*, which pierced Jerome's thigh, and he screamed in pain. He balanced himself using the gun. She threw another one, which pierced his shoulder. This time, the gun fell out of his hands, and he hit the floor. His screams reverberated through the room, and Victor looked terrified and helpless as he was cornered. His only bargaining chip now was threatening to kill Mike, which was not working. Victor watched in dismay as Jerome was squealing on the floor. He had never seen his brother squirm and grunt in pain, and he was overcome with emotion.

Mike felt Victor's grip loosen, and he took this opportunity to instinctively drive his elbow into Victor's ribcage. Victor's body moved to one side, and his eyes shut tightly for a moment. The pain made him let go of Mike, and even with all his injuries, Mike somehow managed to move out of the line of fire. The coast was now clear for someone to aim and shoot Victor.

Chapter 40

A clean shot at Victor was the exact opening Asha needed. As she saw Mike move out of the way, she took a shot at Victor's leg while Carter shot a bullet, which pierced his hand, and he let go of the gun while falling to the ground. They rushed upstairs and cuffed Jerome and Victor. Although the brothers were resisting arrest, Gordon and Asha squeezed their wounds, which made them scream in agony. They realised their efforts would go in vain. They were forced to give in, and they were arrested. Both Victor and Jerome were dragged down the stairs, and they noticed their entire gang had been killed and even dismembered.

Gordon contacted Vikram and Walter and said, "It's the end of an era. The *Draconists* have been captured, and the icing on the cake is that Mike is alive as well."

Walter and Vikram breathed a sigh of relief, and they felt a huge weight being lifted off their shoulders. Walter informed Gordon that if there were any issues while transporting Victor and Jerome, he was free to execute them in cold blood.

Walter then called the President and informed him, "Sir, you can ask your office to update the accomplishments section of your election manifesto."

The President was euphoric at hearing this. He asked, "Does that mean what I think it means? Please don't play frivolous mind games with me now, Walter."

"Yes, sir, the *Draconists* have been defeated. We have captured Victor and Jerome alive, but injured. We will begin our interrogation process," responded Walter.

"Great work, Walter! I'll get in touch with the District Attorney and push them to try this case as early as possible. I need them sentenced or executed immediately," said the President.

Walter agreed with the views of the President. He, too, was a firm believer in making hay while the sun shines. He responded, "Sir, the hard work in the battlefield is complete, and with it, another chapter of arduous legal work will begin. We will work diligently along with our friends at Roth & Gotham to prepare the case and ensure there are no loose ends Victor and his legal team could capitalise on."

"Sounds like a plan, Walter!" responded the President.

The President triumphantly punched the air. He contacted the Prime Minister, and the two of them congratulated each other on the accomplishment of a lifetime. No matter what, now the President was sure he would be in office for a second term. His media team would sing his praises throughout the campaign, and he believed the people of the United States would see the benefit in voting for him. His election manifesto always read, "I promise a crime-free America." And now he had the results to back it up.

Victor and Jerome were transported directly to a high-security prison and were kept in isolation. A prison doctor treated their wounds, and they were constantly being watched by three guards each, who perennially pointed a gun at their heads.

A single wrong move and the guards were instructed to execute them. The guards also beat Victor and Jerome before the doctor arrived to make it clear that the two of them were not kings within the prison. They would now have to wait for their trial and sentencing. They both realised it was probably the last day they tasted freedom.

Walter and Vikram welcomed the team with jubilation, and everyone was ecstatic. Everyone's hard work had paid off, and they believed this task force would become permanent. Mike, too, was welcomed, but he was not happy at being treated as the bait. A doctor examined his wounds and bruises and said none of them were fatal, and he would make a full recovery in a few weeks.

Walter set up a meeting between the partners of Lions Star Capital and Roth & Gotham and provided them with the details of the events that had unfolded. Damien and Gary were delighted to see their old friend Mike once again. They were relieved to know he would make a quick recovery. Mike was able to get back his stolen watches and his BMW. He gloated that had it not been for his quick thinking, Victor would probably not have been captured. Asha heard the narcissism in his voice but did not respond directly. Instead, she massaged his ego sarcastically, which he understood but did not appreciate. He responded, saying, "You should thank my opportunistic mind, which urged me to injure Victor and provide you the chance to take a clean shot."

Asha looked back at him dead in the face and said, "What makes you think I would not shoot you in the process. You were always accepted as collateral damage, so be happy, your life was spared."

Mike looked repulsed and was about to say something derogatory, which is when Raymond jumped and diffused the situation. He turned to both and said, "We've all had a stressful few weeks, but we should remember we won. We're all alive, and the *Draconists* are captured. It is a time to celebrate and not point fingers at each other."

Mike and Asha agreed and shook hands to bury the hatchet. Walter was happy because, for once, he didn't have to play the mediator.

The UK courts decreed Pierre and Paul from Downforce Capital would face the maximum sentence of fourteen years for money laundering, ten years for investment fraud, and a fine of fifteen million pounds each. Paul faced an additional two years' imprisonment for manipulating Formula One results, a lifetime ban from accepting any role connected to Formula One, and an additional five-million-pound fine. The father and son duo stepped into oblivion with their tail between their legs. The Chief of Design at Ajax Racing faced a five-year ban and a one-million-dollar fine for bribery and unsporting conduct.

The owner, team principal, and two drivers of Trinity Racing were tried by the Motor Sports Council and found guilty of unsporting conduct and bribery. As a result, the drivers were prohibited from racing for five years, while the owner and team principal were barred from all motorsport activities for ten years each. In addition, all four were fined two million dollars. Following the scandal, Trinity Racing's sponsors withdrew their funding, forcing the team to shut down and list its assets for auction. However, the auction failed to generate enough revenue to cover the owner's debts, leaving him no choice but to declare bankruptcy. A lien was placed on all his assets, which were subsequently liquidated to recover the outstanding amounts.

Raymond and his team helped the District Attorney and Walter build the case against the *Draconists*. There was enough evidence to secure a conviction against Victor and Jerome. The evidence against the two brothers was insurmountable. There were a plethora of charges against them, which ranged from bribery, murder, extortion, illegal weapons supply, human trafficking, smuggling and sale of illegal drugs, and money laundering. They were presented in court, and the jury unanimously sentenced them to death for all their vile activities.

Although their lawyer tried to defend them, his efforts were in vain, and even though he promised he would challenge the judgement, he knew the minimum sentence they would get was life in prison. The two of them had discussed killing themselves, but they did not have the stomach to commit suicide. While being transported to a maximum-security prison, they reminisced about their good times and how they ruled the world of crime. They also cursed their father, who abused and ill-treated them for years, which scarred them so deeply that they welcomed the world of crime as a means of escapism. The sight of their perished gang lingered in their mind, and Victor remembered Hector's severed head and shed a tear in condolence.

Damien, Mike, and Gary entered the San Francisco office of Lions Star Capital and immediately started feeling at home. The three of them hugged and popped a bottle of champagne. Raymond and Andrew entered their office and were greeted with pomp. The five of them shared some champagne, and Raymond informed them that they and their families needed to sign a non-disclosure agreement for their safety. They were not to mention the details of the events that took place over the last few weeks to anyone.

Mike decided he would take a couple of weeks off and visit his parents in Charlotte. A visit home was long overdue, and he longed to spend time with his family. The horror of the past few weeks made him realise money was not everything and true happiness was to be found in the relationships that stood the test of time.

Celebration was overdue in the Roth & Gotham camp. Raymond had just completed a case of a lifetime and had secured about four million dollars in client billings, which was to be paid by Lions Star Capital. Additionally, the US government agreed to a bill of $500,000 as well and decided to outsource a few government projects to Roth & Gotham.

Andrew and Ron were elated with the result and were glad Raymond and Mike were safe and alive. The next day, Raymond was invited into Ron's office and presented with the firm's partnership agreement. He signed the agreement instantly and was presented with an Enzo Ferrari Mont Blanc special edition pen and a bonus check of $300,000. The pen was carefully chosen by Andrew as it related to his favourite Formula One team, Ferrari. They told him to take the next few weeks off, as he had more than earned his leave. Andrew also let him in on a little secret and said, "Raymond, we lied to you about one thing."

"What is it?" asked Raymond.

"Your car and house were not bugged. We wanted to ensure you don't venture out in the open unnecessarily. We had a hunch of how dangerous the case could be. We felt it could turn on its head, and we wanted to guarantee your safety," said Ron.

Raymond looked a little disappointed, but then remembered the beautiful Californian sunset he and Giovana witnessed while they sipped wine. He responded, saying, "Well, the case did turn on its head, and I understand it was all for the greater good."

"Glad you understand and sorry once again."

"I think Roth & Gotham have more than made up for this. Plus, this was the first time Giovana enjoyed being out of the house, so I guess it was a win-win," responded Raymond.

The three of them shared a light moment, and Ron decided he would take Andrew and Raymond to the most expensive dining place in San Francisco to celebrate the win.

The dangers of this case had taken a toll on everyone. The President made Sentinel a permanent task force, and each of them was given a medal of honour by the President and presented with a check of $30,000 as a one-time special bonus. Also receiving a medal of bravery was Raymond for his heroism in England.

Raymond reached The Ritz Carlton, and he and Giovana packed all their belongings, thanked the hotel staff for their hospitality, and left a generous tip of $1,000. Upon entering their humble abode, they realised they had forgotten the feeling of living in their own home, and the butler service at The Ritz had spoiled them. Raymond hugged Giovana and thanked her for all the support over the past few weeks. This case had tested everyone's emotions, and they were looking forward to a holiday at home. Raymond showed her the Enzo Ferrari Special Edition Giallo Modena Mont Blanc pen and broke the news of his signing the partnership agreement. She hugged him tightly and said, "The pen looks great, and it's a generous and thoughtful gesture from Andrew. However, now you're a partner at the firm, make sure you send someone else on these dangerous missions."

Raymond laughed at hearing this and agreed that the drama they endured was more than what they had bargained for. He and Giovana looked forward to their stay-at-home vacation away from the rest of the world. While cuddling on the couch, they decided they would go for a holiday to a new country at least once a year to rejuvenate themselves and explore the world. Life was short, and they wanted to make the most of it while they could.

Acknowledgements

The journey of writing my first novel has truly been eye-opening, introspective and self-exploratory. It made me realize how fortunate and blessed I am, because it is a product of all the support I received throughout the journey. Therefore, I would like to express my heartfelt gratitude to everyone who made it possible.

At the onset, I would like to thank my family who believed in me right from the day I took the first step. To my parents, Naveen and Winky Aurora, your continuous support as well as constructive criticism pushed me to dig deeper. To my brother, Vikram, and soul sister, Virken, thank you for always being my cornerstones and hearing the story develop into what it has finally turned into. A big shout out to my sister, Saugat, who introduced me to the team at Nu Voice Press. My deepest gratitude to my adopted family from the Cayman Islands—Shyam, Pavithra, Mukul and Sahana, who patiently listened to snippets of the story and encouraged me to continue writing even on days when it felt impossible. To my oldest friends, Jatin, Rishi, Veronica and Aditya, who never backed down from reassuring me that I should follow my passion. I am sincerely grateful to Disha, Kalrav and Riya who were some of the few to get a glimpse of the novel in its most raw form. Their unwavering support helped me realize my goal was always within reach. To Prashanth, thank you for diving into the story and providing me with your productive feedback which significantly improved the quality of my novel. Your guidance has been priceless.

No novel is ever complete without the editors, literary agents and publication & distribution teams. I would like to thank Sakshi, who first edited the manuscript, and whose insights laid the foundation for this book. This novel came to life through in-depth contributions from Prity and Sukanya, the Chief Editors. A special thank you to the entire teams at HubHawks, Nu Voice Press and Penguin

Random House India who collectively made it publication and distribution possible.

From the deepest corner of my heart, I extend a special leaf of gratitude to my paw-some friends, Kehwa and Billie, who proved to be the perfect stressbusters when the going got tough. Finally, and most importantly, I would like to thank you, the readers and booklovers. Your enthusiasm and passion for stories inspired me to carve this one and share it with you. I appreciate you joining me on this journey and giving me a part of your life through reading my novel.

About the Author

Aditya is a Chartered Accountant from India who recently completed his stint as an Audit Senior Manager in the Cayman Islands. Outside the world of numbers and asset management, he is deeply passionate about two things: Formula One racing and writing. *Formula For Crime*, his debut novel, is a unique fusion of both worlds—an attempt to channel his lifelong love for motorsport through the lens of his professional expertise. His love for Formula One began when he was just two years old, and over the years, it became more than a sport—it shaped his values. Michael Schumacher, the seven-time world champion, remains his all-time favorite racer, and he proudly wears his logo tattooed on his arm. Watching him race taught him lessons no classroom ever could: resilience, grit, and relentless determination. He's skipped birthdays, playdates, and risked many scoldings just to watch races at odd hours. In 2024, he fulfilled a lifelong dream by watching the Italian Grand Prix at Monza, where Ferrari clinched a historic victory. The memory of Charles Leclerc crossing the finish line and running onto the track to hear the Italian national anthem echo across the circuit will be cherished forever. His journey as a writer began in 2015 with a whiteboard in his office. He'd ask colleagues for a word and craft a quote around it each day. What started as a private creative outlet eventually became public in November 2017, with the launch of his Instagram page, @the_white_board_series. This leap of vulnerability came after a personal battle with anxiety and depression—writing became both refuge and release. Encouraged by the warmth and support of readers worldwide, he began to write poems on themes like love, grief, friendship, determination, and even a tribute to Michael Schumacher and Chester Bennington. Most of these poems remain unpublished, but close to his heart. In the summer of 2024, he wrote his first and only song, 'The Roads', which quietly lives on his laptop. Probably a piece waiting to be released at the right time. Most recently, in December 2025, one of Aditya's poems, titled *The Soul*, was published in *All That Wasn't Said*, an anthology.

The idea for *Formula for Crime* came to him during a flight back to the Cayman Islands in January 2025, while reading a book he'd picked up at the airport. It felt like divine timing. Despite the demands of audit season and 65-hour workweeks, he found time early mornings, late nights to build the story. What began as a fleeting thought became a manuscript, completed by the end of April 2025. The process revealed just how far he could stretch creatively, even through self-doubt and writer's block. Writing this book reminded him that when passion meets purpose, no dream is too far-fetched and that sometimes, the boldest journeys begin with a single page.

About the Author

Aditya is a Chartered Accountant from India who recently completed his stint as an Audit Senior Manager in the Cayman Islands. Outside the world of numbers and asset management, he is deeply passionate about two things: Formula One racing and writing. *Formula For Crime*, his debut novel, is a unique fusion of both worlds—an attempt to channel his lifelong love for motorsport through the lens of his professional expertise. His love for Formula One began when he was just two years old, and over the years, it became more than a sport—it shaped his values. Michael Schumacher, the seven-time world champion, remains his all-time favorite racer, and he proudly wears his logo tattooed on his arm. Watching him race taught him lessons no classroom ever could: resilience, grit, and relentless determination. He's skipped birthdays, playdates, and risked many scoldings just to watch races at odd hours. In 2024, he fulfilled a lifelong dream by watching the Italian Grand Prix at Monza, where Ferrari clinched a historic victory. The memory of Charles Leclerc crossing the finish line and running onto the track to hear the Italian national anthem echo across the circuit will be cherished forever. His journey as a writer began in 2015 with a whiteboard in his office. He'd ask colleagues for a word and craft a quote around it each day. What started as a private creative outlet eventually became public in November 2017, with the launch of his Instagram page, @the_white_board_series. This leap of vulnerability came after a personal battle with anxiety and depression—writing became both refuge and release. Encouraged by the warmth and support of readers worldwide, he began to write poems on themes like love, grief, friendship, determination, and even a tribute to Michael Schumacher and Chester Bennington. Most of these poems remain unpublished, but close to his heart. In the summer of 2024, he wrote his first and only song, 'The Roads', which quietly lives on his laptop. Probably a piece waiting to be released at the right time. Most recently, in December 2025, one of Aditya's poems, titled *The Soul*, was published in *All That Wasn't Said*, an anthology.

The idea for *Formula for Crime* came to him during a flight back to the Cayman Islands in January 2025, while reading a book he'd picked up at the airport. It felt like divine timing. Despite the demands of audit season and 65-hour workweeks, he found time early mornings, late nights to build the story. What began as a fleeting thought became a manuscript, completed by the end of April 2025. The process revealed just how far he could stretch creatively, even through self-doubt and writer's block. Writing this book reminded him that when passion meets purpose, no dream is too far-fetched and that sometimes, the boldest journeys begin with a single page.